I0671034

VAUGN

GEORGE TERRAN

Fried Brain Productions

www.friedbrainproductions.com

For my family ~ thanks for your patience

The subject of suicide is the catalyst, and lingering shadow in the story of 'Vaugn'. Though I may use it for narrative purposes, it is a subject I take very seriously, and believe should not be considered taboo, or 'off-limits' in any way.

During the editing process of this book, one of my very close friends ended their life. He was, and remains, one of the best, kindest, and gracious people I have had the honour of knowing.
It felt so sudden and shocking to me because of how he presented himself to the world every day. I couldn't help feeling like a poor friend for not being more attentive, or seeing any signs that he was fighting on a regular basis to make it through a day. Knowing him the way I did, he probably wouldn't have wanted to "burden" me with his problems.
I failed him there too. I failed to express to him that I was more than willing to listen to anything he needed or wanted to say, or share.

In the time since his passing, I have come to the complexly simple conclusion...
We need to listen to each other more, and better.
We need to shake off any feelings of shame, or weakness that may be attached to someone asking for help, or suffering any form of mental illness.

I'm rambling and, for that, I apologise. I just felt the need to express these thoughts and musings.
There are so many wonderful organisations across the world who offer free assistance to anyone who might be feeling suicidal, anxious or depressed.

www.beyondblue.org.au - Australia
www.papyrus-uk.org - United Kingdom
www.suicidepreventionlifeline.org - North America
www.crisisservicescanada.ca - Canada

chimera

/kʌɪˈmɪərə,kɪˈmɪərə/

noun

a thing which is hoped for but is illusory or impossible to achieve.

doomed

/duːmd/

adjective

likely to have an unfortunate and inescapable outcome; ill-fated.

the doomed priest

LUKAS I

The catacombs of Paris were a fantastic, death-drenched underground arcade of twists and turns. Over the centuries, these corridors had been home to countless vagrants, criminals and general lowlifes. With centuries of history, hidden secrets and untold mysteries, the tombs had taken on a character of their own. Over six million people called this grotesque, beautiful mausoleum their final resting place. It truly was the Empire of the Dead.

Depending on the way the winds were blowing, the tunnels assumed different characteristics: sweet smells drifting in from the Northern markets; dry, ammonia-tainted air blown back topside from the deepest bowels of the sewers. When the wind was just right, one could discover an infinite number of unexpected aromas. Since the construction of the Straights, more and more sections of the sewer system below ground had become unofficial extensions of, and thus colloquially named, 'The Catacombs.' In March of 2037, Remy La Bouffe and his new business partner, the mysterious Mr Cipher, were using such extensions of 'The Catacombs' beneath Paris as a base of operations.

***

A distinct fragrance of freshly baked bread permeated the section of 'The Catacombs'. Along with the heavy stone architecture and bleak atmosphere of the sewers themselves, it made for a frightening but homely environment. The aroma was in stark contrast to the surroundings and the things that happened within them these days. Remy La Bouffe had gone to great lengths to convert this particular stretch of the sewers into a set of makeshift prison cells. There was no style, grace or artistry to their construction. It was simple, cold and sterile. Hard metal with large bolts held the cells in position; clinical and serviceable. Covering the ceilings, and no doubt behind the temporary walls too, was densely woven, chain-link fencing — one of the many precautions Mr Cipher had demanded during the 'renovations'. He would not allow cellular signal to be transmitted, or received whilst in 'The Catacombs'.

There were ten prison cell door along this particular stretch of passageway. Four of them were open, and vacant. The other six were closed, and locked firmly, trapping unfortunate occupants. There were screams. There were slams and knocks. There was inane babbling. The sounds alone in this godforsaken place were enough to bring to mind similarities to the barbarism of a mental asylum from the nineteen-forties. There used to be a time when the kids of the Straights would dare each other to venture into the tunnels to prove their bravery, but not anymore.

In one of the cells sat Lukas Vaugn, a shell of a man. Beaten to a bloody pulp and dragged through the sewer for good measure, he looked like a crack addict at the very end of his rope. He was painfully thin, with heavy black bags under his sunken eyes. The fact these features could be seen despite the low light spilling into the cell spoke to how pale his flesh had become.

The limited illumination came from a slight gap under the door. Lukas hated that crack of light. It suggested the distant possibility of hope and salvation. He felt certain that this torture was the intent. Lukas was kneeling on the strangely cushioned ground of the cell. It was made of the same material used in children's play areas to ensure safety.

"I know the moves," he muttered, as bloody spit fell from his bruised mouth. "I . . . I have to get out of here!"

The words screamed with an unknown pain from Lukas's mouth before he could catch them. The realisation of his situation hit him once more, like a demolition ball destroying any safeguard or delusional notion of control. Dejection weighed heavily on his shadowed and beaten face.

His mind raced as he attempted to find something, anything to grab onto, to ground him. He breathed in deeply, closed his eyes tightly and pressed his hands firmly together. He tried the only thing he had left . . . he prayed, but not to God.

"Come for me. Come for me. Come for me."

ELIZABETH I

Meanwhile, walking down the stone corridor was Elizabeth García. She was around five feet tall and slender. Her long, vermilion hair hung lackadaisically in gentle waves across her shoulders and down her back. Her face was graceful but full of character that was hidden amongst a sea of freckles atop a rich, dark goldenrod skin tone. She was wearing tight, black denim pants, a black top and a pair of simple pumps.

One of the few pieces of this woman's construction that did not fit with her beauteous nature was a painfully raw rope-burn scar around her neck. It was an old scar, but time had done nothing to quell the burn. Yet Elizabeth always showed it off proudly; a badge of honour from her storied past. The confidence in her scar suggested a hidden volatility to her personality.

She walked purposefully down the corridor, determined not to be sidetracked from her immediate task. Elizabeth was already being pushed to her mental limits fulfilling her promise. She was afraid of anything else pushing her over the edge. Through the cacophony of the underground asylum one voice resonated louder that the others.

"Please . . . kill . . . me . . ."

The plea fell on deaf ears. Elizabeth's stride remained strong and focused. Coming to a stop outside of Lukas's cell, Elizabeth's hand hovered around the lock. A barely visible, uncontrolled twitch of her eyes defied her stalwart, dangerous demeanour as tears begged to form and flow. Elizabeth denied them. The man behind this door had delivered unto her a world of pleasure and contentment. She never believed she was going to receive anything like it in her unusually long lifetime. She certainly didn't believe that she deserved it. Elizabeth took a deep breath and held it in briefly. She allowed her eyes to close for a moment as she forcibly controlled her racing heart.

Finally, she opened the door.

LUKAS II

Light flooded into Lukas's room, revealing the true, disgusting environment of the cell. There was a pile of dried faeces in one of the corners, while a mess of blood and vomit had contaminated the floor and walls. When he had been thrown into the cell, Lukas's captors had stripped him of his own clothes and left only shit- and vomit-stained rags as a replacement. He had refused to put them on until about an hour ago. When he did, he couldn't help throwing up from the smell emanating from the rags, or the way they felt against his bare flesh. They did a terrible job of concealing his manhood, but that was the last thing on his frenetic mind.

Lukas's vision blurred as the light burned into the back of his eyes. For the briefest of moments, the sensation reminded him of his first Chimera trip. But then reality hit hard and fast — just as it always did after the high. He looked up at Elizabeth as she stood in the doorway as a weak smile crept onto his face. His smile revealed shattered teeth — evidence of a fairly recent, torturous beating.

"I knew you'd come."

He noticed Elizabeth wince slightly at his words and he understood why. They sounded a little too much like a prayer for her tastes. The feelings they had awoken in each other made them both feel so good, and yet at the same time, so terrible. The things they had done, what they had become — they believed that pain and suffering were what they deserved. Their relationship was the perfect torment for them. Hope and pain inextricably entwined. But it was made all the more terrible because of their plan and the item Lukas hoped Elizabeth was holding. Some hitherto unknown sixth sense informed him that the item he was so hungry for was hidden in her right hand. His craving irresistibly drew him to it, like a moth to a flame.

He watched the hand reluctantly reach out towards him as the fingers slowly unfurled. Resting perfectly within her palm was a hypodermic needle filled with a cloudy, yellow fluid. Chimera.

"This is your last chance to back out" she said flatly.

Lukas looked at the needle hungrily, the first true sign of life he had displayed in days. Elizabeth knelt next to him and cupped his face with her left hand. He paid her no attention. He couldn't see her staring intently into his eyes, trying to find anything that remained of the man she had fallen in love with. He offered her his left arm automatically. His breathing became more eager. He barely noticed the beautiful woman inches from his face. There was a map of ageing needle track marks along his vein; the "tattoo" of a junkie.

"Let's do this" he said hungrily.

ELIZABETH II

Seeing him like this, Elizabeth desperately wanted to save him, but fought to bury the urge. Even though she hated it, she understood there were greater things in play here than their relationship. She scowled at the needle in her hand and silently cursed the fluid inside. Lukas was the one good thing to have come out of Chimera's creation, and yet it had utterly destroyed him. Once more she looked into the shadowy face of her lover. Tears were silently rolling down Lukas's cheeks as his eyes finally met hers.

"I'm sorry for everything . . ." She wasn't sure who said those words, but they echoed in her mind for a second.

Before either of them knew it, the needle was in his vein, and a drop of blood swam up into the syringe.

I love you, they thought together, without speaking. Their relationship had always been passionate and unusual. It seemed strangely fitting that it should come to an end here and in this manner. They had agreed this would be the end of their odd romance, but not their love.

LUKAS III

In an instant, the entire contents of the needle rushed into Lukas's bloodstream. He could feel Chimera moving through his system, along the vein, up his arm and into his chest. As soon as it hit his heart, an explosion went off inside his soul. It took no time for the effects of Chimera to command and warp his reality. The pain that had wracked his body moments ago was gone. His heart pounded in his chest as Chimera burned through his system. His breathing became deeper, as his mind demanded more oxygen and his muscles pumped with energy and adrenalin. There was a tingling in his fingers and toes, heightening his sense of the surroundings to extreme levels. Euphoria rushed through his entire body. Despondency was replaced by joy in the blink of an eye.

The sights swirling into his vision were unearthly. The world around him seemed to mutate; to deform and reform in a way he had never imagined possible. It was glorious to behold!

Describing the effects of Chimera on a person was like describing each individual snowflake ever created. It was simply impossible. Chimera allowed its user to actually experience Heaven. It wasn't simply psychedelic stimulation presenting itself like Heaven. It _was_ Heaven. One's own, personal interpretation of the Afterlife. Pure Contentment, whatever that may be.

Lukas finally stood up, completely at ease, calm and collected. Elizabeth rose to her full height again. No matter who shared a room with her; no matter the situation, people always stopped and took a breath as they received the sight that was Elizabeth. She loved and hated it all at once. She could never usually disappear into a crowd or live a normal life being who she was. But right now Lukas didn't see her. She was invisible to him and it wounded her.

"It's so beautiful," Lukas said in awe.

ELIZABETH III

Given their surroundings, Elizabeth couldn't tell what was so beautiful. Chimera didn't work on demons. But she couldn't deny a morbid curiosity. Gritting her teeth, she cracked her knuckles and forced Lukas to focus on her.

"Lukas! It's a lie." She repeated his own mantra back at him. "You know what to do. You know the moves."

As Lukas looked at her, she could tell he was wrestling with the euphoric high, whilst simultaneously fighting to concentrate on what he knew he needed to do. The alluring, Chimera-induced visions were intoxicating. Lukas knew he looked terrible, withered and rotten. There was old, congealed blood splattered along his limbs and around his neck. He was barely recognisable as a human being.

". . . Right" he said after catching his erratic breath.

Lukas ran. It was time for the plan to complete. He ran out of his shit-stained cell and through the corridors. He was focused, and his mind was clearer than it had been in weeks. He ran for the only place he knew his message would get out before his body fell apart. Still, Lukas ran as if the Devil himself was chasing. He ran from the catacombs and the home of the dead.

Elizabeth watched him make his escape, disappearing from sight. After a few moments, she snapped to, realising she had been staring at nothing. Her mind refocused. She double-tapped the thumb and middle finger on her right hand to reveal her heads-up display. There was no reception this deep in the catacombs, but she had wasted far more time than planned. There were many things she needed to do, chief among them was making contact with Loki.

Elizabeth hated "the ritual" with a fiery passion. Add the fact Loki was an emotional rollercoaster and sanctimonious pain in the ass, and the next twenty-four hours were going to be a nightmare in more ways than one.

foreboding

/fɔːˈbəʊdɪŋ/

noun

a feeling that something bad will happen; fearful apprehension.

a foreboding vintage

REMY LA BOUFFE I

This is the best part! Remy La Bouffe thought, as he gazed down at the two helpless prisoners before him. The defenceless men, though dressed in impeccably tailored suits, were bound and bloodied. They had been forced onto their knees amidst the grape vines at the La Bouffe estate. Were it not for the animalistic savagery emanating from the pack of men surrounding them, it would have been a picture-perfect Provence evening.

La Bouffe stood before the two downed men, caressing an old but well-kept Walther P99 handgun in his clammy hands. The feel of the metal, the weight in his hand, the promise of violence aroused him. He relished toying with his mark. And he intended to feast on this sensation for as long as he possibly could. Richard Strauss, his opponent for over eight years, was finally in his clutches.

People privately referred to Remy La Bouffe as "The Feline" because of his mannerisms and similarity to those of a cat. He didn't look particularly dangerous, but always fought dirty. He believed he was better than everyone, and everybody was there to serve him. He was forever scheming, with a calculating look always in his eyes.

He felt confident when flanked, as he was now, by his security team. La Bouffe was wearing one of his tailor-made white suits that had recently been adjusted to suitably fit over his swollen belly. Despite being just under six feet tall, he remained unimpressive and rather unimposing. His face, on the other hand, was memorable, distinguished beyond his years. Wrinkles wove their way across his gaunt face. He was healthy, but from the dryness and inhuman shade of his skin, he clearly liked fake tanning a little too much. There were four tiny scars just above and below each of his eyes — the telltale markings of a HUD system and cybernetic enhancement.

***

Technological advancement had become an art form — not just science — during the years of peace. "Professional" scientists and inventors had been given carte blanche to "improve the world" when the World Council was formed at the beginning of 2028. Ethical walls disappeared, and funding became plentiful. Especially huge leaps had been made in energy, genetic modification and computer AI in a relatively short period of time.

With these mighty leaps in tech came a sub-genre of science, "Garage Physicists" — people inspired to develop or utilise modern science for alternative purposes, the most popular being cybernetic implants and augmented reality.

La Bouffe was a huge proponent of this technology. The enhancements provided by his implants included a heads-up display (HUD), which had a multitude of functions ranging from point-of-view video broadcasting and augmented reality navigation to communications and even — given the right modifications and technical know-how — hacking. In his younger years, he'd broadcast an entire year of his notorious party-boy lifestyle — sex, drugs and all.

***

La Bouffe's excitement was at its peak. He quickly reminded himself of certain guarantees he'd made to Mr Cipher. Those included a promise to keep a low profile. Broadcasting this would not go unpunished. He bit his lip in frustration and pledged to himself to remember every single detail and savour it.

"Do you remember the last time we got together, Richard? The Black Moon Bar. Two years ago." La Bouffe leaned ever-so slightly towards the older of the two men before him. "Whisky did a good job negotiating, right? It was a fair deal, wasn't it?"

La Bouffe hated that even after taking a vicious beating; even with blood still flowing from a freshly broken nose and congealing in the rugged salt and pepper beard of his prey, he was still jealous of Richard Strauss managing to somehow look impressive in spite of it all. Richard even wore a thoughtful, considered expression on his face while stoically denying La Bouffe what was so desperately craved for. . . a reaction.

The moon glowed brilliantly in the pitch-black sky above. But the light offered no comfort tonight, promising only one thing, violence. La Bouffe was keen to oblige. With the slightest of glances, he indicated to his bodyguards that he wanted to see the prisoners beaten more, suffer more, beg more.

Blood-stained knuckles the size of anvils collided with the already pulverised faces of the victims. Blood flew. Teeth fell. Stars were seen. La Bouffe smiled devilishly. His bodyguards were ex-French Special Forces and exuded a deep-seated volatility in their physicality and demeanour that explained why they were dishonourably discharged ex-COS operatives. They had the same HUD scars as La Bouffe. With grizzled smiles, they watched the Feline delight in their torment of his prisoners. They'd grown accustomed to his sociopathic tendencies and ha quickly taken to the twisted delight in watching others suffer, and in inflicting injury.

From the shadows came the semi-broken voice of a male trapped in the arduous period between child and manhood.

"How long are you going to keep doing this? Mr Cipher hates waiting."

La Bouffe tried to hide his frustration and slight fear, but even he knew it hadn't worked. He wanted the torment to continue for many more hours. He cast a dark look towards the source of the voice. La Bouffe always kept his thoughts closely guarded around this youth. He couldn't shake the feeling as if the young man might be able to read his mind somehow. Something about the boy was unnerving, and that pissed him off to no end. He hated not being the scariest person in the room and recently that feeling had been happening more frequently. It was infuriating.

The boy spoke again, remaining carefully hidden in the shadows of the grape vines. There was more authority in his tone when he spoke next. "Well?"

"Fine, Styx" La Bouffe replied.

In the blink of an eye, he shot Richard's beaten bodyguard. The bullet passed through a swollen eyeball and shattered the poor man's skull from the inside out. The corpse collapsed to the dirt. The body twitched slightly on the ground as life seeped into the soil. La Bouffe turned his gun on Richard Strauss and smiled gleefully.

"Two years I played nice. Two years I gave you the opportunity to leave. You didn't, because you're a stubborn asshole. Now you will die. Your family will die. The Strauss name will die thanks to me. I beat you!"

Through the ecstatic mania overtaking him, La Bouffe never saw Richard brake eye contact with him. He watched as anger spread into every facet of Strauss's demolished face.

Finally! A reaction! Thought La Bouffe excitedly.

"Fuck you, Kitten!" Spat Richard Strauss, determined to piss La Bouffe off one final time. "Fuck you." he finished with a satisfied smile.

La Bouffe had an infamous short, violent temper. He couldn't contain himself, and in response his gun spoke. The bullets ripped Richard apart. His body sagged, remaining in a loose kneeling position. To anyone passing by, the poor man might have simply been resting on the ground between the vines. Nobody ever admitted it to La Bouffe, but he was a truly terrible shot. Where it not for the close quarters range, there was a fair chance the shot might not have been fatal, or missed entirely.

La Bouffe continued pulling the trigger despite having emptied the clip into his helpless foil. His weapon clicked repeatedly as he tried in vain to unleash more death.

"Fuck you!" La Bouffe raged.

"And so ends the life of Richard Strauss" said the boy.

Breathing heavily, La Bouffe eventually gathered his thoughts. He looked at the corpses before him. He saw the blood spilling on the ground and slowly running towards him. In the moonlight, it looked more like oil than a vital part of human life.

"I guess this batch will be a red wine vintage. Rich, earthy notes, with a hint of lead."

The bodyguards laughed politely, as La Bouffe smiled at his own joke. They knew better than to not follow his lead.

Finally, the youth stepped out from the shadows. As always happened around the boy, the hairs on the back of La Bouffe's neck stood up; he likened it to being trapped inside a dark room and knowing a deadly creature was with him, somewhere nearby.

To La Bouffe, nothing about the boy added up. Styx appeared as though from a different time. His clothing was tatty, but had a certain ageless style to it. Everything was a little large for him, like he was wearing his father's attire. Though his face and overall shape seemed to be youthful and still maturing, his eyes suggested the knowledge and wisdom of someone well into the winter of life. Unlike the other men, Styx had no cybernetics. La Bouffe had once asked him why, to which Styx replied, "I don't trust the technology and preferred to be unplugged."

La Bouffe and his men refused to look away from Styx. Each step the young man took towards the pooling blood was more like a choreographed dance. He seemed acutely aware of his balance and weight at all times. There was none of the slouching that was so common in younger generations. He knelt down next to the puddle and dipped his hand into the violent liquid. He inhaled deeply, steadying his heartbeat. "Waste not."

Styx lifted his bloodied hand to his mouth and licked the gore hungrily. His tongue darted across his palm, not missing a single drop. A happy light glowed behind his strangely ancient, evil eyes. La Bouffe watched in stunned silence, his stomach turning in disgust, though his eyes refused to.

The boy rose slowly to his full diminutive height again. "Now, seize control of the Straights."

La Bouffe glanced at the two dead men over the boy's shoulder as Styx purposefully stalked towards him. "Don't worry about those two. You killed them. They're not coming back" stated Styx.

He took a nervous breath. "Err . . . Not until I've spoken to Whisky." The boy kept moving towards him. "But my men are on it as we speak." he finished uncomfortably.

Sensing the domineering presence emanating from Styx, La Bouffe instinctively took an awkward step backwards; just far enough so that his bodyguards were between him and the young man. He knew they were seasoned veterans of violence and were paid handsomely to keep him safe. They had been trained to sense the subtle changes in a person's tone and posture that preceded an act of ferocity. Styx was on a wholly different malevolent level to anything they had previously experienced. La Bouffe could see them grow more tense than usual as their hands moving to their holsters.

Styx turned his back to La Bouffe and eyed the dead men hungrily. "Mr Cipher will deal with Whisky personally." There was a moment's silence before he continued. "Now go enjoy your niece's party. I will deal with these two."

La Bouffe and his men needed no better excuse to evacuate the area.

By the time Styx had knelt next to the two cadavers, he was very much alone. He balanced on his hands and knees and began consuming the blood.

With the scene played out, the moon slowly disappeared behind a large cluster of clouds. The promise of blood had been fulfilled. Styx disappeared into the night. All that remained of that bloody scene was the faint sound of liquid lapping in the dark; of something grotesque devouring the remains of lives now extinguished.

disquiet

/dɪsˈkwʌɪətɪŋ/

adjective

    inducing feelings of anxiety or worry.

a disquieting night

VAUGN I

The night markets of Lyon always drew scores of people, locals and tourists alike. Tonight was no different. The street was still bustling, despite it being close to midnight. Stalls were lined up along the roadside, and vendors were happily performing their sales pitches at the tops of their voices. Street entertainers were putting on their shows, including juggling, singing and playing a multitude of instruments. Beautiful smells filled the air seducing the patrons to sample every delight. It was a veritable cornucopia of pleasures ranging from incredibly sweet fairy floss and fresh toffee apples to hot-dogs, burgers and flame-grilled chicken tenders.

From one of the uglier homes on the street burst forth the siren of a security system shouting out into the night over the atmosphere of the market. A red light on the side of the building began flashing, determined to get someone's attention. A few people close to the property momentarily looked up with instinctual concern. Concern quickly changed to determined avoidance and hurriedly moving away when they realised which house was making the noise.

The locals knew the building very well. They knew about its owner and about the sort of "business" that took place within its walls. The community learned years ago to pretend that 26 Quai Saint-Antoine wasn't there and certainly to never, ever interact with the people who visited or occasionally resided in that house. Number 26 was one of the many homes across France that belonged to Remy La Bouffe. And everyone knew of the La Bouffe legacy of blood and of his personal motto: "Dominate those with less, destroy those with more".

People did everything they could to remain unseen by the house of La Bouffe. However, well-believed rumours and here-say engulfed nearly every single La Bouffe property. In spite of their best efforts, locals couldn't always tune out the building. Noises would occasionally escape and pique curiosity. A gunshot here, a screaming plea for mercy there. Nobody ever said anything, and nobody ever contacted the police. They knew there was no point and it would only bring further trouble. It was a matter of public record that La

Bouffe had a personal relationship with Président de la République Française Alain Durand. A popular conspiracy theory hypothesised that this relationship protected La Bouffe from law enforcement, and was a large factor in their mutual rises to power.

But the building alarm going off was something new, and every single local thought the same thing:

"Who would be stupid enough to break into La Bouffe's place?"

***

Inside 26 Quai Saint-Antoine, a well-armed, and cohesive six-man team burst into the building via an adjoining door which separated Number 26 from Number 24 Quai Saint-Antoine. A rotating security team was on site at Number 24. It had been less than thirty seconds since the alarm had been tripped that the unit penetrated the building and begun their sweep.

The interior of the house was as "shake-and-bake" as the exterior, no personality and excruciatingly tidy. The smell of cleaning products still hung obnoxiously in the air. Obviously, nobody actually lived there. It was a shell house. The unit quickly made their way upstairs, searching for who, or what, had set off the building alarm

"Where's the alarm coming from?"

"It was the safe alarm. In the study!"

The team clambered to the top of the stairs and swung to the right, heading towards the study on the second floor.

"The Feline's gonna kill us if anything's—" began one of the team. But, before he could finish the sentence, they all saw a man at the far end of the hall with a sheaf of papers in his hand. Shrouded in shadow and a long, dark coat with a high collar, the mystery man's features were perfectly disguised in the gloom.

Before anyone could move, the intruder pulled out an antiquated Beretta M9 pistol and fired off two warning shots, one bullet hitting the wall on the left, the other on the right. The security team clamoured for whatever cover they could, as the assailant disappeared back into the study and slammed the door shut.

"Holy shit!" exclaimed one of the men, as he flattened himself against the wall.

As the door shut violently, the man ran towards a large oak desk at the far end of the study. The lights of the night market cast unique, almost supernatural rays of colour into the room through large windows facing the desk. With a great effort, he tipped the desk over to create more suitable protection from the impending counterattack.

The office was filled with old "stuff". There was an actual, physical book collection on one of the walls (which must have cost a fortune in its own right). Old guns and swords were proudly displayed on the opposing wall. There was a forced ostentatiousness to the whole room — like someone was desperately trying to prove they had style and taste.

As the man took cover behind the desk, the security team burst into the room. The door flew off its hinges and crashed to the floor. A human wrecking ball had shattered the door and ducked back behind the wall.

"You broke into the wrong house!" yelled someone from beyond the entry.

The security team's many years of training and experience took full control of their faculties. Two quickly entered the study, while another two covered them from the doorway. Eyes meticulously scanned the room, checking the darkened corners and behind doors. The guard deepest into the room cautiously edged her way towards the upturned desk. Her gun tracked continually around the room, but her eyes remained focused on the makeshift barricade.

"Do you know whose house this is?!"

"Actually, yes! I do!" came the jovial reply.

From behind the desk erupted a flash of gunfire; the ear-piercing blast of a bullet as it was unleashed from its prison. In an instant, the guard crashed to the floor with an oozing wound in her chest, becoming just another body to dispose of in the morning.

The remaining members of the security team opened fire on the desk. The bullets began gnawing their way through the woodwork, like ravenous wasps devouring a tree. As the man behind the desk hunkered down and waited to return fire, he was doing something highly unusual for anyone in his position: he was smiling ecstatically.

"You tripped the alarm on purpose, didn't you," stated an annoyed female voice through the man's HUD.

His smile broadened with just a hint of devilish charm.

"You're smiling, aren't you?" came the accusatory voice.

"He needs to know it was me. When he gets pissed off, he makes mistakes." replied the man confidently as the hailstorm of bullets finally subsided.

That was when everything went to hell.

The man reached into his coat and pulled something out of the inside pocket. Releasing a small metal pin, he tossed the now-live grenade over the desk in the direction of the advancing squad.

CLAIR I

Outside of the La Bouffe building, a small crowd of tourists had begun to gather. Two police officers were standing a short distance away from the building unenthusiastically attempting to move the crowd along. Though not technically paid off, they were used to turning a blind eye to La Bouffe events. But even they were curious about this rather unique incident.

"Can't you do anything about this?!" demanded a crusty old woman who reminded one of the officers of his grandmother — and of the disgusting candy she would always offer him as a child. "It's ruining my evening!"

The officer looked at the old woman defiantly, turned on the spot and moved away without a word. He felt a surge of pride for finally standing up to his dominating Gran — even if only symbolically. He smiled as the old woman scoffed incredulously. "How dare you!" she barked.

Parked just behind the police car was a bright yellow original 1965 Volkswagen Beetle in pristine condition. It was rare to see a car this old still being used. Petrol-engine cars needed a special (and expensive) licence for road usage since the Clean Air bill had passed ten years ago. The car and the wonderful condition it was in were statements. The owner and driver of this beautiful car was Clair Bobak. She had inherited the Volkswagen, as well as a deep love of classic cars from her father. It was her pride and joy.

Clair had been told she was classically attractive. She never fully understood what people meant by that, but assumed it had something to do with her small button nose, fair, dewy skin and long, wavy brown hair. All together, it gave her the appearance of a Jane Austin heroine. At this moment, she wore a worried expression typical reserved for when her partner "went off book". This had all the hallmarks for one of those situations.

"'Let's go to the market,' he said. 'It'll be romantic,' he said," Clair fumed.

From the corner of her vision, she noticed a passerby stopped in front of the car and gaped happily at the Beetle. She subconsciously watched the young man as he held his hands out in front of him creating a frame with his thumbs and forefingers. When he was finally happy with the shot, he said, "Click."

"Your car's beautiful!" commented the photographer.

Clair smiled uncomfortably at the young man. "Thank you."

#

Clair had been a member of Interpol for a little more than five years. She had been recruited into the agency after excelling as a National Police Officer while based in Marseille. With an impressive closure rate, high attention to detail and a hunger to progress professionally, it was only a matter of time before she was promoted to Interpol and the world stage. On multiple occasions, Clair had been noted as something of a prodigy.

Then she met her new partner. Things started to shift and change quickly after she met Gabriel Vaugn.

#

Clair's gaze returned to the La Bouffe house while her hands drummed absentmindedly on the steering wheel. She double-tapped her thumb and middle finger.

"Why's it gone quiet?" she asked, already having a sneaking suspicion.

There was no reply.

"When you go silent—" But she wasn't able to finish her statement, as a window-shattering explosion came from the La Bouffe house. A flaming figure crashed through the second-floor windows with a long, dark coat flapping behind him. The ends of the coat were burning, leaving a smoke trial as he plummeted towards the ground. Every witness had the same thought: "What the fuck?!"

The small crowd of people in front of the building fled in panicked screams. The locals finally took notice of 26 Quai Saint-Antoine. Nothing like this had ever happened before. Explosions and gunfights at a La Bouffe location? To the best of public knowledge, there was nobody powerful or foolish enough to stand up to La Bouffe. Who was this burning idiot that was standing so proudly amidst the broken glass?

The man appeared very pleased with himself, as he looked back up to see the remains of his handiwork.

Clair was still looking up at the window. Unlike the growing crowd, she was not shocked at all by the explosion, fire or general destruction. This was, tragically, typical of Gabriel Vaugn. Although she would never admit it aloud, she couldn't deny being mildly amused. Her gaze finally met Vaugn's as he walked towards her car with a big, childlike grin on his face.

Gabriel Vaugn stood at nearly six feet tall. He was slim but athletic, with mid-length, light brown, wavy hair. His tanned, leathery complexion belied his age and showcased his vagrant years living on the streets. During that time, he had developed a particular confident and brash way of moving; it told anyone who saw it that he was not to be messed with. Along with his charred "duster" coat, black combat pants with the pockets filled to bursting, a yellowish T-shirt and dirty, white Converse trainers finished his "uniform".

"I got the information we needed," Vaugn said, bright with victory.

He slid into the passenger side of the VW as Clair turned the key and started the engine. In spite of the intense frustration she was feeling at that moment thanks to her partner's actions, the rumble of the car sent a wave of joy through her body.

"Did you really have to do that?" she asked while pointing towards the still smoking, broken window of 26 Quai Saint-Antoine.

"Yes, I did." He laughed confidently.

Clair shot Vaugn an accusatory side-glance. The VW casually pulled out into the road, calmly accelerated down the street and moved away from the ruckus Vaugn had created.

"Why did you have to do it?" Asked Clair, attempting to remain as calm as possible.

"Check your HUD. Reports are coming in from all over Europe. La Bouffe's openly wiping out Strauss. So he needs to know that someone is opposing him."

"...fuck..." said Clair.

#

Through the smouldering window of Vaugn's grand escape, two men watched the car drive off down the street. They were both covered in dust and tiny pieces of exploded wood. Remnants of Vaugn's grenade.

"The Feline's gonna be pissed!" said one.

A short, poignant silence followed. Finally, "I'm not tellin' him," remarked the other disheveled guard.

violent

/ˈvʌɪəl(ə)nt/

adjective

using or involving physical force intended to hurt, damage, or kill someone or something.

a violent night

LUKAS I

Following the Great Religious Surge (G.R.S) of 2027, the world found itself in a social climate never seen before. The Christian, Islamic, Jewish and Bahá'í faiths had each earned strong political and social power without bloodshed or open conflict. The various religious groups were peacefully co-existing and — to a certain extent — informing each other for greater faith parity.

There was arguable proof for the very existence of God. A steadily growing acceptance of a "Higher Power," thanks in part to a YouTube "miracle-worker," known as Jonah, coming out of Mogadishu, Somalia.

Religion in the modern world was a strange creature. Millions had watched Jonah's supposed miracles on YouTube, but the church had yet to confirm or deny the rampant speculation. Even with this new religious symbol for the new age, there was still an undeniable power in the icons, rituals and procedures of the old, for those who believed. Then again, there were also huge numbers of people who mocked the idea of faith in the modern world at all.

***

Since the G.R.S, churches worldwide remained open twenty-four hours a day, without exception. It was all they could do to control the massively increased numbers of people who wanted to attend. Notre-Dame was no different despite the ridiculous hour. A repeating, all-channels government broadcast requiring citizens return to their homes for safety due to sudden gang warfare had done little to reduce the crowds. The church still had hundreds of people milling around outside the fantastic entrance doors. There were street vendors selling their wares: food, drink and a lot of vaguely religious paraphernalia. There were T-shirts, mugs and commemorative plates with a picture of a young boy plastered on them. The tagline "In Jonah We Trust" was written over the merchandise.

What should have been about an hour's walk for Lukas to reach Cathédrale Notre-Dame, actually took him nearly two. Bundling down the street, he looked like a raving lunatic between his clothes, his smell and his seemingly inane babbling about Heaven, Hell and Demons. He was still under the heavenly effects of Chimera, but his awareness of his surroundings was returning to him. He knew where he was and why he had forced himself on to Notre-Dame. He needed as many eyes on him as possible. He was shouting incoherently to get more attention. It worked. People watched with morbid curiosity. Some of them began streaming Lukas's madness to social media channels via their HUDs.

It wasn't unusual to see teams of priests in the bigger cities. They would walk the streets offering support, mediating arguments and even getting in the middle of fights. They were known as the Soldiers of Christ and there were many, many rumours about what their actual agenda was. Yet they seemed content to simply help whomever and however they could, never asking for anything in return.

The queue slowly heading into the cathedral became painfully aware of Lukas's presence when he purposefully collided with them in almost comical fashion. As verbal and physical frustration from the masses quickly grew thanks to Lukas's actions. As he stumbled towards the Notre-Dame entrance he saw, through the haze of Chimera, that an increasing number of police roaming the area had obviously taken an interest in him. Being arrested wasn't the plan.

#

Inside, the cathedral was brightly lit and ostentatious beyond compare, save only for the Vatican. A rather handsome priest, with accompanying salt-and-pepper beard was positioned in front of a bank of microphones. Six drone-controlled cameras with small, red lights indicating they broadcast and live on all channels. He led the congregation in a sermon that, even he agreed, would have been more fitting being delivered but the eternally crotchety Priest, Pierre Vaugn. Yet the congregation was far more invested in it than he'd expected. So he continued.

"You will be cursed in the town and cursed in the field. A curse will be on your basket and on your bread-basin. A curse will be on the fruit of your body, and on the fruit of your land, on the increase of your cattle, and the young of your flock. You will be cursed when you come in and cursed when you go out. The Lord will send on you cursing and trouble and punishment in everything to which you put your hand, till sudden destruction overtakes you; because of your evil ways in which you have been false to me.' Deuteronomy 28:16-20."

"Amen." Came the solemn response.

It was at that moment the sound of Lukas's commotion from outside undeniably filtered into the cathedral. Some of the congregation to the rear of the hall started turning around and began reacting with snide looks and remarks. But the younger, more curious members on the masses laughed at the prat-falling as it occurred. Lukas careened into the nave like some junkie version of Charlie Chaplin. His ruined, naked flesh made an almost comics squeaking, screeching sound as it skidded across the tiled floor. The sound silenced the mighty cathedral and everyone watched. As Lukas wearily pulled himself to his feet, he saw the drones spin in the air and quickly hover towards him. He noticed the red broadcasting lights. A slight smile cracked on his rotten face.

"I made it."

Lukas stumbled to the front of the church and began crying and muttering aloud at the feet of Jesus. His eyes were blood-shot, with his pupils heavily dilated. The effects of Chimera had completely subsided. The weight and despair of the world lay heavily on his shoulders once again. Somehow, within a few short hours, his condition had deteriorated further. Anaemic and exhausted, his body was not going to last much longer. Lukas could hear the buzzing of the drones as they spun around this way and that. He knew they were attempting to capture his actions and the responses of the congregation. It was exactly what he wanted. Tragically, his plan was finishing up perfectly.

"Father, forgive me . . . I . . . I . . . It's the only way."

The priest and his congregation watched in stunned silence, growing more invested into what this madman would do next. Recognition slowly grew in the handsome priest's mind. "Lukas?"

Lukas pulled a large piece of a broken brown glass from inside the folds of his ragged clothes. It was the remains of beer bottle and he used the neck as a makeshift handle. The snapped point of the bottle body momentarily reflected the powerful lights from above. It was like the flash of a camera going off and everyone in attendance saw it. They saw the lethal-looking piece of glass. Lukas actually heard audible gasps as realisation of what was going to happen next dawned on his audience.

"Please…help me, Gabriel." He dug the tip of the shard deep into his jugular and dragged it across his throat as his final word weakly fell from his lips.

"Lukas!" Yelled the priest as he ran towards Lukas.

". . . Chimera . . ."

The life of Lukas Vaugn came to a perfectly executed, public, grotesque end. Blood spurted from the wound and splattered on the feet of Jesus on the cross. Lukas's body collapsed as the bottle shard fell from his hand and scattering into tiny pieces on the hard floor. His message had been sent, and his final hope had been that Gabriel would understand it.

favour

/ˈfeɪvə/

noun

approval, support, or liking for someone or something.

a favour

WHISKY I

Five months ago; The Straights.

Because of the G.R.S — as well as the end of open global warfare and years of peaceful, albeit tense, prosperity — every major city in the world had become overpopulated and home to at least one gigantic shantytown.

The "Straights" was one such shantytown. Built under the Eiffel Tower in Paris, the Straights stretched the full distance of the Champ du Mars and was one of the most high-density living blocks in Europe. The Straights was a perverted throwback to a bygone era — as if the people had been gripped with an urge to re-enact random moments of French history. Paris was experiencing an artistic, sexual, scientific and metaphysical renaissance the likes of which hadn't been seen in centuries. Drugs were rampant, alcohol flowed like a river and a perpetual fog of dirt hung in the air, lending a sepia filter to the city. In spite of — or arguably because of — the nefarious, roguish reputation of the Straights, there was a thriving economy.

The Black Moon Bar was the place to go in the Straights — probably in all of Paris, and arguably the whole world. It was certainly the place to go if you wanted an adventurous night. If you had no fear of potentially disappearing for days or weeks on end, you could return with one hell of a tale to tell. It was a rite of passage for the underage kids of Paris to try and sneak in.

Its well-deserved reputation only increased the allure of the place. The Black Moon Bar promised mystery, fun, excitement and legend. Every single night, a long queue stretched into the streets as eager patrons waited to have the night of their lives.

#

Inside, the main bar — about forty meters long and thirty meters wide — was situated in the centre of a large warehouse space. It was a massive pillar reaching all the way to the ceiling. The structure inside the warehouse was vaguely reminiscent of a tree with a main trunk and off-shooting branches. It was rare for someone to visit the bar and not question its structural integrity. The simple truth was that it had actually been "designed" by Whisky's then-three-year-old son, Solomon. It took a great deal of money and effort, but the child's vision was made into reality.

At the far end of the main bar floor was a large stage with an enormous Holo-wall showing every possible form of recorded media. Even explicit content would play if that was what the customers wanted, which was basically the unofficial tagline for the Black Moon Bar. Scattered throughout the main bar floor were gambling and arcade machines. In one of the darker corners of the floor there was even a classic games area.

One element of the Black Moon Bar that wasn't visible, but everybody was slave to, was that the entire building was a broadcast blackspot. There were no incoming or outgoing data signals anywhere within the walls of the Black Moon Bar. During its construction, Whisky had installed an enormous Faraday cage around the entire establishment. It was one of the primary reasons the bar had become a hub for any meetings where privacy was paramount. It also helped Whisky stay tangentially involved in every meaningful business endeavour.

On top of the peerless security, the bar offered an unsurpassed range of drinks; specialising in whiskies, stouts and cocktails. The employees behind the bar were more like performers than tenders, spinning bottles in their hands, tossing glasses and ice to each other. It was a song and dance routine delivering a spectacle for the punters. If the bar couldn't serve your choice of drink, you would never have to buy a round for yourself again. Ever!

The Black Moon Bar catered to an extremely broad patron base. In any direction within its walls — up, down, left or right — there was something different to witness: groups of suit-clad professionals of varying ages arguing the latest stock figures, New Spartans debating the personal benefits of their beliefs, technophiles showcasing their latest enhancements and inventions, even bounty hunters bragging about their highest value targets. Venturing deeper into the recessed pockets of the Black Moon Bar would test a person's strength and fortitude, as the lines between the natural and supernatural realms disappeared. Even within the infamous walls, most patrons avoided these areas that were so shrouded in myth and fear.

The bar itself was labyrinthine. There were platforms of varying sizes on numerous levels. Many of the platforms were reserved for special clients or private functions, some had been personalised with unique furniture and decorations. Considering the Bar's exterior and its location in the Straights, there was an unusually strong sense of aristocracy to some of the clients and their spaces. The hierarchy was built into the platforms: the higher you climbed, the more lavish and impressive it became.

At the very top of the multi-tiered construction were two very different segregated platforms. The first was small and completely walled off, with a basic plaque on the door reading "Private". The doorframe featured unusual scratched-in graffiti — it looked like stylish Norse runes or funky hieroglyphics.

The other platform was large and expensive-looking with screens on each side. This was the only area in the whole bar that had windows. A spiralling iron staircase rose up above the screen walls towards a dome-shaped atrium. The glass ceiling was a beautiful mosaic of random shapes and colours; it was also the only place where Whisky's Faraday Cage was visible — lending the atrium a birdcage-like appearance. The space at the top of the stairs was minimal, with only a small platform and a two-seater leather Ottoman. From this exalted position, there were lines of sight for the entire bar, as well as a fantastic panoramic view of The Straights outside. Two titanic, bald-headed bodyguards stood watch over the door to the platform. The entrance was designed like a small, but fashion-conscious fortress and wouldn't have been out of place in a high-roller Abu Dhabi nightclub. Merely through its appearance — and the looks on the security guard faces — it said, "Keep Out. Not Welcome."

#

Whisky resembled a mole thanks to his thick, bottle-end glasses, bad skin, wispy moustache and larger-than-normal front teeth. He was short and fat, making the mole similarities all the more apparent. But in spite of his appearance, he was a hugely popular, respected and influential figure in many circles. He described himself as "a purveyor of professional neutrality". Whisky was instrumental in ending the brutal gang warfare between the Strauss and La Bouffe crime families when it bled onto the streets of Paris two years ago. As payment for his services, the Black Moon Bar and the surrounding district became an official neutral zone, controlled and protected by Whisky and his allies.

Though it didn't appear to be the case, Whisky was sitting cozily in an old leather armchair nursing a wooden cup in his chubby hands. No matter how he sat, there was always something uncomfortable about the position. It wasn't uncomfortable for him, but always looked slightly disturbing for anyone sitting opposite. Many people rightly believed it was purposefully done. Whisky spent a great deal of time and effort cultivating his persona. "You've cer'ainly made my life more even'ful" he said, with a hint of frustration.

Cipher sat opposite Whisky, just as at ease and enjoying himself. Relaxed and calm. "I aim to excite and delight!" he commented with his usual, genial accent.

"Jus' remember I'll always remain neutral. I'm sure you can apprecia'e th' power of reputation."

Whisky made sure to stress the friendly, yet threatening tone as he took a sip of an eighteen-year-old Glenmorangie from his wooden cup. He tapped his foot to the beat of the music playing downstairs. Taking moments like this was "therapeutic for the soul," as his father used to say.

Suddenly, the sound of glass smashing and a fight breaking out somewhere below shattered the calm of the scene. Broken property and fighting was highly irregular for the Black Moon Bar — everyone knew the rules:

1) Always pay your bill before leaving.
2) Never start a fight in the building. Take that shit outside.
3) Don't break anything.
4) Whisky's word is law.

Whisky let out a sigh of disappointment. He reached down the side of his armchair and pulled out a double-barrelled shotgun. Without a single question or quizzical look from Cipher, he stood up, walked over to the edge of the platform and glanced down to where the fight was starting up.

Below, five young men were causing a scene. It wasn't serious, but it was annoying and against the rules. They were hurling poorly constructed insults at each other, along with inaccurate, drunken fists.

Whisky aimed his shotgun at a huge metal bell hanging from the rafters. It was old and peppered with small impact dents. Two signs hung next to the bell. One detailed the four bar rules. The other simply read "You get one chance". He fired his shotgun. The ringing of the bell (which was slightly distorted from the dents and blast) silenced the whole bar, and the fight immediately stopped. Everyone looked up. It was one of the rare occasions where Whisky wasn't smiling. It made everyone in the building feel embarrassed.

"If you can' 'andle ya drink, I suggest stickin' to our wonderful array of teas 'n' coffees."

The patrons turned their attention to the five fighters without uttering a single comment or criticism. Without the inane drone of loud dialogue happening all at once, the bar music sounded strangely ominous. It highlighted to void of conversation making it all the more excruciating. A limp, childlike apology eventually echoed up the rafters. "Sorry, Whisky."

Whisky huffed angrily. "So ya should be. Get ou'. Ya done for today. Everyone else can enjoy a round on th' house."
Instantly, the atmosphere was pumping again. Excitement resumed, as everyone rushed to get their free round at the bar — it was chaos. Whisky's trademark smile reformed to his odd face. He watched the patrons return to their more genial ways. "An' don' try ta trick th' system. We always know!" he shouted.

With his curiosity sated, he finally turned and walked back to his seat. "So, aside from th' excellen' array of drinks and my wonderful company, what' brings you to my humble home?" said Whisky, slumping back into his seat.

He noticed that Cipher hadn't let the scene interrupt his appreciation for his fine cigar and beautiful Scotch. Whisky had never seen Cipher unsettled, which concerned him. He believed he couldn't trust someone who didn't get surprised or rattled from time to time. The concept felt alien to him.

"I was hoping you could do me a favour?" asked Cipher, sniffing the delicious aroma and enjoying the smoky, earthy, yet delicate taste of his drink.

Whisky unapologetically scratched his crotch as he waited for the favour. Cipher smiled courteously and leaned forwards a little. He looked directly into Whisky's eyes. So few people could look him in his dull, comically magnified eyes, without feeling awkward. Cipher always looked, and with an intensity that actually made Whisky a little nervous.

"I need you to kill a man."

Whisky raised an eyebrow at Cipher incredulously. "Nope!"

He made quite a show of shutting his eyes and taking a long, considered sip from his cup. A pronounced, agonising quiet followed as neither man was willing to be the first to speak.

Cipher eventually bellowed, "I'm just messing with ya!"

Another awkward silence stretched out, as Whisky leaned back into his seat once more, letting out a slight groan. *This is my house. You play by my rules,* he thought confidently.

"But seriously, what do you know about priests in the Straights?" Cipher asked.

interloper

/ˈɪntələʊpə/

noun

a person who becomes involved in a place or situation where they are not wanted or are considered not to belong.

interloper

MARIA LA BOUFFE I

The La Bouffe estate sat regally on the side of the Provence hills, overlooking a huge vineyard. Fairy lights had been hung elegantly on either side of the driveway leading from the drive entrance, all the way up to the house. The châteaux was positioned near the very top of the hill while the rows and rows of grape vines cascaded down onto various levels surrounding the property. The estate was picturesque and made any oenophile jealous. It was hard to imagine the soil encircling this gorgeous environment so frequently drenched in the blood of La Bouffe's enemies.

On this particular night, the châteaux was bustling with people, largely inside the house, but guests would occasionally attempt to wander through the grape vines, only to be quickly turned around and redirected back to the house. Armed security patrolled the estate, as yet another grandiose car pulled up to the main entrance, waiting for valet parking. A chorus of "Happy Birthday" echoed out from the open windows in painfully terrible quality, fuelled by drunken rapture.

#

Inside the main ballroom of the châteaux, over a hundred people and live drone-cams surrounded the evident birthday girl. Everyone was heinously inebriated and seemed to be having a great time, none more than Maria La Bouffe. Maria had just turned eighteen and was obnoxiously drunk. She had long, flowing blonde hair that reached to the small of her back. Although it was a mess now, it was easy to believe that great effort had been spent to ensure it looked incredible at the start of the festivities.

Maria was an average height for her age, but almost always wore some form of high-heeled shoe or, like tonight, thigh-high, leather boots. She adored people having to look up to her, and relished looking down on everyone — particularly men. She was wearing a sleek, black dress with slight white flecking that stopped just below her ass. Her outfit and demeanour screamed for constant attention.

She raised her champagne flute for a toast; so enthusiastically that she nearly fell over. While she managed to regain her balance, the contents of her glass was thrown high into the air, arched overhead and splashed all over the floor. The typical birthday paraphernalia was strewn around her: balloons, party poppers, streamers, crates of beer, wine and bottles of champagne were everywhere.

The people in attendance were an odd lot. There were only a few of Maria's peers nearby, perhaps twenty at most. The rest of the attendees appeared much older and likely only there to fulfil dutiful requirements to her uncle, Remy La Bouffe.

Some guests had clearly consumed too much of everything and had crashed anywhere they could. One had even fallen asleep next to the speaker system and the loud music was not remotely phasing them.

There was certainly a stereotypical "Maria party" vibe to the event. Anyone who had been to one of her soirees in the past (or had watched any of her broadcasts) knew exactly what that meant: excess and hedonism worthy of Emperor Caligula. As the saying goes, "The apple doesn't fall far from the tree". Maria was a La Bouffe, after all.

"Happy Birthday, Maria!" came enthusiastic screams from her friends. Everyone else commented far more politely and with far less exuberance. Their civility and reservedness was completely lost on Maria — she wouldn't have cared anyway. Being the centre of attention was all she wanted; the power of her celebrity, the idolisation, it was intoxicating to her. She spun on the spot with a huge smile, as the alcohol and adoration flooded her senses. She was barely keeping herself upright.

"Thank you all! Iwannabeall . . ." Maria slurred. "I can honestly say . . . this is the best birthday ever!" She pointed at the drone-cam directly in front of her and yelled, "This is for my fans!"

Maria downed her drink and everyone followed suit, some with far more youthful exuberance than others. She reached out and drunkenly hung around the neck of an older gentleman who had the misfortune of standing beside her at just the wrong time. He had been smoking the remaining stump of a large cigar and having a conversation with an attractive older woman before Maria slumped into the discussion uninvited.

"Where is my Uncle?!" Maria let out a raucous holler: "Remy?!"

The poor gentleman couldn't protect himself from Maria's shouting. It pierced his ears like hot pokers and stung his brain. Worse, when his head stopped spinning, there was no sign of the older woman. . . and he hadn't gotten her number.

REMY LA BOUFFE I

Remy La Bouffe was standing in front of the windows of his conservatory office. It was almost identical to that of 26 Quai Saint-Antoine. It, too, was decorated with antiques of a bygone era, including old record sets, leather recliners and an impressive collection of whiskies and cigars. An ornate crossbow hung on the wall behind a large mahogany desk. As in the Lyon office, everything was meticulously preserved and well looked after. But they were tools to disguise La Bouffe's natural vulgarity. A glamour, so to speak, of sophistication.

He was on an ancient wired phone with someone. The phone was a black turn-dial model with a cradle on top of the dial for the receiver. The wired phone, and the idea of using the office, had been offered to him by an associate. It was a futile attempt to eliminate his bad habit of broadcasting everything. La Bouffe was an avid poker player, but he was terrible at hiding his tells. Now, on the phone, he was again failing to hide his emotions: he was cracking his knuckles.

His mind kept snapping back a mere two hours to him gleefully murdering Richard Strauss. Aside from Styx cheapening the mood, he had felt invigorated as he returned to the châteaux. His blood had been pumping and, as was his prerogative, he had viciously taken one of his staff members. It was a known fact amongst La Bouffe's staff that he would, on occasion, sexually assault workers. But there was nothing they could do about it. He preferred it if his prey fought back; if they didn't, they would disappear soon after the incident.

But this phone call had utterly ruined his evening. A voice trembled through the old receiver. "Sir, I'm sorry—"

La Bouffe had just finished a brutal tirade directed at the underling on the other end of the line. Belittling his subordinates was usually one of La Bouffe's favourite past times, but the severity of this particular situation tarnished it.

"I don't give a flying fuck if you're sorry! Do you have any idea how much of a fuckup this is?! Of course you don't, Lucien — you're a fucking retard!"

La Bouffe knew he had to calm down, so he did his usual routine.

He assumed a power pose, puffed out his chest and assessed his reflection in the glass. He looked strong, confident, in control — or at least so he thought. La Bouffe invested his strength into a veritable perpetual engine of violence, domination and power consolidation. Even though the remaining pockets of Strauss supporters were being exterminated at that very moment, he was still being called "The Feline" and knew the name wouldn't die anytime soon. He was obsessed with eradicating anyone who used that nickname. He was more prone to tantrums when he didn't get his way or something didn't go quite to plan. This had resulted in a more strained business relationship with Cipher than ever before. La Bouffe hated anyone with less power than him, but loathed those with more power even more damningly. His relationship with Cipher was an ever-growing unpleasant one.

La Bouffe rested his head against the windowpane. The cool glass soothed his forehead. His breath created condensation on the window pane, the swirling and misting having an almost hypnotic effect on him. For the briefest of silent moments, La Bouffe felt calm and like a normal person. It was one of the most boring moments of his life.

Lucien's voice cautiously emanated from the phone, instantly ruining La Bouffe's calm. "There's only one place he'd go—"

"We already fucking know where he went! He's fucking trending online!" barked La Bouffe.

"I'm sorry," Lucien mumbled, unconvincingly.

La Bouffe slapped his palm violently against the glass. It stung his delicate skin and he had to resist letting out a whimper of pain. *I'm strong! I am dangerous! I'm a fucking God!* La Bouffe screamed at himself in his mind. "Pass me to Reynard!"

UNDERLINGS

On the other end of the line, two men walked along a makeshift thoroughfare of the catacombs. It acted as a connection between the outside world with the realm of the dead. Light, sound and smells from the street were drifting in to them through the open entrance door at the far end. The shorter of the two men, Lucien, had a physique more befitting a professional jockey than hired muscle. He had a lit joint hanging loosely from his lips, his eyes were red and he was slightly bent over, cradling his stomach with his free hand. His facial features looked swollen and unusually large for a man of his size. His nose in particular was incredibly crooked and malformed. A mess of long black curls framed his puffy face.

The other man, Reynard, was a stocky gent with a heavily scarred face and military issue buzz cut. Reynard and Lucien had been friends for many, many years, but their relationship was far more antagonistic than a traditional friendship. For example, Lucien had stabbed Reynard in excess of ten times over the past few months alone. Reynard, on the other hand, had broken Lucien's nose so many times they had both lost count. Reynard was watching Lucien nervously as his compatriot held out his left hand towards him.

"Boss wants to talk to you." said Lucien.

"Is this about the priest?" Reynard asked cautiously. There had been a knot in his guts ever since he heard about Lukas's escape.

After a second of uncomfortable silence from Lucien, Reynard finally clapped his right hand with Lucien's left, transferring the call to his HUD. Lucien continued mopping the floor. Reynard looked worried and proceeded to keep careful watch of Lucien. There was barely any trust or camaraderie between the two men. Reynard liked Lucien, but they were both keenly aware that each would sell out the other without a moments thought if it meant saving their own hide.

"Yes, sir?" Reynard asked professionally.

Reynard could hear La Bouffe straining to control his breathing. After working for him for over a decade, Reynard knew exactly what the silence and breathing meant. La Bouffe was calming himself down, weighing and calculating his next words.

"Shoot Lucien." La Bouffe commanded.

Without skipping a beat, Reynard pulled out his gun, smiling devilishly. A great wave of relief swept over him, knowing that he was — at least temporarily — safe from La Bouffe's wrath.

"Oh, shit." Lucien responded resignedly.

REMY LA BOUFFE II

La Bouffe had moved back over to his desk and picked a fresh cigar from a beautifully carved, dark wooden box. He happily sniffed the roll of tobacco as a scream emanating from the phone. Where most people would have felt discomfort from the pained yelp, La Bouffe only felt a soothing calm. The weak whimpering of Lucien on the other end of the call continued sadly. As the sound echoed comfortingly in his mind, La Bouffe held the phone in position with his right shoulder and easily removed the capped end of the cigar with a set of ornate clippers.

He fumbled in his jacket pocket momentarily for his book of matches. In an unexpected display of finger dexterity, La Bouffe removed a single "strike-anywhere" match from the sleeve, returned the book to its pocket and, using his thumbnail, ignited the match. He then gracefully lit the cigar.

"Now get back to work."

He slammed the phone back onto its cradle and stomped over to an old, worn-out leather armchair. As he moved through the study, the cigar smoke trailed behind him. He slumped into the chair and puffed agitatedly. Smoke lingered overhead like little storm clouds, perfectly capturing his mood.

"Fucking assholes!"

From out of nowhere, Cipher appeared, looming behind La Bouffe's chair. There weren't many occasions where Cipher would allow himself to be seen publicly, but no mater the gathering size, he always put everyone on edge. There was something undeniably dreadful about him. That feeling of dread was only heightened by an uncanny ability to seemingly appear and disappear at will.

Cipher smiled, leaning on the back of La Bouffe's armchair apparently without a care in the world. He sniffed the smoke cloud that floated about him, savouring the rich flavours and textures he expected had been lost on La Bouffe.

In spite of his cavalier pose, there was a stern and considered look on his face. Partnered with an exquisitely classic pin-stripe suit,

Cipher looked as if he was constantly weighing up every possibility of any situation he might be in and how he would successfully dominate that situation.

"Is the wired phone helping with your . . . bad habits, Remy?"

The voice had an undefinable American South accent to it, and a healthy dose of baritone that heightened its allure, creating a hypnotic speech pattern.

Startled, La Bouffe looked over his shoulder straight into Cipher's frightening eyes. His mouth hung loose, allowing the cigar to fall into his lap and quickly begin singeing his suit pants.

"You're crotch is on fire, Remy."

Cipher watched the realisation dawn on La Bouffe's stunned face. Frantically La Bouffe tossed the stogie away. Cipher smiled, but put no effort into hiding the face there was no genuine fondness.

"Hi," Cipher said, easily.

Cipher reached into his jacket pocket, removed a cigar of his own and clicked his fingers. A flame appeared on the end of his thumb. Cipher enjoyed doing little tricks such as this in front of people because, like now, it helped to build a reputation of disquiet. Fire from nowhere was just another item on the list of inexplicable things regarding Cipher. He sat down next to La Bouffe and crossed his legs underneath him, even though it was a traditional armchair almost identical to La Bouffe's own. It looked an uncomfortable pose to sit in, but Cipher retained a casual smile and consumed his cigar.

Lurking just behind La Bouffe's armchair was Styx — a scheming smile ready to reveal itself at a moment's notice. With intense, intelligent eyes, high-collared white shirt and heavy, woollen dark green three-quarter length coat, his appearance seemed Victorian despite his youthful look. There were elements of working with Cipher that Styx really enjoyed; intimidation was one of them.

La Bouffe watched Cipher's every move as fear crept up his spine.

"Uh . . . Cipher . . ."

La Bouffe uncomfortably watched Cipher sitting opposite with his eyes closed. He could feel the colour draining from his face. It felt like his energy was being leeched from him and consumed. He felt sweat leaking from every pore. La Bouffe already knew that as soon as Cipher's eyes opened again, he would look away in shame. He gritted his teeth and tried to fight against the rising sense of submission within himself.

Weakness. Disgusting. Pathetic. Thought La Bouffe chastising himself.

There was no sound. The noise of the party seemed incapable of penetrating through the walls. Not even the water filter of the fish tank in the corner of the office could be heard. The environment was devoid of noise. After what felt like the longest thirty-seconds of his life, La Bouffe saw Cipher open his eyes and glare directly at him. Instantly, he looked away. The Silence continued longer. He knew why. Cipher was waiting for him to finally look. Swallowing hard and still gritting his teeth, finally La Bouffe met Cipher's gaze. La Bouffe swore he could feel Cipher strangling his soul with his powerful glare. He watched Cipher lean forward ever so slightly, remaining in his cross-legged position. He could feel the threat and knew there was nothing he could do to avoid the danger. La Bouffe hung his head in shame.

"I don't like my business being public. It leads to questions." Cipher's voice remained excruciatingly calm and balanced; the detached tone of someone beyond mere anger. "I had my reasons as to why Lukas was locked up."

He tilted his head to one side and squinted aggressively. Cipher stood up, crossed his hands behind his back and scowled at La Bouffe in a manner reminiscent of so many of his childhood tutors.

"I delivered the Strauss family to you. I made you a lot of money." The gentle American voice stated.

Styx rested his hand on La Bouffe's collarbone and exerted the smallest amount of pressure, pinching the bone in a vice-like grip. In the instant before the pain hit him, La Bouffe couldn't help but be impressed by the huge amount of power within the boy's grasp. Cipher stepped away from La Bouffe, and Styx eventually released his grip. A wave of relief swept over La Bouffe as the pain in his shoulder subsided, but the sense of relief was short lived. La Bouffe watched Cipher calmly make his way towards the door.

"You monopolise the drug industry within the Straights and

across Europe, Mr La Bouffe." In the literal blink of an eye, Cipher was mere inches away from La Bouffe's face. "Why are you fucking with me now?"

Just then, Maria burst into the room, followed by one of the drone-cams. There were many things that terrified La Bouffe, but Maria meeting Cipher was certainly one of the worst. There weren't many people he actually cared about, but he had a great fondness for his niece. The idea of her getting involved with Cipher or Styx worried him immensely.

"Uncle! You're missing my party!"

Cipher smiled politely at Maria as she passed him. Styx finally followed Cipher towards the door. Behind the two dangerous men, La Bouffe massaged his wounded pride and shoulder.

Without asking for permission, Cipher casually grabbed Maria's right hand as she strutted past and kissed it gently. Completely confused by the sudden interaction, Maria almost fell over. Cipher quickly held her up graciously. La Bouffe twitched involuntarily — he desperately wanted to pull his niece away from Cipher, but he knew it would come to nothing. Maria smiled happily. She was getting attention again; not just from her Uncle, but the two other men in the room as well. "Happy birthday, my dear," commented Cipher, politely.

Maria looked at her hand where Cipher had kissed it. "Ha ha! Thanks!" she said.before moving over to her Uncle.

Cipher and Styx left the room, but as Styx slid out of the door, he smiled a nasty grin toward the two. Maria never saw the look, but La Bouffe certainly did and Styx wasn't disappointed by the look on his target's face. Maria leant on the edge of the desk, looking completely at ease. Ignorance is bliss, as the saying goes.

"Who were they?" She asked energetically but not really caring.

"You don't want to know." replied La Bouffe.

La Bouffe's phone rang, making him jump. Maria got up and started back towards the party, fully expecting her uncle to follow unconditionally. "Uncle! Join the party!"

He wasn't going to miss this opportunity to vent some of his returning anger on the poor, unsuspecting on the other end of the line. He snatched up the phone. "What?!"

Maria looked aghast at her uncle, shocked he was talking on the phone rather than pandering to her every whim. "Remy!"

From the phone, Maria could hear a worried voice of someone. "Sir, Agent Vaugn . . ." came the very professional voice.

Looking confused and angry, Maria stormed out of the office. "You never have time for me!"

The voice on the end of the phone continued, "He blew up Quai Saint-Antoine."

La Bouffe slammed the phone down so hard it broke apart. He erupted in pure rage. "Fuck!"

STYX

Cipher and Styx made their way confidently through the crowded party, smiling warmly even though most of the people who acknowledged them watched with apprehension and kept their distance. Cipher looked in his element as he snatched up a glass of champagne from a passing waiter. Even in the highest of high-society events, human waiters were a rarity. Most remedial jobs had been taken up by machines. Any time a real person was used for a "service" job, it was a show of money and power by the host.

"I'll stick around here," Styx confidently proclaimed.

Cipher suddenly grabbed Styx with his free hand. "Don't trust them. Even if they do fear me. Don't. Trust. Them."

"Don't worry. I'll keep things under control."

"Why is it I simply don't trust you, Styx?"

Because you're not as stupid as I'd like, thought Styx.

Cipher continued walking through the party, while Styx remained in the middle of a group of drunk men and women.

tender

/ˈtɛndə/

adjective

showing gentleness, kindness, and affection.

a tender moment I

VAUGN

Nances, France.

Having grown up living on the streets, Gabriel Vaugn was commonly described as rough around the edges. Typical social graces and opinions didn't hold much weight with him. His education and development came from fighting for his life and learning "on the go" as he would put it. From a very early age, Vaugn demonstrated a strong sense of justice that arguably got him into more trouble than it ever solved. Gabriel Vaugn was the quintessential revolutionary rebel.

Vaugn was a man born with the fire of combat in his blood. He was found abandoned at the entrance to Pierre Vaugn's little church in Paris as a newborn. Even then he proved he lived for the fight. But in recent years he found himself searching for something different, a quieter path — this was thanks to Clair Bobak.

Old habits, however, die hard.

Vaugn's mission in Lyon had been a success, albeit a convoluted and surprise one. He and Clair had gathered information they sorely needed to build a stronger case against Remy La Bouffe. But he had fallen back into his destructive habits, and people had died. Vaugn felt no guilt for killing La Bouffe's men, but knew he had unintentionally disenchanted Clair. He had broken his promise to her and now, removed for the immediacy of the situation, felt terrible for his formerly beloved maximum carnage attitude. He was acutely aware that it was thanks to Clair's general high standing within Interpol (and their teams reputation for maximum results) that he had only been threatened with disciplinary action and nothing more severe.

It's a strange thing how opposites so frequently attract. A man who legitimately enjoyed the thrill of violence found solace in a quaint little suburb just outside of Nances. The house, a small, personal and personality-dripping cottage in a quiet little cul-de-sac, was not designed for someone so energetic and larger-than-life as Vaugn, but it was the old family home of Clair Bobak. Vaugn called Clair his home. Wherever she was, his place was beside her.

Vaugn was fast asleep in front of the Holo-wall with his arm around Clair. Clair was flicking through wedding websites in her HUD. She would have far preferred an old-fashioned magazine, but the paper medium was too costly. She had an athletic figure and was wearing comfy jogging pants and a hoodie. They were huddled into the corner of a well-loved green fabric sofa. Sleeping peacefully, stretched out on the other end of the sofa, was Socrates, a slender, adult golden-ginger Siberian Husky with electric-blue eyes.

#

Vaugn had been living on the streets for nearly six months. One night, he had taken refuge from the rain under Pont Royal when he noticed a woman toss a wriggling sack into the River Seine. Vaugn had heard sickening tales of people casting unwanted babies into the Seine and gut instinct overtook him. He dove into the water after whatever was struggling within the slowly sinking sack. After struggling against the river flow, Vaugn finally managed to drag himself and the sack back to safety. His cold, wet hands fumbled with the swollen rope knot to finally extricate whatever was inside. Socrates (barely three weeks old at the time) was furiously fighting for life and drenched. Ever since that day, Socrates refused to leave Vaugn's side. They grew up on the streets together, protecting each other and being each other's most trusted ally.

#

As was painfully evident from the living room, this cottage was no way near big enough for the people it housed. The living room was almost bursting with clutter: stacks of old newspapers that no longer held any purpose other than as collector's items precariously loomed in corners, movies were scattered around the Holo-wall, and books of every possible subject covered the largest wall. Heavy, dark green curtains were drawn, and a large wooden table led out into a small conservatory and the back garden of the house beyond. Vaugn and Clair had initially bonded over their love of physical media. Neither of them felt completely comfortable in the digital age. Were it not an

Interpol requirement for all Agents to be fitted with HUD systems, they wouldn't have had them implanted.

A large, black monstrosity of an old-style phone began to ring, waking Vaugn with a start. "Whazzat?!"

The sudden movement also woke Socrates, who didn't look happy about it. Clair patted Vaugn on the stomach reassuringly as she wriggled off him, further disturbing Socrates as she moved. "It's just the phone." She said calmingly.

Socrates begrudgingly got up and stretched on the spot. He let out a long, moaning yawn, his tongue curling and stretching out. Vaugn saw it and laughed to himself for a second, but then the ringing of the phone brought him out of his post-snooze stupor. Clair spread herself out across the entire sofa, attempting to snuggle up to Socrates. Socrates wasn't entertained and unceremoniously kicked Clair with his hind legs, just enough to let her know that she wasn't going to win the sofa war.

The phone continued to ring. Vaugn reached over and answered it sleepily. "Bonjour?"

"*Gabriel.*" Pierre Vaugn's ancient, gravel-and-cigar voice echoed through the phone and crashed into the pit of Vaugn's stomach. Vaugn's adoptive father always spoke "The Old Tongue," and it instantly sickened him.

The smile on Vaugn's face abruptly disappeared. It seemed that Vaugn's past wasn't done with him, and long-fought rivalries, like bad habits, were hard to kill. The sound of Pierre's voice screamed through his mind, stimulating savage, cruel memories from his childhood. It immediately returned him to a more feral state of mind — one he cultivated to withstand the permanent onslaught of oppression he had to endure as a child.

Darkness exploded within him and emanated outwards. Hate, pure and vicious, filled the immediate atmosphere. Vaugn was furious in only the way a returning enemy from your past could make you feel. "How did you get this number?"

Vaugn sat stiffly in his seat; his muscles had instinctively tensed up, ready to attack. Socrates's ears pricked up instinctively. Clair and Socrates looked at him, concerned. "Who is it?" Clair asked.

"I'm sorry to call so late~"

"How'd you get this number?!"

He refused to give Pierre any more time than absolutely necessary. Blood pumped violently through Vaugn's veins, throbbing in his ears. He was well aware of his anger issues; he just chose to embrace them more than most, or than was probably healthy. Clair watched Vaugn in inquisitive silence, her hand reached out and rested on Vaugn's leg, but he was too incensed to even feel it.

"Gabriel . . . Please . . ." Pierre's words got caught in his throat.

He never gets choked up on words, through Vaugn, and for a split second, his hatred gave way to concern. "What's happened?"

Pierre cleared his throat and stoically continued with his message. His stoicism was one of Vaugn's greatest hatreds of Pierre. *"Lukas . . ."*

That was all Vaugn needed to hear. Even though he and his brother hadn't spoken for almost a year, their bond remained strong. Given their childhood upbringing and the tyrannical dominance of Pierre, the brothers learned quickly to trust and support each other in order to survive. Pierre knew the bond between the brothers. He knew to not interfere in their relationship. Pierre mentioning Lukas unsettled Vaugn further.

"Lukas just killed himself."

There was a long, painful silence.

Vaugn's rage demanded to lash out at something. He remained frozen on the spot as a battle raged within him for control of his functions. Socrates' hackles bristled and he released a deep, chesty growl that momentarily caught Vaugn's attention. He then glanced at Clair who was studying Vaugn's face intensely, attempting to read every line of his unreadable expression. He knew her obsessive mind and aggressive empathy drove her compulsion to find an answer to the current situation.

"Gabriel?"

Clair sat up properly and continued to study Vaugn. "What's the matter?"

Vaugn got off the sofa, picked up the phone cradle and started moving around the room; the long cable tracing his movements. He was a man torn. A large part of him was desperate to find out why his brother would commit a mortal sin. On the other hand, he really hated Pierre and relished the idea of denying him assistance.

Pierre's voice rang out again. This time with his typical, commanding tone: dominance and certainty, befitting a priest and stubborn bastard.

"Did you hear me, boy?"

He wiped his hand down his face while carefully weighing the next step. The detective in him began analysing the scenario, working out the next plan of action and lining up the questions that would need to be asked. Vaugn absentmindedly ran his fingers over the spines of the books on the shelves. Their tactile feel helped to centre him.

Pierre's voice boomed from the phone once more. Vaugn remembered hearing that same tone so frequently as a child. Especially on the day he liberated himself and ran away from home.

"Gabriel!"

Vaugn finally spoke and used Pierre's own tone against him. "I'm coming over." He abruptly hung up the phone.

Clair and Socrates had continued watching him. Vaugn stared into nothingness while his mind began compartmentalising. It was instinctual — especially when his family was involved — to remove his emotions from a situation. Cold, hard facts were best when dealing with a Vaugn. The conversation had really happened. Pierre wouldn't joke about that sort of thing. But Lukas killing himself made no sense. ". . . Lukas is dead."

Clair let out an audible gasp. Even though she and Lukas had never met, Gabriel had spoken well of his brother. She, like Vaugn, couldn't understand. From everything she knew about Lukas, suicide didn't make sense. He was a faithful man of the cloth. "What?!"

Vaugn sat on the coffee table in front of the sofa and looked directly into her eyes, which made her even more concerned. It was the first time she had ever seen Vaugn in true pain. He was hurt and didn't know how to deal with the feelings. They had been through some insane situations — some as recent as a few hours ago — but she'd never seen that much heartache in her partner's eyes.

Vaugn flicked his fingers in the direction of the Holo-wall. "Find Lukas Vaugn." The wall burst into pixel-perfect life and, almost instantaneously, was replaying Lukas's violent death, care of onlooker HUD videos.

Clair wanted to pull him into a deep embrace and tell him things were going to be okay. But she knew he wasn't into that kind of consolation. What made her the perfect partner for Vaugn was her analytical nature. She could read him well. He never broke eye contact with her. She instantly understood what he needed.

"We can still make the midnight Pod." Clair said comfortingly.

Socrates growled argumentatively. That, and the expression on his adorable face, made Vaugn smile despite the seriousness of the situation.

"Yes, Socrates. You can come too."

hostile

/ˈhɒstʌɪl/

adjective

showing or feeling opposition or dislike; unfriendly.

hostile

CLAIR I

The Pod system had revolutionised public transport in Europe. It delivered fast, clean and reliable transportation across the European continent. The journey from Nances to Paris used to take over five hours, but now took less than one. It was a modern marvel of technology and had been copied in every major city across the globe. What with the population booms in places like the Straights, those who could afford it had opted to move further afield and commute.

***

In what seemed like no time at all, Clair, Vaugn and Socrates were standing in front of a pair of heavy mahogany church doors. There was a very simple A4 piece of paper affixed to the doors that read, "CLOSED". From the moment Vaugn had answered the phone, Clair had noticed his body had remained in — for lack of a better description — attack mode.

Clair watched her partner stare intensely at the entrance. Most people would have thought he was preparing himself for the emotional minefield that came with familial tragedy, but not Clair. She knew it was far more than that. He was resisting the urge to burn down the building. The topic of his adoptive father had come up only a handful of times and she had, in no uncertain terms, been vehemently shut down. What she had gleaned from these brief and aggressive nuggets of information was that the level of hatred he had for Pierre was frightening. Early on in their relationship, Clair demanded Vaugn seek professional help for his anger management and general psychological wellbeing. Particularly in the last eighteen months, Clair had noticed a huge positive improvement in Vaugn. He was being less destructive and more positive. They had even started casually talking about a future together that involved children.

But she hadn't seen him this way before and it was deeply unnerving. She worried what he might do in this state. Clair gripped his hand tightly. With her other hand, she turned his head to face her and smiled determinedly. She knew the best way to help him was to keep him focused and on task.

"Remember, you're here for Lukas. I'm here for you."

Vaugn had told Clair multiple times that one of the biggest reasons he loved her so much was her ability to read and understand him without having to actually talk about his feelings and emotions. She got him with nary a word spoken. He knew she was one-in-a-million and refused to mess up what they had.

The gothic, mahogany doors slowly opened ominously with a clichéd, creaking moan. Standing in the arched entrance was Pierre Vaugn dressed in crisp, clean habits and resting on a walking stick. His slight frame and thin features were aggressively pronounced because of a painfully low fat percentage and high muscle mass. His thread-like fingers were partnered with knuckles forged from a thousand fistfights. They were a testament to his preferred fighting method, and he displayed them proudly.

The tension between them was palpable. Clair and Socrates could feel the mutual disdain. Vaugn wasn't one to exaggerate; he had cleanly relayed facts about his uncomfortable relationship regarding his guardian. Knowing everything Vaugn had told her still didn't fully prepare her for the ferocity between them.

Clair was not surprised to see that Pierre had made no attempts to join the modern world. He had no enhancements — the clearest indicator of this was his use of a cane. Genetic medicine was advanced enough that he wouldn't need the walking stick if he so chose. Clair theorised that he was a man proud of his injuries and their history. That he revelled in displaying his experiences.

Socrates followed his animal instincts and growled angrily at the older Vaugn. Pierre watched his adopted son with contempt. Vaugn glared back with a hatred only a bad father can draw from a son. Clair was still holding Vaugn's hand, watching and reading his mood.

The husky decided to finally break the silence by pissing on Pierre's robes. It did the job. The urination seemed to reboot everyone. Pierre looked at the fresh wet patch on his clothes.

"Wonderful . . ."

Clair was taken aback by Pierre's voice. He spoke in a dense, old dialect. She recognised it as one simply referred to as "Old Tongue".

It was an ancient Christian dialect that was now used only by a select few. She remembered Vaugn telling her that Pierre had been a part of some "secret" society that followed archaic practices. "Bullshit," as Vaugn called it.

Vaugn smiled at his canine partner with as much pride as he could muster. Socrates always knew how to help. That, and his urination had gotten them both out of some bad situations in the past. "Good boy."

Clair took the initiative and introduced herself by grabbing Pierre's hand. She looked him square in the eyes and gave him a polite "don't fuck with us" look.

"Hi, I'm Clair, Gabe's fiancé. I'm so sorry for your loss."

"*Please, come in,*" Pierre said, with no real sense of welcoming. Clair and Socrates silently followed Pierre inside.

#

Unlike Notre Dame, the streets in this particular part of Paris were far, far quieter, with nary a person in sight. There were fewer street lamps and so the environment seemed more dangerous; more threatening. Hiding in the shadows across the blackness of the street were Styx and Elizabeth. They watched quietly as Clair, Socrates and Pierre entered the church. Just before crossing the threshold, Vaugn turned round and squinted his eyes attempting to penetrate the dark shadows. But eventually Vaugn also moved inside, and the church doors closed behind him.

"Who are those two?" asked Styx with a growing sense of amusement.

Elizabeth strongly presumed she knew the answer, but remained silent. She'd heard Lukas repeat his plan so many times it was as if he was right beside her, running through it one final time. *He doesn't trust anything that's too easy. You must let him seek you out, or he won't trust what you have to say.*

Styx never attempted to disguise his excitement. "Looks like trouble to me. Good. I was getting bored."

#

Vaugn and Clair were led through the relatively small church, into the back and beyond where Pierre and Lukas had private rooms. Pierre had directed them through to a small, unimpressive kitchen where he immediately picked up a cup of tea from the counter and began stirring it. Vaugn leaned against the doorframe, looking neither comfortable or happy. Clair surveyed Pierre with great interest. It was a habit of hers, to record every facial gesture and hand movement of people she didn't know. It made her a very successful poker player, but it also meant she often unsettled those she studied with her intense gaze. Meanwhile, Socrates trotted into the kitchen with one of Pierre's slippers in his mouth. He purposefully brushed up against Pierre and left a smear of fur on the otherwise pitch black gown then lay next to Vaugn and happily began chewing the slipper. Pierre watched Socrates with condemnation.

"*Must it do that?*"

Vaugn smiled impudently. "Good boy."

Clair felt the tension in the room was, somehow, about to turn even more venomous. With every piece of information she had gathered surrounding who Lukas was — and his death — she had one question that demanded to be asked. She knew that question would bring both men to step.

"What would trigger Lukas to kill himself?"

She watched as Pierre placed his spoon carefully down on the counter and give himself a moment to gather his thoughts. Clair could see the confrontational relationship with Vaugn was physically taxing. The old man looked drained.

"*Lukas had been spending an increasing amount of time in the Straights.*"

At the mere mention of the Parisian shantytown, they knew and understood the nefarious possibilities that could have drawn Lukas into its clutches. They'd heard the stories. Drugs, debauchery, organised crime and a near-epidemic level of missing person cases.

Vaugn scoffed angrily. "Of course he'd make his way there."

"*Given your occupation, I'm sure you are aware of the rising suicide rate within the Straights? The archbishop required us to investigate.*"

Unlike Vaugn, Clair hadn't been raised with any form of religious imperative. She felt out of her depth and needed more information. "Why would the Church be concerned with something like that?"

Almost instantly, she felt a distinct air of superiority emanate from the older Vaugn. A hostile, self-assured smile grew on his crotchety face. The look told Clair — unquestionably — that he relished speaking down to those he deemed inferior.

"*Suicide is still a mortal sin. More than ever, the church is taking matters like this very seriously.*"

"Because of Jonah?" she asked.

"*Of course.*"

Clair was surprised by the reply. "Does that mean the church is confirming—"

"*~The church is saying nothing regarding Jonah. But innocent people are in pain and taking drastic actions. We want to help.*"

She recognised the comment as an official PR line from the Vatican — it had been liberally shared online and was hard to avoid. Pierre momentarily looked as if a foul taste had caught on his lips. Given his instinctual reaction, she presumed that, in spite of his salty persona, he did actually care about his parishioners. Having to use a bullshit quote was insulting to him. She was already acutely aware that Vaugn men were notoriously stubborn and antagonistic (even more-so towards each other apparently).

"What about Lukas's life?! How did you help him?!" Vaugn snapped.

"I would exchange places with him in an instant if I could!" bellowed Pierre. He was so furious he even briefly forgot his own language habits, as tears and rage welled up in his eyes. He breathed out hard, forcing himself to control his emotions once more. Clair recognised this trick; Vaugn used it earlier in their partnership.

"*He committed a mortal sin.*"

Clair took out a notepad from her pocket and prepared to write down anything of value. "Tell us everything you know."

Pierre glanced over to her and couldn't hide his surprise. She understood the look; it wasn't the first time that her note-taking had caused surprise in older generations. Most people would either just broadcast or record things with their HUD's. They didn't make physical notes. As she glanced up from her notepad, she could have sworn she caught a very brief, very slight smile on Pierre's face.

desperation

/dɛspəˈreɪʃn/

noun

a state of despair, typically one which results in rash or extreme behaviour.

desperation

WHISKY I

Following the freshly renewed hostilities against the Strauss family, Lydia Strauss had immediately reached out to Whisky seeking assistance. He wasn't the sort of person to be a hero; he was master of one thing: being the consummate middleman. However, he was a fierce father-figure and when Lydia begged and pleaded for him to protect her daughter, Alex, he couldn't turn her away. He took young child under his protection and the safety of the Black Moon Bar. Protecting Alex was the right thing to do, even though he knew it would cost him dearly at some point in the future. But it was worth it.

When Alex had been dropped off at the bar by her mother, she was understandably crying and screaming, begging for her mummy to stay. After nearly a full hour of tears, Alex wore herself out, and with the gentle assistance of Solomon, she was taken to bed and fell asleep.

***

Whisky was tucking his rambunctious son, Solomon, into bed. The bedroom was quite small, but well decorated, and toys were strewn all over the place. There was another bed in the room with a young girl fast asleep in it. Solomon Colliard still had dirt on his bright, lively young face and one of his front teeth was missing. He had mousy-brown hair that hung in an unflattering mop, quite possibly due to it having been recently (and unprofessionally) cut by his father.

"Will you be out late again tonight, Papa?"

Whisky gently coaxed his son under the bed sheets, but his gaze drifted over to the sleeping girl as she let out a slight moan of discomfort. "'opefully no', monsta," he said quietly. "Now sleep. 'n' don' wake Alex. She's been frew enuff."

"Sleep well, m'boy," Whisky whispered, kissing his son on the forehead.

He silently walked over to Alex. Her long, messy brown hair had covered her face and she was unconsciously eating it. He reached out and gently brushed her hair back behind her left ear where she was less likely to choke on it. He then walked towards the bedroom door.

"Remember th' routine?" He asked over his shoulder.

"Kill the burglars. Hide the bodies." Solomon replied confidently.

Once more, he turned to face his son and the sleeping Alex. They both looked at her as she slept peacefully. Together, Whisky and Solomon finished their new routine: "And look after Alex."

"Sho'gun shells are in th' usual place." Stated Whisky.

Whisky quietly left the room and shut the bedroom door behind him carefully. He was fighting to hide the emotions welling up inside him. He loved his relationship with Solomon, but the amount of pride he felt for his boy on this night took it to a whole new level. Solomon had so graciously and genuinely accepted the unexpected arrival of Alex into his life. As the door clicked shut, Whisky released a small sign of happiness.

"Aww! That's cute! I've never seen this side of you before, Whisky." Came a familiar American drawl.

Leaning against the wall a few paces away from the bedroom was Cipher, looking as casual as can be. Whisky managed to hide it, but was undeniably surprised and worried. He was unaware just how much his composure pissed off Cipher. Whisky actually felt the instantaneous disappearance of cordiality as a nervous rumbling sensation in his belly.

Over the last few months the burgeoning friendship between Whisky and Cipher had been poisoned somehow. There was an unquestionable sourness between them. Neither Whisky, nor Cipher ever truly trusted the other, but there had been genuine friendship. Now thought, each was waiting for the other to betray them without a moments notice.

"You know Anamaria Jeunet?" barked Cipher.

Whisky gritted his teeth and casually walked up to Cipher, being sure to keep his expression as calm as possible. Deep within the recesses of his mind, he began plotting, planning and calculating. It deeply shook him that Cipher was inside his house, uninvited and without warning. It should not have been possible, and yet there he was. More extreme steps would have to be taken. His subconscious continued working on the problem as he attempted to control the present situation.

"Lovely girl. Very high profile. Wha'eva ya plannin', I'd sugges' ya don' do i'." Whisky politely warned while placing a hand on Cipher's shoulder, trying to direct him away from the children's bedroom. Cipher smiled halfheartedly and paused for a moment, watching the children's bedroom door.

"So you know her!" Exclaimed Cipher happily while his attention remained on the bedroom door.

Whisky fought his paternal instincts. He was no fool and knew Cipher was a dangerous man; if they were to come to blows, he had no hope in hell of winning. He understood exactly why Cipher had chosen to linger near the children's bedroom. The certainty of the threat was indisputable. The only option he saw, was to redirect Cipher's attention. The surest path to success was refusal.

"I'm no' doin' i'. Wha'eva i' is, I'm no' doing i'."

Cipher finally looked back to Whisky confusedly. "I'm sorry?"

"I don' care wha' i' is. I'm. Not. Doing. It." Whisky declared.

CIPHER I

Cipher recalled this moment as when he abruptly ended the friendly partnership with Whisky; there was something about the look in his bulbous eyes that unnerved him. That in itself was reason enough to break any bonds of friendship. There was a fortitude to Whisky — not something Cipher had expected. He appreciated strength of character in a person. But that didn't mean he liked it, as it meant a certain level of incorruptibility. This relationship with Whisky had been fun while it lasted, but Cipher had noticed a weakening in his own resolve as the friendship had developed. That simply wouldn't stand. Cipher stood defiantly baring down on Whisky.

"Then I'll have to use your son." He said matter-of-factly.

There it is! Thought Cipher gleefully. There was the look he craved to see. Fear. Hatred. Pain. Desperation. He was a proud monster, and these emotions were his sustenance. He had previously shown restraint with Whisky because of their friendship. Thankfully, he had finally given up that silly notion. His power in this arrangement had returned.

"Or perhaps the Strauss girl you're trying to hide."

WHISKY II

All sense of self-preservation and strategy vanished as Whisky stomped towards Cipher until they were standing toe to toe. Whisky proudly retained control of his "persona" at all times. This was one of the very rare occasions where he lost control.

"Don't . . . you . . . dare!" snarled Whisky, with a ferocity he'd never found within himself before.

"You can't stop me. I need to make a statement. Anamaria has caught my eye. Get her for me." A devilish grin spread across the Texan's face.

Tears of rage burned in Whisky's eyes and streamed down his cheeks as Cipher calmly placed a hand on his shoulder. But through the rage and fear, his sub-conscious mind was planning once more, and with more focus and drive than ever. There was nothing Whisky was unwilling to do for his kids. He had to hope rumours and legends held some truths. Whisky needed to visit the Swedish National Library. He needed a specific book. The Codex Gigas.

"Wha' are ya gonna do with her?" he asked flatly.

omniscient

/ɒmˈnɪsɪənt/

adjective
    knowing everything

omniscient

LUKAS I

Four months earlier.

The growing cloud cover in the sky above Paris was quickly cutting off the last rays of sunlight as dusk settled onto the city. Lukas was returning home from another funeral. He felt dejected; the number of funerals he and his father had overseen over the last few weeks had been rising steadily. Even more tragically, so many of them had been suicides.

Lukas had never been very good at handling death that was not natural. A natural death, he could explain away and cultivate some form of resolution. But violent death, especially suicide, was hard for him. A therapist would have probably assumed it was related to Lukas witnessing his mother's suicide when he was a baby. But Lukas knew better: he simply valued life and mourned an existence so sad that death was a release.

On his walk back from the graveyard, Lukas had decided to discuss his concerns with Pierre. That was a serious enough sign for him to know that he was not okay. Lukas generally agreed with his brother's assessment of their father: that he was a bigoted, cantankerous old son of a bitch, but a good person to talk out problems with. One of the reasons Pierre was so abrasive with the many people he encountered was because of his bluntness and attitude of "do or do not."

Upon entering the church, Lukas could hear muffled voices echoing from one of the antechambers to the rear of the building. As he got closer to the source of the voices, he recognised them. One was Pierre; the other was Monseigneur Edwards.

Lukas knocked on the door and waited for a reply. The voices stopped suddenly, and a suspicious sound of rustling paper could be heard from behind the door. It was a common sound from Pierre's rooms. Pierre had a lot of secrets, and though he was very good at keeping them, everyone knew that he knew . . . something.

"*Lukas, come in, please,*" said Pierre, through the door.

Lukas entered the room and saw the old, chiselled visage of

Monseigneur Edwards smiling up at him. There was thick cigar smoke lingering overhead and the Monseigneur was doing his best to look genuinely pleased to see Lukas. But that in itself was enough of a give-away that these two old men had been discussing some form of cloak-and-dagger operation.

"Lukas!" exclaimed Edwards, joyously.

"Good evening," Lukas politely replied. "Another night of reminiscing over old war stories?"

As he spoke, he quickly surveyed the room and table that the two men were sitting around. There were a bunch of old books and manuscripts strewn across the tabletop in a manner so overtly it practically screamed, "Don't look under here". He realised Pierre was watching him with a look of either annoyance or calculation. He couldn't quite tell which, but that was fairly typical. Lukas knew Pierre didn't like to be disturbed, especially when friends from his "Vatican days" visited. They didn't visit often, and when they did, it was always secretive and behind closed doors. They always felt traditionally clandestine to Lukas.

"*What's the matter, Lukas?*" enquired Pierre, with barely any care to his tone.

Instantly, Lukas knew that Pierre was in one of those moods. A new tactic would be required. Lukas let out a perfectly balanced, sorrowful sigh, dropped his gaze, and purposefully waited exactly nine seconds before speaking. As he counted off the seconds in his head, he could feel the frustration quickly building in his father.

"I'm concerned by the massive increase in suicides in the Straights." Lukas proclaimed. "Something is happening, and we aren't seeing it."

Lukas spotted Edwards gave Pierre a knowing look. He decided to run with his gut instinct; something he had learned from his brother. He began to piece together the strands of the narrative.

"You know something about it," he said, without making it a question.

"*There is nothing we can do for those poor souls now,*" said Pierre, aiming to shut down this line of conversation as quickly as possible.

Lukas, like his brother, did not like that their father absolutely refused to speak to anyone with a modern dialect. He and his Vatican friends' insistence on speaking in the Old Tongue annoyed everyone. Growing up hearing it every day meant translating the thick accent was second nature to Lukas, but it still sounded strangely isolating and took energy to decipher — energy he was rapidly running out of. Either Pierre couldn't see that Lukas wasn't in the mood for any bullshit, or he simply didn't care. Lukas buried his anger and frustration and refocused his mind to the task at hand.

"What do you know about the suicides?" he commanded.

Edwards looked at Pierre nonchalantly. He shrugged his shoulders, signalling that bringing Lukas into the fold or not was up to Pierre. Edwards made it very clear that he would not take the blame for the outcome. He took a long, thoughtful drag on his cigar, letting the smoke fill him up so he couldn't speak for a moment.

Lukas turned his attention fully on his father. Pierre took a deep, strained breath. He tapped absentmindedly on an old piece of parchment. The subtle crackling sound of the paper drew Lukas's attention. For Pierre to be doing anything absentmindedly was very, very rare. He controlled and commanded his mind and body so aggressively, it took an incredible amount of stress and pressure for it to manifest physically. There were maybe three occasions in Lukas's whole life when he'd seen Pierre react this way. It sparked memories in Lukas's mind.

Each of those three times, Lukas had seen an old page like what he was toying with now, and whenever he had, Pierre would disappear for weeks or months at a time. When he returned, he would simply say he'd been doing God's work and discuss nothing more on the topic. The last time was just before Gabriel left. On that occasion, Pierre had taken Gabriel with him, and whatever occurred during their father-son excursion changed everything forever.

Now, here was a fourth piece of parchment, and a fourth physically stressed Pierre. Things must be particularly unsettling. Finally, Pierre lifted the parchment and placed it in Lukas's hand. The faint scent of dust and some kind of incense — frankincense, perhaps — still lingered on the document. Lukas's eye was drawn to the Papal symbol in the top corner. Curiously, it wasn't formed in the traditional gold. This one was different somehow. It was almost burgundy red, like dried blood.

He rubbed his thumb over it automatically. It was slick. It felt viscous and warm. Lukas began to read the page. The first lines were written in the Old Tongue and needed to be translated.

"*Hear my words. The words of the One True God.*"

As soon as he finished reading that line, a sensation swelled up and engulfed his soul. His mind was transported. He had the odd feeling of greater understanding. A wave of light-headedness swept over him, and he was sure he would pass out at any moment. But as quickly as the sensation had come upon him, it vanished.

***

He didn't know where he was. He recognised the atmosphere of the place he found himself: it was just like the orphanage from his early childhood. A strict, challenging environment. Learn or suffer, a sentiment that had always stuck with him. That feeling of dread weighed on him now.

"Hello?"

As the sound left his voice it seemed to be consumed. The words didn't carry. They escaped his mouth and almost instantly died in the air. A etherial, androgynous voice emanated from somewhere within the darkness.

"*Welcome, Lukas. You have questions. I hope I can guide you.*"

Lukas tried to find the source of the voice, but it was no good. He was surrounded by the deepest, blackest darkness imaginable. The voice seemed to echo all around him. Lukas felt an air of foreboding. He could only describe it as supernatural.

"*Please, take a seat,*" said the voice.

Lukas suddenly realised that he was standing in front of a table and chair. They were unassuming, but there was a sense of age to them. Aged, but still a young vitality. In a strange way, it felt like the table and chair were almost sentient . . . The source of the voice remained elusive, giving the impression that it was the place itself that was talking to him rather than some hidden person.

"Thank you," said Lukas, as he cautiously sat down at the table. "Now we can begin. We have much to discuss."

PIERRE I

Pierre and Edwards had returned to their conversation. Neither seemed concerned about Lukas's current situation. Lukas had been stretched out on the floor in a more comfortable position by Pierre. A small cushion had been placed under his head and an old blanket was wrapped around his body. Except for the studious look on his face, onlookers would have assumed he was simply asleep on the ground.

"*Have we all been reactivated?*" asked Pierre.

"*All...*" Edwards scoffed, "*The few of us that remain, yes. There are only three of us left now. Four, if you include Gabriel,*" he finished with a hint of sadness in his voice.

They both became momentarily lost in their thoughts of fallen comrades. For the briefest of moments, the memory of Gabriel learning the truth swarmed Pierre's mind like it was being attacked by wasps. The day Gabriel left. He had never spoken of it, but that day still remained a severely sour recollection for the old bastard.

"*Don't count on him. He knows everything Lukas is learning now, but he does not believe,*" Pierre said matter-of-factly. "*Maybe one day. But I hold no hope for that boy. He is off being his own style of hero.*"

Edwards was stunned. He was one of the few people who knew the full extent of the Vaugn family politics. He knew there was no love lost between Pierre and Gabriel, but Pierre's venom still came as a surprise.

"*You can't mean that, Pierre! You know ~ better than anyone ~ that boy's potential. Nobody blames you for trying to tell him the truth. Even Jesus was challenged with knowledge of his destiny. And let's face it, old friend, who can beat Jesus?*"

Pierre let out a single, mocking laugh. "Ha!" Silence fell between the two men, but the atmosphere between them was palpable. These two comrades had had many confrontations over their long history, but they both knew that right now it was a conversation that most certainly should be dropped.

Edwards pulled a pack of cigarettes and a lighter from his pocket. The packet was beaten to hell, but had only one cigarette missing from the original twenty. He tapped the pack on the table to unleash one from the hole. He raised it to his mouth, resting it gently between his lips.

"*You know it's serious when I smoke,*" said Edwards, with a look somewhere between serious and comical sincerity. He sparked up and took a long, deep drag. He rolled the smoke around in his mouth, taking in its flavour and texture.

Pierre glanced over at his son of the floor. In that instant, the pit of his stomach fell away, and he knew that hell was about to rain down upon him. Lukas was awake.

"What the fuck was all that?!" demanded Lukas.

"*Welcome back, Lukas,*" said Edwards, nonchalantly, as smoke curled around his face. "*I'm guessing you learned a few things just now. Also, watch your language.*"

Lukas looked around and scowled at Edwards. "Just now? Just now?! I've been gone—"

"*—twenty minutes. Lukas, you've been out for twenty minutes,*" stated Pierre, seemingly bored with the whole conversation already. "*You have all the answers you need. So what are you going to do with that information?*"

LUKAS II

Lukas stood dumbfounded, as his newly acquired knowledge flooded his mind. A cacophony of information screamed through his cerebral cortex, delivering a pain he had never felt before. Pure, cold and unconditional knowledge; Lukas never imagined it would be such a painful burden.

He took a long moment of quiet reflection. Pierre slowly picked his way through a shallow bowl of peanuts, still radiating boredom. Edwards stubbed out his cigarette.

"Chimera's responsible for the suicides. Whatever just happened to me . . . you already have all the evidence you could possibly need," snapped Lukas. "So that begs the question: why do you need me?"

Edwards knocked his cigarette packet again and removed one more. He lit it slowly and eagerly took a fresh drag. *"We can't do anything else. The wrong people know who we are. You are a fresh candidate. You have drive and determination. Maybe you can do something we cannot."*

"Basically, you guys have fucked up and need someone else to fix your mess," Lukas spat, but then couldn't help but burst into laughter. "I think you have the wrong Vaugn."

There was a long silence. The atmosphere was as dense as the blackest tar. At least for Edwards. Somehow, he found himself stuck between father and son. The judgment emanating from both Vaugn men was incredible. There was only one thing for him to do. He unleashed another cigarette.

Finally, Pierre rose from his seat. *"You have all the information. What you do with it is entirely up to you."*

Lukas watched his father fume in silence, while Pierre cracked his neck agitatedly. *"I tried to control your brother. You know how that turned out. Can you do better when armed with free will, I wonder?"* Pierre growled down at Lukas.

"And what if I choose to contact Gabriel?"

The thought of his brother and how he would deal with this situation emboldened him. He gathered himself up and rose to his complete height. He was taller than Pierre, and certainly more physically dominating, but the power difference between the two men was not so cut and dry.

Eventually Lukas spoke again, "I shall investigate as I see fit," said Lukas. And with that, he turned and swiftly exited the room.

Pierre watched in silence as the door swung shut behind Lukas. With the posturing finally over, Pierre gracefully lowered himself back into his seat. He reached inside his pocket and pulled out a beaten-up old hip flask, an ornate cross engraved onto the front.

Pierre drank deeply. With his eyes closed, he screwed the lid back into place and dropped his head forward so that his chin rested on his chest..

"Well . . . that was entirely awkward," said Edwards, jovially. *"That's why I didn't take in any orphans."*

***

Lukas walked the streets of Paris, fuming about his father. Oblivious to the torrential downpour and unusually chilly evening, he attempted to calm his mind by surrounding himself with the delights of Paris at night. The sights, the sounds, the smells. It was intoxicating.

A hatred, a venom had, at some point in the past, settled inside Pierre's heart and isolated him from friends and family. Chief amongst them had been Gabriel. As time passed since Gabriel ran away from home, Lukas had frequently been reminded why Gabe had left.

But in recent times, Lukas himself had felt the cold brutality of Pierre's uncontrollable rage. It concerned him. It was as if an instinctive mania was purposefully segregating him in an effort to weaken Pierre.

As Lukas walked, he began forming a plan of action. Whatever happened to him in that room earlier had armed him with every detail of Pierre and Edwards's investigation. They had been working for some time, attempting to gather information, even going so far as to investigate the possibility of supernatural interference.

Lukas's mind quickly catalogued all the data in order of relevance. Then he processed through it, analysing each item for flaws, connections and weaknesses. One connection kept coming up, and that was

The Black Moon Bar.

In the years that Lukas and Gabriel had spent growing up in the Straights, neither of them had ever ventured into the Black Moon Bar, but its reputation vastly preceded it. It was the place to go. Lukas remembered a time when they had dared each other to attempt a break-in but backed out at the last minute when the owner threw someone out of a third floor window and shot him in the back for good measure. They agreed that it probably wasn't a good time to push boundaries.

Lukas's mind snapped back, and he realised where his feet had taken him . . . the entrance to the Black Moon Bar.

disposal

/dɪˈspəʊz(ə)l/

noun

the action or process of getting rid of something.

disposal

UNDERLINGS

Under Paris.

Reynard and Lucien were dragging an obese corpse through the catacombs. Lucien walked with a heavy limp from earlier in the evening. The dead man had blood in the corners of his mouth and many apparently self-inflicted wounds all over his body. Both his wrists had been sliced open crudely. A path of gore followed the corpse like a bloody snail trail. The dead man had taken his own life and been desperate to do so.

Ahead of the not-so-dynamic duo was a huge wooden door. It had the air of death about it, with thick, cast-iron hinges and a handle that looked remarkably like the hilt of a broadsword. A reddy-orange glow was escaping through the cracks surrounding the door, casting ominous shadows that danced devilishly. Both men felt—though they never verbalised their concerns — that they had somehow gotten themselves into a situation they didn't fully comprehend.

Along the corridor were more doors identical to Lukas's former cell. Every door was locked. Every room had sorrowful moans and groans escaping from them.

"I can't believe I've gotta keep working!" Lucien complained. "You fucking shot me!"

"Shut up!" snapped Reynard, as they dragged the body towards the monstrous door.

"It stinks in here!"

"I said, *ta gueule!*"

The catacombs reeked of bodily fluids and death. But the scariest and most perplexing element about it all was the sweet backdraft from the surface markets mixed with the putrefaction of the dead. It created the ideal perfume for a slaughterhouse.

"You'd stink too if you were locked up like these guys."

A voice echoed out into the hallway. "Please . . . kill me . . ."

"Good morning, Anamaria." Reynard said with a smirk on his face. Reynard and Lucien stopped outside Anamaria's door. The smell emanating from her room was enough to make both men physically retch.

"Why don't they let her die? They don't care about any of the others," Lucien choked out through the urge to spew.

"Apparently they need a pure test subject. To see the long-term effects of Chimera," Reynard replied. He had asked the very same question previously.

Reynard kept his distance from the door. He breathed deeply, controlling the involuntary urge to throw up. Lucien clapped a hand over his mouth and nose as the flavour of bile infected his throat and stung in his nostrils.

"Don't need to be a scientist to see Chimera's effects."

Only very basic details could be seen in the room, due to the limited light coming through the bars. Its general layout was identical to Lukas's cell, but there was a morbidly perverse sense of being "lived in". Everything seemed older and — overall — worse.

Lucien continued, "Highly addictive. Two weeks and the user's so dependent they kill themselves to maintain the high. It's fucked up. Why would they create something like that?"

Anamaria suddenly slammed herself into the door like some heinous monster knocking on the gates of Hell. She looked feral, borderline primeval.

"Kill me!"

Both men jumped back at the sudden impact and Anamaria's howl. "Oh fuck!"

Anytime Lucien and Reynard had to come down to this part of the catacombs they morbidly joked about it being a vile human zoo. Though crude, the simile was rather apt. Lucien and Reynard quickly picked up the corpse and continued down the corridor. They both looked shaken but their nausea had passed, thanks to the overriding urge to get the fuck out of there as soon as possible.

"Would you want to see what they've seen?"

"Hell no! I'll see it when I'm dead."

Lucien and Reynard entered an enormous room with a massive, old-fashioned furnace sitting in the centre. Stoking the furnace were two hideously malformed dwarfs in grime-encrusted, flame-grilled boiler suits. They were covered head-to-toe and wore gas masks that completely encased their heads. Extended filter sections stretched down from the mouth area. Given their stature, the shape of their head gear and their far larger than usual hands and feet, it was easy to believe these creatures were not human.

Reynard and Lucien may not have been the smartest people in the world, but they learned quickly to not ask questions they didn't really want to know the answers to. The furnace dwarfs were a perfect example. They dragged the corpse towards the dwarves cautiously.

"Hey, where do you want this one?"

The dwarves stopped stoking the furnace and watched the men dump the corpse. They began muttering to each other in a language that Lucien and Reynard didn't comprehend. But though they couldn't understand it, something about the dialect brought on a sickness that made the nausea induced by Anamaria earlier pale in comparison.

Without warning, the creatures began acting skittish, their diminutive frames dropping to all fours. They looked at the furnace and, a moment later, ran out of the hall, making animalistic noises like feral dogs.

Reynard and Lucien looked at each other confused and deeply unsettled. Lucien scanned the room, trying to find anything that could have spooked the creatures, while Reynard watched the furnace and the hypnotic movement of the flames.

"Fucking bizarre."

"That's an understatement."

". . . Is it wrong I want to broadcast this shit?" Lucien asked, coyly.

"Not if you want a quick death."

The moment those weird monsters began speaking to each other, the fire in the furnace had gotten more vicious and destructive. It was something Reynard was acutely aware of. He was a self-professed pyromaniac and had the criminal record to back it up. He adored fire. He studied it intimately. There was something about the flames in this furnace that was completely foreign to him. The way they moved, the subtle changes of colour, even the noise was different to anything he'd witnessed before. He was captivated.

"This whole thing freaks me out. I miss the good old days. Traditional drug running, embezzling, murder … not this supernatural bullshit," remarked Lucien.

As curiosity continued to grow in Reynard, he ventured ever closer to the flames. Deep in the recesses of his mind, a memory of his grandfather stirred. Something about curiosity killing the cat.

Without warning, the lights in the room snapped off with a loud, quick groan of power failing. They were left standing in the haunting glow of the furnace. The shadows in the room danced like devils, hungrily circling a tasty soul.

"Let's get out of here," Lucien pleaded.

No matter how strictly La Bouffe policed rumours and hearsay, everyone had heard at least one story about the furnace that chilled them to the bone. Lucien and Reynard felt that exact same sensation, abject fear snaking down their spines. A certainty of death reserved only for the most extreme circumstances.

The furnace exploded with the ferocity of Pompeii. Tendrils of fire burst out from the furnace door and stretched out, thrashed about in every direction. Flames wrapped around Reynard and Lucien, as they tried in vain to dodge them and escape. The defenceless men could feel every lick of the flames burning through their clothes and flesh. They were tossed around like rag-dolls, smashed into the ceiling, walls and floor, as their bodies were mercilessly converted to fuel.

The men screamed in fear and pain for only a moment before they lost consciousness from the bodily violation that was being wrought upon them.

The flames from the furnace scattered light everywhere. The impact of the two men's bodies on the walls painted the room with rage, fury and blood.

nightlife

/ˈnʌɪtlʌɪf/

noun

social activities or entertainment available at night in a town or city.

nightlife

VAUGN I

The Eiffel Tower and le Champ de Mars had been overrun by the high-tech shantytown known as the Straights. After its initial construction, neighbouring blocks surrounding the area had quickly become annexed districts as the population (and popularity) boomed. As the years passed, The Straights continued to slowly expand. Its unofficial borders ran down Rue de Constantine and Avenue de Breteuil on its eastern-most side. It then curled westward and up Boulevard de Grenelle back to the Seine with a total perimeter distance of just over seven kilometres. Much of the parklands of le Champ de Mars and Esplanade des Invalides had been converted into — quickly-erected — buildings to satisfy the housing demands and retail potential.

Directly below the Tower was the huge makeshift church of Monseigneur Reynard; with a large halfway house adjacent. There was an enduring line of people waiting outside hoping for a bed, food, and/or spiritual salvation. The line encapsulated the old and young alike, loners and entire families. A worldwide poverty issue remained, and displaced citizens looked for anywhere to call home. The Straights, like many of the super shanty-towns around the world, was a natural gathering site for these poor souls.

On the river side of the Eiffel Tower was a neon sign hanging above the door of the Black Moon Bar. The sign read, "Always Open." There was a queue almost as large as that of the halfway house. It might not have looked like anything more than an abandoned warehouse from the outside, but every single person in line couldn't wait to get in. Two security guards stood at the entrance with shotguns in their hands and smiles on their faces. They were a pair of cybernetic-enhanced individuals — one male and one female — standing on either side of the entrance, scanning and muting all the patrons' HUD systems.

"No online HUDs, people!" Shouted the woman.

"Yeah, turn them off now. They won't work inside anyway," finished the man.

Behind the church and the Black Moon Bar, the Seine represented the northern border between the Straights and Paris proper. The riverside stretches on either side of Pont d'léna could only be described as a wasteland strip, somewhere between a deconstructed Berlin Wall and the apocalypse, if it had been a slow, steady rollout rather than instantaneous. There was no real reason why it looked so terrible beyond simple neglect. During the construction of the Straights, this area was where the building materials had been delivered. Since then, it had never really recovered; The Black Moon Bar and a thriving street-art scene were the exceptions.

#

The first rays of sunlight had not yet begun to penetrate the blackness of the early morning sky. Vaugn was still fuming after his reunion with Pierre. He'd not had any contact with the man in over fifteen years and yet, in a matter of a few conversations, he had regressed to his former self; to a time before he met Clair. It scared him. He didn't want that life any more. He didn't want to fight every God-damned second.

Vaugn and Socrates watched the Black Moon Bar for a moment whilst being bathed in the bright lights of the neighbourhood announcement Holo-walls. They were showcasing footage from some of the more brutal fighting which had broken out across Europe after La Bouffe's attacks on the Strauss organisation. Unlike the area surrounding Notre Dame Cathedral, there was no Police presence in the Straights and nobody seemed concerned about possible attacks. Everybody knew this particular area was controlled by Whisky and therefore neutral. At a time like this, it was arguably the safest place in Paris.

As a Parisian native, Vaugn had heard of the Black Moon Bar growing up in the city, but he'd never been inside. Six months after running away from home, he vehemently refused to return to Paris. And so the unorthodox delights of the notorious bar had eluded him. . . until now.

"You ready for this buddy?" asked Vaugn whilst looking down at his canine partner. Socrates barked confirmation.

Flashing his Interpol credentials, Vaugn and Socrates pushed their way into the building and were almost immediately awestruck by the looming tree-bar towering overhead. Socrates kept his head low; uncomfortable with the atmosphere. He was out of his element, and the bar spoke to the husky in a way that made him incredibly uncomfortable and highly cautious. Vaugn pushed his way through the dense crowd and smoke toward the main bar. Socrates followed him closely. They didn't make much progress before getting stuck behind a loud woman throwing her ego and (substantial) weight around. As he took a closer look at her, he couldn't help but be impressed by her incredible appearance. Detailed tattoos of brilliantly coloured rose vines wove their way up each arm and down both legs. Her skin was utterly flawless — impossibly perfect. Vaugn recognised the slight sheen on her skin instantly. She was a Synth. He looked at his own left hand—the same flawless skin wrapped around his fingers and palm. A barely visible scar line at the wrist revealed where his real flesh began.

A popular trend within certain circles was the replacement of flesh with a synthetic polymer. Its primary functions were within the military and medical reconstruction. Underground fighting organisations had co-opted the technology for their own ends — as battle-ready skin. Picture Perfect, or P.P., skin had also begun infiltrating the fashion scene, making models into living canvases. This woman had taken it to an extreme level, replacing everything with P.P. skin.

Vaugn looked back up at the lofty woman before him. He had heard of people becoming addicted to the procedures and the drugs that accompanied them. But he had never seen such extensive synthetic work before. Then he noticed the group of people she seemed to be part of. They each displayed varying degrees of synthetics adoption.

The Synth was orally sparring with another woman who had a variety of facial scars and metallic protrusions from her eye sockets. From the extent of the modifications, it was clear she was not concerned with her appearance in the classical sense. But she was wearing some of the newest implantable tech on the market. Much like the Synths, there was an entire subculture dedicated to technical modifications. Referred to as Implanters, these people had happily adopted technology into their bodies to (sometimes) extreme levels. Apparently, the dispute had something to do with their differences of lifestyle. Despite the volume of the argument, Vaugn was surprised that it wasn't an all-out brawl. They were purposefully keeping distance between each other. He scanned over the faces of some of the people involved in the verbal sparring and saw them glancing up into the rafters of the bar. He followed their gaze and noticed the large, dented bell and bar rules hanging prominently beside it.

Oh. . . Ok then, he thought to himself.

"Ge' ta fuck outta my fucking face!" exclaimed the Synth, recapturing Vaugn's attention.

Her voice was unusually low and bass-filled. From the pungent smell of cigarettes clung powerfully to her clothing and hair, it suggested to Vaugn that she had purposefully deformed her voice with excessive smoking. Years of intentional vocal cord damage had enriched her deep voice with a gravelly texture. Despite the uncomfortably loud, booming voice, the tone with which she spoke was strangely mesmerising and — Vaugn couldn't deny — sexy.

"Excuse me," Vaugn said, as politely as he could muster.

The Synth turned slowly to face him, and glared. Even taking care to turn slowly, she almost fell over. Her eyes were bloodshot, and she must have been crying very recently, as her cheeks were still wet from the tears. "Wait your goddamn turn!"

She turned back to the Implanter she'd been arguing with and continued her drunken, barely comprehensible tirade. "Bitch don' wanna be fuckin' wi' me!"

One of the bouncers from the front door had begun to move towards the loud Synth. Vaugn cleared his throat audibly, attempting to gain control. He looked down at Socrates, who returned a clear "I don't like it here" expression. He mouthed, "I'm sorry" to his dog, then once more pulled out his Interpol ID and gun. "I said, excuse me."

The woman turned again, this time with more ferocity. Vaugn watched her drunken eyes focus on the Interpol badge in front of her face.

". . . Interpol . . ." she read aloud.

Vaugn fought the urge to laugh at the woman's face as it twisted and contorted. He could see her mind racing through an apparent laundry list of misdeeds that may have afforded the attention of Interpol. She looked down and noticed the gun at Vaugn's side. She swayed slightly and her drunken bravado overtook her once more.

"Like I give a rat's ass! My dick's bigger than that thing!"

Vaugn glared at her. It was a look he had been mastering even before he ran away from home, and he had gotten very good at it. Pierre had been on the receiving end of that look many times. But unlike Pierre, this particular woman submitted, correctly translating the situation and stepped aside. Vaugn and Socrates pushed by like the badasses they occasionally pretended to be. Both Vaugn and Socrates knew this alpha feeling wouldn't last long.

The Synth screamed out one final verbal jab. "Rentre chez la pétasse qui a craché ton cul de merde par sa putain de chatte."

As Vaugn finally reached the bar, he couldn't resist laughing aloud when he heard the same drunk woman happily exclaim, "Oh! A puppy!"

He noticed a small group of attractive men and women drinking, and chatting animated with the nearest bar host. Vaugn recognised the host as genderless and very beautiful; he could see why the drunk party were all flirting with them so enthusiastically. Vaugn and Socrates slipped by and nestled comfortably up to the bar.

SOCRATES I

Socrates sat between Vaugn's legs and watched the entrance as people came and went. The husky watched the loud Synth finally being forcibly removed from the bar. Though it was clear from her overly physical shifting, she had ceased shouting. As she was being escorted out, Socrates overhead the big guy escorting her say, "Leave quietly. You don't want to get banned, do you?"

Early in their relationship, Socrates had learned that Vaugn was terrible at sensing danger and so had taken it upon himself to assume the role of sentry. On countless occasions, he had saved his partner from danger Vaugn seemed completely unaware of or unconcerned with. He didn't mind at all though; Vaugn was the only reason he was alive. They looked after each other.

VAUGN II

Vaugn leaned over the bar, trying to get the attention of any of the hosts.

"Hey!" He shouted.

"Wha' can I ge'cha?" called a voice from the left.

Vaugn turned to see Whisky's short, plump, mole-like physique standing before him; bold as brass. Everyone in the criminal world knew, or knew of Whisky. There weren't too many in law enforcement who didn't either, though most hadn't actually met him. Usually "a friend of a friend" or "an informant spoke to a guy, who spoke to a guy" was about as close as Vaugn had ever gotten, or Whisky ever allowed. This man presenting himself before Vaugn (who, given the limited description he had, he guessed was Whisky) was. . . well. . . grotesquely unimpressive. Vaugn surmised that this was probably the intent, then he realised he'd not replied yet and probably looked somewhat stupefied.

"Have you been here all night?" He asked dumbly, already knowing the answer.

Whisky laughed raucously at the question. "Course I 'ave! I own th' place, Mr Vaugn."

Vaugn was taken aback, not anticipating being recognised. He didn't like it. He'd worked very hard to ensure he and Clair were as autonomous at Interpol as possible. Part of that was to ensure his, and Clair's names were never associated with any press. The only people he wanted knowing his name were the criminals he took down. Socrates was quiet, but continued watching the crowd from between Vaugn's legs. Vaugn felt the dog shift his weight awkwardly, as if trying to physically remove the uncomfortable sensation. Vaugn silently apologised to his partner. *Sorry buddy, I know you're not happy.*

"I'm in th' business of knowin' ev'ryfin'. Didn' ya jus' cause some kind of trouble in Lyon? Th' way I hear i', your bosses are kinda pissed!"

He failed to hide the mild, shamefully proud smile behind his eyes, knowing exactly what "trouble" Whisky was referring to. But there was something in the way the "Master of Neutrality" had delivered his comment. It was almost like he had impressed Whisky during a job interview. Hopeful optimism, perhaps? *Does Whisky not like La Bouffe? Is that it? I can work with that,* Vaugn pondered.

"Now you're just showing off, Whisky."

Whisky smiled broadly. "I don't normally like other people knowing my business. How about, to counterbalance my discomfort that you have <u>unintentionally</u> caused. . ." Vaugn paused for a moment to add a little comical brevity to his current bullshit. "I don't supposed you'd tell me who your contact in Interpol is, would you?" Vaugn placed his elbows on the bar, laced his fingers together, and casually rested his chin on his hands.

Whisky shook his head; his flabby cheeks wobbled comically. "No' even when Hell freezes over."

Good answer, Vaugn thought. "How about you tell me what the best drink you've got is?"

The old bartender turned to the vast array of whiskeys on display behind him and casually chose a bottle from near the floor; part of Whisky's personal reserve as evident from the old, tatty piece of paper hanging beside it. *He likes his signs, doesn't he? A passive/aggressive method of retaining control?* As he thought this, he began to notice more and more small paper notes dotted around the bar. Vaugn then watched Whisky intently, studying him for any weaknesses, faults to exploit or general tells to his character. As he observed the man, he wished Clair had been with him — she was far better at this than he was. But even he could tell that a great deal of thought and effort had gone into cultivating this persona, from his glasses down to his far-too-intrusive butt-crack reveal whenever he bent down. One hundred percent misdirection, intended to discombobulate others.

"Seen anything strange in here the last few nights?" enquired Vaugn, innocently.

Whisky scoffed at the question. "Clearly it's ya firs' visi'."

"Meaning?"

Whisky smiled, leaned in close and pointed his finger off toward the far-right corner of the warehouse. It was cast in deeper shadow than anywhere else in the bar. Through a small crack between heavy, dark-green curtains, Vaugn could just make out something large and white hanging ominously within the room.

"Righ' now, in tha' corner, there're at leas' eigh' folks biddin' on authentic angel wings."

Before Vaugn could ask any questions, Whisky pointed to one of the private platforms above.

"In tha' room, there are people dressed up as Care Bears 'n' Werebears indulging in the fluffiest, eighties-themed orgy imaginable."

He poured Vaugn a measure of Scotch and smiled at the bewildered expression on Vaugn's face . "See tha' sad-lookin' guy at th' end of th' bar?"

Vaugn blinked in a vain attempt to re-orientate himself, then glanced in the direction Whisky had noted. Sure enough, there was a very sad man sitting alone at the end of the bar. He looked to be somewhere in his mid-thirties, with a handsome face and muscular body. Vaugn noticed the man had a fair amount of elbow room on either side, which seemed odd considering how packed the rest of the bar was.

"What about him?" Vaugn knew he was being baited, but he didn't have many options at this stage.

"How old ya think 'e is?" asked Whisky, playfully.

Vaugn signed quietly. "I don't know. . . thirty-five?"

"Add a couple of zeros to tha'."

Vaugn looked back at Whisky disbelievingly. "He's a vampire or something?"

"Nah, they're in th' basemen'."

Whisky laughed and Vaugn politely joined in, but quickly stopped when he realised Whisky wasn't making a joke. His mind fired off a thousand memories from his childhood. Instances of Pierre aggressively reciting passages from ancient tombs. He and Lukas were frequently "tutored" by their adopted father regarding the best methods of identifying and combatting supernatural entities. For their entire shared childhood, the brothers assumed these lessons were a bizarre byproduct of Pierre's supposed PTSD. Based on snippets of overheard conversations with Pierre's old friends, the boys knew that Pierre had, at some point in the past, seen combat.

"I's th' safes' spo' away from dayligh'. Poin' is, I see a lot o' strange shi'. It's kinda my business."

Whisky began pouring himself and Vaugn a drink. Without missing a beat, Vaugn pulled out a picture of Lukas and Pierre he'd acquired earlier and slid it across the bar.

"Take a look and tell me everything."

Whisky barely registered the picture. "Where should I begin? 'Ow far should I go back? 'N' wha's in i' for me?" Whisky asked.

Again, Vaugn sensed something in Whisky's tone that didn't quite fit the overall persona being presented to him. It offered a peek behind the facade of Whisky. Vaugn surmised that Whisky was a man of great power and respect within many circles. But maybe that power had given him a little too much knowledge. Maybe that knowledge was too much to bare. Maybe, just maybe, Whisky needed help. *If that's the case,* Vaugn thought, *I can use him.*

spartan

/ˈspɑːt(ə)n/

adjective

showing or characterized by austerity or a lack of comfort or luxury.

new spartan

CLAIR I

Surfacing during the early years of the Great Religious Surge, many citizens around the world had begun following an unusual new lifestyle methodology. Practitioners were removing "non-essential" elements from their lives, focusing on "living, rather than owning to enrich ones life." These people commonly referred to themselves as New Spartans. Though not explicitly a religious doctrine, it was certainly most popular in the more extreme corners of organised belief.

Lukas's rectangular room was quintessentially New Spartan. It was entirely devoid of personality or any homeyness. Barren, grey walls dominated the atmosphere within the abode and the absence of a natural light source only served to increase the prison-like feeling of the room. A very simple bed (that didn't look particularly comfortable) was pressed up into the southern-most corner; a bedside table had nothing on it except for a small lamp and a well-read Bible. On the opposite side of the room was a near-derelict wardrobe leaning against the wall, with a chest of draws buttressed up on the other side of it. The only "non-essential" item in Lukas's room was a chess set where a now-abandoned game still remained.

Clair couldn't help but feel that Lukas's room strangely stood out when compared to the rest of the living quarters at the church. All evidence suggested that Pierre, like Vaugn, was a pack rat. Even the church itself was messy and cluttered. She found herself thinking more deeply on the variations between Vaugn, Pierre and Lukas. In some ways it helped inform her more on why Vaugn was the way he was; but it also threw up more questions.

Why did Vaugn leave, and Lukas stay? Why is Lukas so very different from his family? she wondered to herself.

Clair was accustomed to being the one dealing with unpleasant or difficult tasks. Thanks to couples therapy early in their partnership however, that sort of disparity had been generally nipped in the bud, and Vaugn had taken more ownership. But Clair felt off-balance. She was still pissed with Vaugn for his actions during the impromptu Lyon operation — as well as the reprimanding from their Section Chief she had endured whilst they travelled to Paris. Vaugn had made a swift escape to the Straights shortly after they'd arrived. Without having a proper discussion about it, she assumed it was to avoid Lukas's room and the unpleasantness of dealing with Pierre any longer than was necessary. Considering everything that was happening all at once, she begrudgingly dealt with the familial situation. But again, Vaugn not talking to her directly about it, had pissed her off.

Clair caught herself stewing on her emotions. She grit her teeth and told herself off. *Now's not the time for this. Talk to him about it later. Deal with this shit first. Focus.* She took a breath and calmed her mind.

"How long had Lukas been a New Spartan?" She asked aloud to nobody in particular.

"*It was shortly after the suicide boom.*" Came the unmistakeable accent and tone of Pierre Vaugn.

Clair did well not to reveal her surprise. "What was he like before?"

She hadn't even begun truly searching and compiling data when Pierre appeared in the doorway, watching her every move. She remembered Vaugn referring to him as "the Spectre," and right now she totally understood the nickname. Pierre had an uncomfortable aura about him. It didn't feel 'good' to be in his presence.

"*Does it really matter?*" He responded bluntly.

Clair glanced over to him and took an educated guess. "So he was a hoarder, like you? Did he ever explain why he changed so suddenly?"

"*I don't understand why you feel this is necessary.*"

"I'm looking for a motive. Why would Lukas — a devout priest — suddenly kill himself?" Clair replied as she began casually searching the room.

"*Sometimes there are no signs that someone is struggling.*" Said Pierre, commandingly before falling silent.

Clair observed the older Vaugn and swore she could see him thinking through what he'd just said.

"*He was. . . a smart, strong boy. I believe that Lukas had his reasons. In his mind, his actions made sense.*"

"Then help me understand them!

"To look for reason in an action as finite as suicide is dangerous, young lady. You will never understand that persons perspective. Never know what and how they truly felt at the end. Nor is it your right to pry into something so personal. Mourn his death, by all means. But do not question it or his reasons. They are none of your concern."

"You don't care about your son's actions? You. . . you genuinely don't care why this happened? Why? Are you afraid it's somehow your fault, and your pompous ego can't take it?"

Clair looked at the old priest aghast. she studied the sullen, stoic face of Pierre for a moment before realising she wasn't going to get anything more from him. She turned and continued checking the room as a silent tempestuousness settled on the scene.

After an excruciating few minutes, Pierre finally spoke. . .

"I have already checked through his things."

From his tone, Clair knew that he was hoping she would stop her searching. Apparently she had not impressed upon him just how little she cared for him or his options. Clair made sure she spoke with grace and calm when she replied.

"Really? You contaminated potential evidence, even though it's not your right to pry into something so personal?"

She could tell that he had no love of her investigation; it helped her focus. One characteristic she'd picked up working with Vaugn was an acute ability to annoy people and use it to her advantage. She began looking through the barely standing wardrobe. There was something off about it. With a double tap of her thumb and forefinger on her right hand, she silently activated her HUD. Then, with a tap on her right palm, she began recording what she saw; a digital video note to return to and investigate further when Pierre wasn't around. She needed to get rid of the Spectre as soon as possible.

Clair walked over to the bed, sat down and looked up at the old man — who had not moved from the doorway. She knew she wouldn't get a thorough, accurate investigation of the room done with Pierre hanging around, so she shifted gears and began cautiously interrogating the old man.

"Why do you speak in the Old Tongue?"

"I presumed Gabriel would have told you. Doesn't he tell you everything?"

he said, with an undeniable condescending tone.

Wow! He's a fucking dick! Clair thought to herself.

Pierre remained in the doorway with a mocking smile on his face. Clearly he didn't trust her and thought she was too smart for her own good. She hid well from him just how on the nose his question had been. It was a frequent point of frustration and contention between her and Vaugn. He was notoriously bad at sharing anything — at times to his own detriment. After finally meeting his adoptive father, Clair felt she had a better understanding of Vaugn and how he handled "silly things" like emotions and freedom of information.

Clair eventually got up and smiled politely to Pierre. "Would you mind leaving me to this? I have work to do."

Pierre stood firmly on his spot. "I *do mind. This is my house.*"

"Isn't it technically God's house?"

"*Same difference*" Pierre snapped back.

Clair walked up to the old man, brimming with determination. It suddenly dawned on her that the same tricks she had developed to 'guide' Vaugn could possibly work for Pierre as well.

"I asked nicely. I could be more forceful if you'd prefer?"

Pierre replied with a measured, but volatile tone to his voice.

"I *told you, no.*"

Clair smiled politely, tilted her head to one side and waited patiently. They watched each other for what seemed like eons, measuring their opponent's reserve. They both had the same thought: Stubborn asshole. Pierre could see why his son liked this woman. Clair clearly understood why Vaugn hated him.

Finally, seeing no chance of success right now, Pierre turned and left muttering something about preparing for mass. Clair watched him go, closed the door behind him and slid the lock into place.

Clair sat on the bed cross-legged and mentally recounted everything she knew about Lukas, all the odd stories Vaugn had told her from their shared childhood. She played back the last few minutes of footage on her HUD repeatedly, letting the visuals wash over her until she was in a hypnosis-like state of rest.

To anyone watching — and she certainly had the feeling she was being surveilled — it might have looked as though she was simply sitting on a bed, staring blankly at a wardrobe and making odd hand gestures. In reality, Clair's mind was moving rapidly. Her brain ran on visuals. Her eidetic memory — something rarely found in adults — could recall anything she'd seen with vivid clarity, and the HUD only helped to improve that ability. As her mind worked, her body took control and directed her to check the wardrobe again.

"What's wrong?" she asked to nobody. "Too many things." She responded to herself.

She automatically began running her hands around the outer frame of the furniture. Her mind remained focused on analysis and character profiling, while her body conducted its own investigation. A tiny part of Clair could feel how strange it was to be out of control of her body and mind at the same time.

She saw her hands open the doors and rummage along the inside walls, ceiling and floor of the wardrobe. Then, just as her hands reached deep inside, her mind and body discovered very similar things. Her mind focused on the fact that Vaugn and Pierre were instinctively secretive men. She had learned that her partner had twisted that instinct to almost comical levels by cultivating it into an odd passion for secret cubbies and spaces.

Meanwhile, her body had discovered that the wardrobe wasn't sticking out into the room as far as its internal dimensions suggested. This was going to be what she was looking for, and it would answer many questions.

"Hmm . . ."

Clair regained full control of her mind and body. She quickly set about pulling the wardrobe out from its hidden cove. She remained cautious to keep the volume down so as not to draw Pierre's attention. She was sure he was lurking around somewhere. After a brief period of nervously worrying that the wardrobe could fall apart at any moment, Clair found that it was actually more sturdy than it looked. Eventually she wriggling and dragging the wardrobe away from the wall. Clair stood in front of a small but detailed "command room" nestled behind a fake wall. There were professional-grade surveillance photos of buildings and people. Each had a small dossier with what appeared to be code names assigned. Bank accounts and timelines had been painstakingly recorded on paper and systematically applied to the walls.

"Investigative priests, huh?"

There was a small, perfectly organised desk, on which there was a large piece of parchment with some form of Latin inscribed around the edges. The Latin acted as a frame for a highly detailed chemical formula that Clair had never seen before. On the top of the page was written "Chimera". Once again, Clair activated her HUD, recording and painstakingly catalogued everything.

"You were in over your head, weren't you, Lukas?"

tale

/teɪl/

noun

a fictitious or true narrative or story, especially one that is imaginatively recounted

tales from the black moon bar

WHISKY I

Even at a young age, Whisky had learned to adapt to changing tides quickly. He was a survivor and understood the need for appropriate information and weapons to control any situation. Whisky was not a religious or superstitious man, but he believed that anything was possible. He did whatever it took to ensure security and safety for himself and his family. In the early years of the Great Religious Surge, Whisky began researching and collecting artefacts with spiritual or mythical significance. The Codex Gigas — also known as the Devil's Bible — was one such artefact, which many believed carried supernatural powers.

Whisky couldn't deny feeling a certain kinship with the legend behind the Codex Gigas. As the story went, a monk violated his monastic vows and was sentenced to be walled up alive. In an attempt to escape this heinous penalty, the monk promised to create — in a single night — a book that included all human knowledge, designed to celebrate his monastery. By midnight, he accepted that he was doomed. In a last-ditch effort, the monk prayed, not to God but to Lucifer. Offering his soul in return for help, the Devil completed the manuscript.

Legend went that the Codex Gigas was one of the most powerful artefacts in the supernatural world. The only others that were apparently stronger were the first editions of the Grand Grimoire and the Bible. If rumour was to be believed, when all three tomes were brought together, it would grant infinite control over God and the Devil. The Bible and Grand Grimoire had been lost in the winds of time for millennia, though tales of their continued existence popped up from time to time. Only the Codex Gigas's location was known for sure.

It was a long shot, but Whisky was desperate for some form of defence. Cipher's appearance on the scene had royally fucked up the power balance in Paris and destabilised Whisky's position. He'd been grasping for more solid ground ever since. He could only hope the legends about the Codex Gigas were true.

***

Whisky's 'trip' to the Swedish National Library had been a success, but the translation of the Codex Gigas was taking longer than anticipated because of the absolute necessity for secrecy. Delays worried Whisky at the best of times. Cipher's recent activities made him all the more desperate.

Whisky had been somewhat prepared for Vaugn's arrival by Lukas and Elizabeth previously. But he had a policy, to never freely gave out information; that was simply business suicide. The turbulent times he found himself in required intelligence and patience at all times. Even so, he could see the growing frustration on Vaugn's face. He knew that if he hoped to bend the current situation to his favour, he would need new allies. Pissing off Vaugn (if the stories about him were true) would be a major problem. But he buried those fearful, doubting thoughts deep down, leaned on the bar, and continued his tale.

"Ya brotha was a nice kid. A li'le screwed up, bu' nice."

"I'm sure you already know that he's dead." Responded Vaugn flatly.

Whisky nodded sadly. He remembered feeling an almost instantaneous kinship with Lukas when they first met, as if it was nearly impossible not to like him. As the bartender's mind drifted through through and memory, he noticed the grimaced expression on Vaugn's face. Vaugn was clearly expending a massive amount of energy controlling his emotions. It shook Whisky back to the here and now. *This brotha isn' as calcula'ed or controlled as Lukas,* he thought to himself with a slight air on concern.

"I really 'oped 'e'd pull through 'n' survive."

"What, life?" Vaugn questioned.

"I guess you'd call it drug addiction."

There was so much anguish in the Agent's eyes. It was the kind of pain beyond simple, physical injury. Whisky understood immediately. It was regret. Regret for things not said or done. The pain of knowing you would never get another moment with a loved one. The words "drug addition" had also visually stunned the young man.

"You didn' know . . ."

". . . No," replied Vaugn.

"Look . . . I don' think anyone knew all sides of tha' kid. There are people who work on a higher mental level than us. I feel like your brutha was one of 'em."

"Is there anything you can tell me that might be useful?" Vaugn implored.

Whisky obliged with the story of Lukas.

"I'd seen yer brutha abou' th' Straights a bi', bu' 'e kept to 'imself mostly. The odd punch-up 'ere or there as 'e 'elped se'le disputes. But 'im comin' in a place like this in full priest garb? Obviously not what my clientele wan' with their drinks. I'm cer'ain it was all a par' of his plan, though," said Whisky.

Whisky remembered the look on many of his patrons' faces when they first saw Lukas enter the bar. He also firmly remembered the look on Lukas's face too: total determination and fearlessness.

"He was always thinking six moves ahead" laughed Vaugn, sadly.

Whisky couldn't help but find it amusing that both Vaugn brothers had made such an immediate impact on him. They were certainly more accommodating than their troglodyte father. At the same time, each of the Vaugn men was very different to the next. Pierre was archaic and an unapologetic ass; Lukas was the steadfast, gallant hero type.

Gabriel, on the other hand . . . Whisky first thought it was pure anger and determination that defined him, but as they talked, that analysis changed. He saw more pain and fear creeping in. Whisky deduced that Gabriel would do almost anything to avoid pain to those around him. "'e asked a lot' of questions openly tha' people in my bar don' like bein' asked in the best o' circumstances."

"You think he was trying to get someones attention" said Vaugn with certainty.

"The Straigh's is essentially No Man's Land. We make our own rules. In 'ere," Whisky motioned to his surroundings, "I'm th' law. Out' there, on the streets . . . you gotta learn t' play by other rules."

Vaugn was giving him a curious look. He didn't know what it was, but for the briefest of moments, Whisky felt like he had just revealed a deep, embarrassing secret. He had essentially confirmed to a near-stranger that he felt trapped within a prison of his own making. He quickly cleared his throat and continued talking.

"So when a pries' comes in 'n' starts shootin' 'is mouth off about illici' activities . . . 'e's bound to piss off some of th' locals. Pissed 'em off so much, in fact, they nearly bea' th' life ou' of 'im.'"

"What stopped them?"

"Me 'n' Günter 'ere." Whisky said as he pulled a 12-gauge shotgun out from under the bar. Etched into the wooden stock with almost preschool handwriting was the name 'Günter'. From all the scratches and obvious wear and tear marks on Günter, it must have been an old, well-used gun, with a bloody history. The old man smiled, but a deep sadness was becoming more and more apparent.

"If you knew your clients wouldn't like it, why'd you let him persist?"

"'e asked permission. I warned 'im, but 'e said 'e knew what 'e was doin'. I also saw i' as a chance t' ban some o' th' more . . . unsavoury of my clientele."

"So you used him."

One of the biggest reasons Whisky had been able to rise to such well-regarded status within the criminal world was his "steel trap" of a mind. It was a huge blessing and afforded him a method of keeping his secrets un-hackable, which he used as a selling point to his clients. It was also one of his greatest curses. He was never able to escape the mistakes of his past.

"There's no way I'm gonna le' someone die in my bar," Whisky said. He took a swig from the bottle he had served Vaugn and himself with. Vaugn looked at his drink, unsure if it was safe anymore. "After tha', I sat 'im down at the bar, gave 'im a drink, and we star'ed talkin'. 'e told me 'e needed information on drugs in the Straigh's. 'e wanted to know if there was anyfin' new on the streets."

"And?"

Whisky rested his hands on the bar and tried to focus on Vaugn. Exhaustion and alcohol were slowly claiming his mind. "God 'elp me, I told 'im 'bou' Chimera."

Vaugn looked confused. "Chimera?"

"Yeah." Replied Whisky, "Strange fing was, 'e weren't surprised 'bout i' like you. 'e already knew 'bout i'."

"Yeah, but why Chimera? Why'd that particular drug come to mind? There's new shit being tested all the time. What's so special about it?" questioned Vaugn.

The two men sat in silence for a moment. Whisky's eyes kept trying to close. "'coz of 'is casual commen' drops 'bou' missing people, an' suicides."

"They started at the same time, or something?"

". . . yeah. . . . They did." Whispered Whisky.

VAUGN I

Vaugn had no idea about Chimera, but he was beginning to see his brother's plan slowly form. Lukas intended to get the attention of the people involved in Chimera's manufacturing. He wasn't going to street dealers or distributors. He was going for the source. And he was using himself as bait. *Fucking idiot,* thought Vaugn, *That's exactly what I would do.*

Vaugn hated knowing that Lukas was so much smarter than he was. It infuriated him how the pieces were coming together so slowly in his mind. He needed to work through his findings with Clair. She was smarter and thought more like Lukas did. Hopefully they'd be able to jump ahead a few steps. Vaugn got out a small, old notepad and began scribbling down all the details he could.

"Lukas said 'e'd been asked to investigate." said Whisky. "Imagine tha', Religious Detectives . . . Mus' run in the family or somethin', huh?"

"Something like that . . ."

Whisky's words reminded Vaugn of something Pierre had once tried to tell him. He resolved himself to having to speak with his father when he returned to the church.

SOCRATES I

Meanwhile, Socrates slowly made his way around the bar, stealthily manoeuvring himself between patron legs and under stools and sticking to the shadows as much as possible. Occasionally a patron would catch a glance of the husky, but he paid them, their stares and their exclamations no mind.

Socrates prowled around, sniffing people occasionally as he moved. His heightened senses were being bombarded with the sounds and smells of the bar. Apart from the booze and sweat, there was a pungent stench hitting the dog's nose . . . an odd combination of fresh mud and sulphur. He looked around at the bar patrons hoping to see some indication that someone else may have noticed the putrid aroma, but there was none. He sniffed at the air and could tell the earthen sulphur smell was coming from one of the platforms high above the central bar.

The husky cocked his head to the side as he looked up at one of the private levels for a moment. Instinctively a low growl rumbled inside his throat, and his hackles bristled violently before he was aware it was happening. There was something up there the part-wolf didn't like; the emanating smell, the instinctual feeling of dread . . .

STYX I

Sitting on the edge of the highest platform, flanked by two men, Styx watched Vaugn and Whisky below. His demeanour had lightened considerably, verging on cavalier. Despite his general distain for Cipher, Styx always displayed a certain level of proprietary around him. He was far more laid back now, oozing an air of calm and youthful power.

Laying on the floor just next to Styx was a thick dossier with Gabriel Vaugn's name on it. Styx had been reading it keenly, leaving pages slightly disorganised in his excitement. The header pages remained crumpled in his hand.

Gabriel Vaugn. You're quite an interesting fellow, he thought with ever-increasing fascination.

"Shall we do something about him?" asked one of the guards.

"I'll let you know . . .," laughed Styx.

revelations

/rɛvəˈleɪʃ(ə)n/

noun

the divine or supernatural disclosure to humans of something relating to human existence.

revelations

PIERRE I

Three months ago.

It was a densely foggy, starless evening as Pierre made his way towards the Straights Church, situated next to the Black Moon Bar. The thick mist was causing an eerie light show up and down the laneways. This was District Two of the Straights, which had become one of the most popular "garage physicist" locations in the world. As a result, it was a very rich area and constantly teeming with people. It was a combination of the high fashion of Times Square in New York, and the technopolis of Akihabara in Tokyo. Even through the heavy smog, the LED light displays of the big brand retailers and labs burned brightly.

Everywhere Pierre looked, his senses were overloaded with vibrant colour displays, booming music that blended together into a cacophony of indecipherable audio, and the musky smell of hundreds of people milling around. The old priest passed Holo-walls that doubled as speciality lab fronts. They blasted adverts into the world for cybernetic augmentation, fashionable genetic modifications, robotics and more. Pierre hated the simulated 3D that came with Holo-walls. He knew it wasn't real, but always felt instantly sweaty when a simulation touched him. Digital Synaesthesia — a neurological phenomenon in which stimulation of one sense leads to automatic, involuntary experiences in a second sense. It was a particularly common occurrence with the older generations.

Passing the Black Moon Bar's entrance, he couldn't help — not-so-silently — judging the attendees queuing for entrance. Visiting Monseigneur Edwards at the Straights church was not a trip he made often, so he always made the most of it. Riling up bar patrons was one of life's free delights for Pierre. It was one of the excruciatingly rare occasions where he would stop speaking in the Old Tongue. He didn't care that many of his well-placed verbal barbs went unnoticed, it just felt good to deride random people from time to time.

Happily ignoring the occasional return insults being tossed his way by the bar patrons, Pierre approached the church entrance (which, like the bar, had a relatively long cue of people waiting to enter). Excited conversation emanating from the side alley that physically separated the bar and the church drew Pierre's attention. Ever the nosey neighbour, he instinctively began listening in on the conversation. Automatically he repositioned himself into the limited shadow and away from the glare of the Black Moon Bar's lights. In many ways, secrets were Pierre's stock-in-trade. To him, this little scene teased that it might be worth something. The source of the enthusiastic conversation was a pallid fellow following another, far more dapperly dressed gentleman out of the bar via a private entrance.

Even with the low light source, Pierre noticed the energetic man's eyes were surrounded by deep, dark circles. He couldn't tell (from this distance) if it was eye shadow, or bruising, or signs of malnutrition, but the thick-rimmed, pure white glasses only helped highlight his odd features. The man wore an old baseball cap with "Respect the Nerd!" emblazoned on the front. From his partial-cover viewpoint, Pierre couldn't see the face of the other man.

"—so we're good to go!" exclaimed the man with a very obvious German accent.

CIPHER I

Cipher had very little respect for Felix Sauer, largely because he hated computer technology, but also because he was an insufferable bore. He did, however, have his uses and necessity often made for strange bedfellows.

"And you're having no problems with the incantations?" asked Cipher. "You're getting them perfect, every time?" He continued, not hiding his disbelieving tone.

Cipher looked fixedly down at the lesser man before him. Felix was unable to meet Cipher's gaze. Pathetic, he thought. "There's a fine line between success and failure, Felix. I abhor fuckups and wasting precious time."

As was Cipher's preferred method of psychological torment, he allowed a painfully long, loaded silence to stretch out. But then a sensation crawled its way up his spine and he involuntarily twitched. Driven on reflex, he spun on the spot and glared directly to where Pierre was hiding himself. "Hmm…"

"Should . . . should I get going?" Felix finally enquired, unable to control the quaking in his voice.

Cipher's eyes never left Pierre's shadowy nook. "Don't let me slow you down."

Felix understood he had just been told to fuck off.

PIERRE II

As soon as Cipher had turned to face him, Pierre's body reacted as if it was suffocating. But, as a seasoned Soldier of Christ, his training kicked in quickly. He began running Bible verses through his mind. After what felt like many painful moments, he eventually regained control of his faculties. Pierre Vaugn had fought enough battles to know true evil when he saw it, and though he was widely regarded a brave man, he first and foremost considered himself as a smart man. This was not fight he would be able to win alone. He quickly turned and pushed past the cue of parishioners.

Pierre entered what he believed was the worst-looking house of God in all human history. The basic internal structure was present, but none of the traditional, gaudy "set dressing" common in so many churches. It was hard to believe that, in the same city that hosted the beautiful Notre Dame cathedral, was this . . . monstrosity. A veritable Frankenstein's monster of religion, architecture and cheap design.

Instead of carved wood or stone pews, there were fold-out plastic chairs. Instead of a pulpit, there was a stack of milk crates with a loose wooden board on top. The altar was made out of reconstituted wooden pallets. Though it was a church held together with industrial-strength packing tape — quite literally in some areas — there was a somewhat quaint, handmade quality about the building that belied its obvious ugliness. The church was packed to the rafters with people from all walks of life and stature. Along the edges of the nave were additional, raised seating areas; construction scaffolding holding up patchy platforms. Even these more dangerous-looking areas were filled to capacity.

Lighting some altar candles was an old priest who — like everything else in the church — looked harder and more decrepit than was normal, healthy, or safe. Monseigneur Edwards was brutish and — in Pierre's opinion — purpose-built to head the Straights Church and district. Edwards was a patchwork quilt of liver spots, scars and cuts all over his face and hands. He resembled a Russian thug who'd grown old disgracefully and inexplicably found religion.

"Monseigneur Edwards, may I speak with you?"

Pierre walked straight towards the older priest. Some of the parishioners overheard Pierre's unusual speech, but quickly returned to their prayers. Edwards put down the lit candle and uncomfortably turned to face Pierre.

"Don't speak in that tone. It ages me!" The crackling English voice demanded.

"*The fact you're old ages you, Edwards.*" Pierre replied as he looked into the old man's foggy, barely open eyes.

He watched Edwards squint and scowl at him for a moment. Pierre wondered if his old friend realised the comment had been made in jest, no matter how truthful it also happened to be.

"It is good to see you, old friend," said Edwards, as a knowing smile finally revealed itself on his face. They shared a comrade's embrace — a stiff handshake and robust pat on the shoulder.

"*I just wish it was under better circumstances.*"

Pierre and Edwards had been a part of the same brotherhood for over forty years and had quite a reputation within certain circles. They'd even been given a nickname: "the Hell Hunters". Pierre was known by his peers to be an intelligent, if paranoid, fellow. His persistent use of the Old Tongue was the strongest indication of his psychosis. Legend said that speaking the Old Tongue meant others would not understand your words; a religious, audible encryption of sorts that had long been debunked.

"You're still using the Old Tongue?"

"*I see you're not.*"

As they walked towards the rear of the church, Pierre glanced back to the entrance. Standing just outside, barely visible through the flocking churchgoers, he noticed Cipher watching him.

"You're here about the suicides, aren't you?" Edwards asked with a tone of certainty. "I was expecting you sooner. When they reach these levels, the Church always takes notice. Isn't this kind of issue right up your alley? You're getting old too, huh? Letting things slip."

"*Maybe so, but I intend to help. Do you still have fight left in you?*"

tail

/teɪl/

verb

    follow and observe (someone) closely, especially in secret.

hopes and tails

VAUGN I

Vaugn looked down as the husky returned to and brushed up against his leg. He quickly noticed the dog's slightly bared teeth as the canine looked towards the upper platforms. Vaugn followed the dog's glance overhead but couldn't make anything out. He dropped his hand down and scratched Socrates behind the ear. Then he returned his attention back to Whisky.

"Did you find anything out for him?" Vaugn asked as he finally acquired a barstool and was scribbling furiously in his notepad.

"You kiddin'?! I'm Whisky! I know a li'le bi' of everyfin'! Told 'im wot I knew. La Bouffe's backrollin' Chimera somewhere in th' ca'acombs-"

"-Did you say La Bouffe?" Vaugn asked, stopping his mad scribbling as Whisky took a moment to drain his glass.

Of course, Vaugn thought. The decimation of the Strauss crime family over the last few hours meant that La Bouffe was essentially unopposed in Europe. A criminal superpower. But few people knew La Bouffe or his organisation like Vaugn. In fact, now he thought on it, it was strangely suspicious that the showy, cocksure Remy La Bouffe — the dickhead who used to tweet about successful drug deals and murders — was being so secretive about his newly acquired power and wealth. Vaugn made a note of this and told himself to talk with Clair about all this when he next saw her.

"Did you meet with Lukas again?"

"Hell yeah! 'im 'n' Beth were in 'ere all the time!" Responded Whisky as he finished his drink, slammed the glass down and hollered like Santa. Clearly — Vaugn presumed — Whisky loved telling a good tale, and knew that right now he had Vaugn's complete attention.

"Beth who?" asked Vaugn, as frustration began to build.

Right then, Vaugn watched as the colour drained from the bartender's face. Something he'd said had put the fear of God into the otherwise genial Whisky. His eyes darted towards the upper platform, where Styx had been sitting. *Who the fuck is up there?* Vaugn though as he too looked up to the rafters. There were, as before, no signs of life. Vaugn looks back to Whisky, who let out a a deep, stress-relieving exhale.

"Mind if I pop up there? Take a look around?" Vaugn asked as he got to his feet.

Whisky spluttered a little. "Ha! Sorry, i's priva'ely ren'ed."

"By whom?"

"Anonymity is my business, my friend."

"Is it Beth?"

"Na. Beth was Lukas's partner," Whisky explained, quietly.

"Partner how?"

"Sexual" blurted Whisky, wincing as he obviously chastised himself. "Sorry. I'm no' feelin' m'self today."

Whisky was obviously embarrassed. Vaugn couldn't help thinking that it was more akin to a mole attempting an embarrassed look, which resulted in his face contorting in a truly bizarre manner. Followed by a difficult silence.

Finally Vaugn asked, "Well?"

Whisky signed frustratedly. "They'd been t'getha bou' two months. I guess you could say they were serious," replied Whisky.

"What happened to her? Where can I find her?" Vaugn rattled off. "I have a lot of questions for her."

"She's normally in District Seven, near tha' old fabric factory."

Vaugn got off his barstool. In his mind, the story had ended. He had a new lead to run down. Whisky also left his seat. Vaugn wasn't up to date on Straights businesses, but everyone knew District Seven was the bordello district. *So Beth's a prostitute, huh?* thought Vaugn. The notion ran through his mind like wildfire.

"What was Lukas up to?" he asked aloud.

Whisky remained silent as he tidied away the whisky and glasses they'd been using. "Beth would be th' be'er person t' ask."

"How will I know her?" Vaugn demanded.

"She's fuckin' stunnin'!"

Vaugn couldn't help smiling at the statement just as much as Whisky. Their relationship had been born, Vaugn could feel it. He knew, with absolute certainty, they understood each other and there was a fair amount of respect.

"Anything else slightly more descriptive?" he asked, confidently but with more humour than he'd revealed throughout their entire interaction thus far.

"Grea' legs too . . . and ass!" said Whisky, cheerfully. "Although I wouldn' try anyfin'. She's more powerful than you can possibly imagine."

Vaugn stepped back from the bar, smiling. He was re-energised with confidence. Socrates instantly got to his feet and walked through the crowd to the exit. Vaugn watched his canine partner leave and understood. He'd kept his friend waiting in an uncomfortable situation for too long. He'd have to make it up to him somehow later. People quickly began to fill the gap between Vaugn and the bar.

"Keep me updated in if anyone asks questions about Lukas?"

"Gimme ya number."

Vaugn pulled a business card from his pocket and successfully tossed it toward the bar. Some of the nearby bar patrons watched the card fly at Whisky. In their inebriated minds, it was one of the coolest things they'd seen, if for no other reason than the nostalgia of passing a number physically; it was usually just done via HUD. Even Whisky would have admitted it was a neat trick.

Whisky fumbled catching the card and couldn't help giggle childishly at his own failing dexterity. Vaugn turned and headed for the exit. His meeting with Vaugn had given him a renewed feeling of hope, that his little family might—just might—be okay.

"Good luck!" he called to Vaugn.

STYX I

Styx was, once again, sitting at the edge of the highest platform and watching Vaugn and Socrates leave the bar. Standing just behind him was La Bouffe sweating nervously, though even he wasn't entirely sure as to why. Ever since he partnered with Cipher, more and more things were unsettling him. A small part of him wished he had someone to talk honestly with about the things concerning him. What was even more telling to him, was how it was becoming more and more difficult to shake those feelings off.

"Mr La Bouffe, your mistake is getting worse," Styx said mockingly.

From below, La Bouffe faintly heard Whisky's obnoxious accent echo up to the platform. "I'm gonna check on Solomon."

"Enjoy the rest of the evening, Mr La Bouffe. I'm sure Cipher will be in touch very soon." Styx remarked.

La Bouffe gritted his teeth in frustration. Styx's ability to perfectly merge cordiality and threat was uncanny. Styx casually headed for the private exit with a smile on his face.

WHISKY I

Whisky left the bar and made his way to the far corner of the ground floor. There was a screen door with the words Keep Out etched into an old plank of wood over the top. He went through and climbed to the top of a flight of stairs. It was the same stairwell where Cipher had threatened Solomon not too long before. The memory still gave him horrifying chills down his spine as he looked on the children's bedroom door. The door was ever-so-slightly ajar. *The little bugger!* thought Whisky.

"Solomon, I know you're awake," called Whisky.

Solomon mischievously stuck his head out of the bedroom; there was a cheeky grin on his young face.

"Sorry, Papa. Couldn't sleep," he said, earnestly.

"Tha' doesn' give ya license t' sneak into th' bar, though, does i'?" commented Whisky, climbing the last few steps.

"Sorry," Solomon replied quietly whilst doing his best impression of a sorrowful puppy. Whisky knew this routine very well, and yet it still worked. It pulling on Whisky's heartstrings with a power nothing else in the world could manage. Without another word, Whisky pulled his son into a big hug. The memory of Cipher's threat instantly vanished as he squeezed his son tightly in his arms.

"It's okay." The bartender said. "Hey, guess wha'?"

"What?" asked Solomon, attempting to snuggle deeper into Whisky's chest.

Whisky always wanted to tell his son the truth. The only way he felt he could do that was to look him right in the eyes. He found it impossible to lie whilst looking into his son's face. He gently turned Solomon's head to face him.

"I think we're gonna be okay."

"Are you sure?" said Solomon, with great trepidation.

In spite of Solomon never telling his father, Whisky knew that his son hadn't been sleeping properly for weeks. One night, nearly two weeks ago, Whisky had come across a thick note pad tucked behind a loose air vent in the darkest corner of the Black Moon bar. He instantly recognised the handwriting as Solomon's. Solomon had even created a rudimentary encryption for certain notes. Though Whisky was unwilling to break the code, it was fairly clear that Solomon had started to build his own repertoire of contacts. Given the clientele of the Black Moon bar, Whisky proud-fully considered the impressive potential this list could hold, even for such a young boy.

Whisky took a moment to weigh his answer. "Pretty sure."

Solomon understood. Without another word, he turned on his heels and disappeared back into his bedroom.

"Study well, Papa," called Solomon, from behind the closing door.

torment

/ˈtɔːmɛnt/

verb

cause to experience severe mental or physical suffering.

torment

CIPHER I

Cipher wandered casually along the passages underneath Paris, passing cell after cell. Each held a generally willing consumer of Chimera, though they were at varying stages of the drug's effects. He loved walking those "hallowed" paths. It reminded him of how far he had come and — in a morbidly comical way — how many people's lives he'd shaped. The self-aggrandising Cipher couldn't resist likening his current endeavour to his legendary defiance of God. All he was doing was offering choice; free will. His "customers" were perfectly entitled to save or destroy themselves.

As his mind drifted from one "I'm amazing" thought to another, he finally stopped outside the cell of Anamaria. He took a deep breath, consuming the putrid stench of his surroundings. Even for one such as he, it was *almost* more than he could bare. Cipher enjoyed taking tiny moments like this to appreciate the world that surrounded him. In his oddly delusional thought process, he believed it brought him closer to Mankind, and so brought him more understanding and a twisted sense of camaraderie. He looked through the small metal bars in the door.

A pair of blood-soaked palms tore through the gaps, pawing at Cipher's face ferociously. The stumps of Anamaria's hands were poorly wrapped with bandages and grossly splattered with coagulated blood. Cipher moved his face far enough away in time, and a little, childlike giggle escaped his lips. He wasn't shocked or scared; he was happy seeing the fingerless hands reaching out for him so desperately.

"Fuck you!" she screamed.

Cipher had chosen Anamaria Jeunet as somewhat of a guinea pig for Chimera. He was curious what someone who had become addicted to Chimera would do if they were denied more of it, but also forced to remain alive? Anamaria continued to showcase — what Cipher considered — entertaining and innovative results. Anamaria's fingers had been removed recently following one such unique suicide attempt. Cipher watched her through the bars with a grotesque smile on his face.

"Well, you're certainly feisty today!"

His saccharine voice made most people want to throttle him for being so damn cheerful. Such was the case with Anamaria. He had observed that she displayed less suicidal tendencies whenever given the remotest of chances to kill him. *I wonder if revenge cures Chimera,* he thought to himself. *Hmm, I'll test that theory some other time. I have too much to live for.*

"Kill me!" she demanded through the bars.

There was a delight on Cipher's smiling face so few people ever experienced in their lives. The excitement and joy derived from extended application of pain and torment on others.

"Can't do that, I'm afraid. I've gone and grown fond of you, Anamaria."

"Screw you! I just want it to end," cried Anamaria. Her swollen, stumpy hands finally pulled back through the bars. The momentary energy she had expended was gone, replaced by chronic fatigue and deepest depression.

"We already 'screwed,' didn't we, what . . . two months ago? Wow, time sure flies! Care to go again?" joked Cipher, without an ounce of sympathy.

He leaned with his back against the wall opposite Anamaria's cell. The euphoric memory of the degrading things he had persuaded Anamaria to do to, and for him in return for the promise of ending her life . . . It was bliss to his evil, twisted mind. For the briefest of moments he thought, *I am a monster.* But as quickly as the thought had come, it was gone. He returned to his usual feeling of self-satisfaction.

"Would you actually kill me, if I said yes?" asked Anamaria weakly, already knowing the answer.

Cipher genuinely gave the idea a moment's thought before replying. He looked through the bars at the poor woman's degraded face and began laughing. The list of her self-inflicted brutality ran through his mind.

"Sorry" he said with a chuckle. "It's too much fun seeing what new method of suicide you'll attempt next! I've gotta admit, I'm genuinely impressed with your innovation."

Anamaria came right up to the bars. Cipher finally saw her face in all its heinous glory. She had bloodied bandages over her eyes, with crimson oozing down her cheeks. Anamaria's mangled hands lunged out furiously at Cipher again as she screamed.

"Argh!"

As Cipher turned away from Anamaria's flailing palms, he noticed Felix heading his direction. Felix was wearing a white lab coat with safety goggles resting on his forehead, and a face mask hanging around his neck. The pleasure of tormenting Anamaria quickly evaporated as he watched the scientist freeze mid-stride as they locked eyes.

"Oh shit" said Felix instinctively, and just loudly enough that Cipher heard it too.

This fucking guy, thought Cipher.

"Boss, we've got a serio—," began Felix.

"—Don't finish that sentence," interrupted Cipher. "It would be an absolute downer on my otherwise cordial mood."

Felix walked uncomfortably towards Cipher. For Cipher, it was already too late. He knew he wasn't going to like whatever Felix had to say and his mood had changed accordingly. Cipher's moods were always quick to change . . . dangerously so. As Felix moved closer, Cipher thought, *I really fucking hate you.*

Felix finally closed the space between them and stood in front of Cipher, but remained silently fearful, like a child being chastised by a parent. Cipher's face twitched ever-so-slightly as he desperately attempted to retain composure. *Look at his stupid fucking face,* he thought angrily, *I'm gonna enjoy killing you!*

"I have a . . . concern?"

Both Felix, and Cipher knew the attempt to soften the bad news blow had come out pathetically, but he continued regardless. "The technical schematics for Chimera are missing."

A huge vein thumped angrily on Cipher's left temple, and his eyes burned. In spite of the fire erupting from his eyes, his face was perfectly still. When he finally spoke, his tone remained level and controlled. However, pure, unadulterated rage had sprung up inside him. For a moment, Cipher could even hear Anamaria cower away to the furthermost corner of her cell. In recent times, rumours of Cipher bursting into a fiery, violent rage had spread quickly. "New employment opportunities" as Cipher put it, would present themselves soon after these outbursts.

"Why is this the first I've heard of it?" Cipher said through gritted teeth.

"I only just found out myself. There were only three logged entries: myself, Mr La Bouffe, and . . . you."

Cipher watched Felix sheepishly take a step away from him and closed his eyes, likely expecting to never open them again. "I'm hardly going to steal my own formula, am I!"

"So it was Mr La Bouffe!"

Cipher recognised the desperation in Felix's tone. Felix was hoping he could throw anyone else under this particular bus instead of suffering himself. He clasped his hands to his head, as if trying to stop it from exploding. For a few painful moments, he actually started hitting himself, like an ASD individual desperately attempting to stop an over-saturation of sensory information. Felix watched and realised something about his employer: Cipher possessed no emotional filter, suffering sudden psychological outbursts.

But as suddenly as the self-injury had started, it was over. Cipher leaned his head against the Catacomb walls. There was something about the texture of the walls against Cipher's skin that helped to soothe him. "La Bouffe's trying to copy Chimera in Berlin, he doesn't need the original formula." he said, matter-of-factly.

There was a moment's silence, which Felix seemed more than happy to accommodate if it meant he wasn't about to be killed. The Catacombs remained deathly quiet. The history of the tunnels surrounding Felix offered no comfort. No wonder silences seemed so fitting down here. When Cipher spoke again, it was with a certain level of admiration and resignation. "She was right."

"Sorry, who was right?"

"Elizabeth said she caught Lukas snooping around near the labs. He must have had them on him the whole time he was locked up." Cipher remembered. "Eww, where'd he hide them?"

There was an undeniable air of amusement to his comment. He was honestly impressed. Cipher had apparently returned to a more "business-as-usual" mood. "I want you to do me a favour." commanded Cipher.

Felix couldn't help but think those might have been famous last words or something. Cipher was smiling happily again. It was truly a rollercoaster ride, trying to keep up with his mood swings.

"Kill that useless, old fart, Pierre Vaugn. Take the brothers with you, they need to be run out occasionally. It'll do them good," continued Cipher.

"Huh?" asked the scientist, nervous and befuddled.

"It's possible Lukas got the plans to him. Regardless of whether Pierre has them or not, kill him. He and his kin are to be wiped off the face of the Earth. I've grown tired of their irritating buzzing." Cipher monologued. From his tone, Felix could tell that he hated having to explain everything to everyone. Excitedly, Felix ran off. Kill someone and stay alive? Hell yes!

Cipher let out an audible sigh of frustration, as he found himself thinking ancient thoughts. *Perhaps God was right to splinter emotions? His plans always seemed to go pretty smoothly.* "Ugh!" he exclaimed, realising what he was thinking. As he walked further into the Catacombs, he physically shook himself to be free of the horrible thought.

question

/ˈkwɛstʃ(ə)n/

noun

a matter requiring resolution or discussion.

questions

CLAIR I

Clair sat in Lukas's hidden office, holding together her two thumbs and forefingers, framing elements of the room and taking pictures with her HUD. The photos, the documents, everything was being catalogued in the finest detail. This was Clair in her element; minute detail was her forte. And, according to the cataloguing on display in this room, it was Lukas's too.

"This is fascinating," she proclaimed, triumphantly.

As she carefully excavated Lukas's desk, Clair uncovered a small digital camera with a note wrapped around it. She took a picture for her records, then opened the note. It was barely more than a piece of trash with a name written on it: Loki. Clair had expected to see Vaugn's name on the paper. She looked around the room again at the highly detailed and meticulous documentation Lukas had displayed, literally on the walls. Who, she wondered, was Loki? This was undoubtedly an orgy of evidence, designed to point any who found it in a particular direction. Clair remembered Vaugn remarking that Lukas was an expert Chess player.

"You wanted to get your brother's attention. How far past your death have you planned?" she voiced in equal parts excitement and frustration.

At that moment, Clair's left hand started vibrating gently. The sudden exclamation from her hand scared her. She had fallen into one of her typical habits of getting so lost in the details she was recording that she forgot about the world around her.

"Oh shit!" she yelped.

She double-tapped her right thumb and middle finger together, and Vaugn's name popped up into her HUD.

"Vaugn. I was just about to call y—," she began.

Vaugn's voice boomed into her ear with clear excitement and energy, interrupting Clair without any form of apology. "I've got a lead I'm going to need your help with!"

Clair knew her partner well, and from the level of excitement in his voice, she was certain Vaugn would be moving fast in his investigation now. He didn't assess situations. He was more of an impulsive investigator, and it frequently meant he was getting into troublesome situations, which could have easily been avoided if he'd simply taken a moment to consider his movements. *At least Socrates is with him,* she thought.

"Well . . . you aren't going to believe what I found."

"Tell me later. I've picked up a tail," said Vaugn.

Vaugn's cavalier attitude to potentially having a tail immediately concerned Clair. Three people ended up in hospital the last time Vaugn thought he had a tail. Vaugn had to undergo a psychological evaluation. Straight away, Clair reprioritised; she needed to be with Vaugn to ensure nothing got out of control.

"Where shall I meet you?" she asked.

"District Seven at seven."

"Seven at seven. Got it," confirmed Clair.

"I love you," said Vaugn, excitedly.

"I love you t—" Clair began, but the call ended abruptly.

"Please don't blow anything up," Clair pleaded.

VAUGN I

Vaugn was looking straight at the large, dilapidated church next to the Black Moon Bar. Standing far in the distance was Styx, cloaked in shadow — as he always preferred. Socrates bared his teeth and growled, instantly recognising the earthy sulphur smell emanating from the figure. Vaugn trusted Socrates's quick assessment of threats. It had rarely steered them wrong. Socrates was very good at his job.

"Rrrrr!" growled the old husky.

"What's your connection to Lukas Vaugn?" Vaugn called over his shoulder to the unknown person. He wasn't expecting a response, but he wanted this person to know they'd been identified. After the Grenoble fiasco, Vaugn had promised Clair that he'd try to behave— conveniently forgetting the mayhem of Lyon mere hours ago.

As expected, no reply came.

Vaugn and Socrates continued into the church. Many of the parishioners waiting outside looked highly affronted by Socrates's presence. One anonymous comment rang out louder that the others — something about dogs not being welcome in the house of God. Vaugn couldn't help but think if God lived in this church, Christianity was more fucked than he had given it credit for.

Grudgingly, Vaugn stopped Socrates at the door. "Guard the entrance for me, ok buddy? You wouldn't like it in there, anyway."

Socrates huffed to signify he agreed, and it was probably for the best. Vaugn scratched him behind the ears, then turned and disappeared into the church. Socrates moved over to the less crowded side of the doorway, sat and waited. The husky let out a low moan as he tuned out the parishioners and focused again on the shadow of Styx in the distance.

The line of waiting parishioners from the outside of the building stretched through the interior of the church and along the back quarters of the meeting house. Vaugn noticed the train of people were waiting to be served food rations at a ramshackle cafeteria. Vaugn looked up to the ceiling and saw scaffolding holding up a very basic second level. Though it wasn't open to the public right now, a number of kids had snuck up there and made sleeping areas.

Vaugn barged his way through a makeshift security line to officially enter the church. A middle-aged priest watched him, aghast at his bullish behaviour. He wasn't confident enough to confront Vaugn himself, but he did motion to Monseigneur Edwards about the rude gentleman.

"Full house this evening," Vaugn said in wonder.

Vaugn watched Monseigneur Edwards confidently stride over to him; they contemplated each other for a moment. When the ancient Monseigneur finally spoke, it was with such a condescending tone, Vaugn momentarily thought it was Pierre.

"Can I help you at all?"

Vaugn only recognised the voice as not Pierre's. As such, he responded per usual method—he refused to dignify any religious representative with his full attention. Vaugn asked automatically, without looking at Monseigneur Edwards, "Do you know a fellow priest called Lukas?"

Edwards was infamous for not being a "people person" and never had time for stupid questions — it was one of the reasons he and Pierre had gotten on so well in the past. "If you consider a junkie drunkard whore-lover a priest . . .," Edwards replied, emotionlessly.

"I'd trust them more than the classic paedophile stereotype," replied Vaugn.

Edwards' right hand instinctively rose, ready to deliver a painful "reply". Vaugn had heard Pierre mention the ugly rumours that had followed the Monseigneur for many years. Edwards' instinctual response clearly showed that he had never learned how to deal with the accusations well.

The sound of the old Priest's gravelly voice and his battle-hardened demeanour was painfully familiar to Vaugn from his oft-denied childhood. Vaugn watched the Monseigneur's sense of embarrassment disappeared quickly, as he apparently remembered the level of hatred he held for Vaugn. Even as a young child, Edwards never hid the level of distain he had for Pierre's eldest adopted son. The sense of purpose and superiority — only held by those in high positions of religious power — clearly returned. Vaugn felt his anger swelling once more.

"I'm sorry for your loss, Gabriel," said the gruff, old bastard.

Vaugn was furious. *One of their own died, and none of them seemed to fucking care! Not Pierre and not this bastard, at least,* thought Vaugn. "Your concern is . . . touching. Sorry. Poor choice of words. . . . I meant appreciated. Did you see him at all before he died?"

Vaugn could see that questions and sarcasm were exactly what Monseigneur Edwards didn't want. Apparently the priest didn't see why the death of one should require any particular attention.

"The last I saw of that . . . rogue, he was out of his mind and raving about a chimera. He was a lunatic and a fu—," began Edwards. He wasn't able to finish his insult. Vaugn punched the bastard perfectly in the jaw. The sound ricocheted through the church like a monstrous, fleshy bell. Nobody in the congregation cared about the fight. Fights happened frequently at the Straights Church; everyone knew Monseigneur Edwards could handle himself. Some angry dickhead wasn't going to ruin their prayer time.

Monseigneur Edwards hit the ground hard, but quickly looked back up at Vaugn. Vaugn glared down at him, keen to land another blow. Though the punch had knocked the old priest down, it apparently hadn't done any serious damage. If the scars and general damage to the old mans face was to be believed, Monseigneur Edwards been hit harder.

As Vaugn fought to regain his composure, a shiver ran down his spine. Instinctively, he turned and found Styx standing right behind him. There were fresh, bloody scratches on the young man's face that Vaugn knew to be injuries dispensed by Socrates, when the need arose. They stared at each other in silence. The man-child was smiling excitedly, and aggressively at Vaugn. Monseigneur Edwards remained on the floor, looking at the boy with confused fear and anger. Vaugn surveyed Styx, taking in every detail of his appearance.

This was the guy following me? A kid? thought Vaugn.

"That was cool!" exclaimed Styx with youthful exuberance.

"I don't like the clergy," Vaugn said, cautiously.

As Monseigneur Edwards slowly got to his feet, Vaugn's attention snapped back and forth between the two. Edwards never took his eyes off Styx. The man-child's appearance evidently surprised the priest infinitely more than Vaugn's punch. "You . . . You can't be in here!" Edwards commanded. "You are not welcome!"

Styx sneered at the felled Priest. "You honestly think God's present in this . . ." His eyes glanced around the make-shift church before finishing his condescending question. ". . .hovel?"

The timeless man looked back at Vaugn and continued smiling. The shiver that had alerted Vaugn to this boy's presence hadn't abated. Every nerve in his body was tingling with apprehension. "I don't like them either, friend," Styx said, jovially, in his pubescent voice.

"Why have you been following me?" demanded Vaugn, stepping closer to the young man.

"I want to know who you are. What makes you tick."

Vaugn ran through the list of clues and leads...

Lukas' death got a lot of attention. That's not good for business, so maybe Whisky and Pierre were being watched by this guy. He's following me now because I was asking questions. Lukas was asking questions about Chimera, which might be driving users to suicide. But why, and to what ends? Why make a drug that kills your customers? What's the benefit?

"How well did you know Lukas?" Vaugn asked as he felt the familiar surge of excitement as his investigation gained more ground.

The young man smiled uncomfortably. An ominous silence grew between the men for the better part of a minute. Eventually, as the quiet continued, Vaugn began walking away. But in a flash of movement Vaugn didn't even see, Styx grabbed onto his hand and applied a surprising amount of pressure for such a young man.

"If you value your life, I'd suggest dropping all interest in Lukas Vaugn. Just saying!" suggested Styx, laughing quietly to himself.

"Take your hand off me," Vaugn demanded.

Vaugn glanced down at Styx's unusually strong grip. Styx smiled and squeezed his arm more forcefully. Vaugn gritted his teeth against the pain shooting up his arm. He had never felt a grip like it before.

"I just want to know you. Don't you want to know me?" Styx said, in a tone that chilled Vaugn's blood. The pain continued to intensify.

Vaugn couldn't help but let out a small, barely audible whimper of agony. Styx heard the tiny grimace and smiled gleefully. Vaugn grabbed the back of Styx's head with his free hand and gripped it tightly, attempting to gain some leverage on his situation. Styx smiled broadly and applied yet more pressure to Vaugn's hand.

"You're out of your league," whispered the boy.

"Yeah, well I'm also pretty stupid," Vaugn replied.

From seemingly nowhere, water aggressively splashed into Styx's face. Instantly, the young man's skin appeared to melt, as if it were doused in hydrochloric acid. Styx immediately let go of Vaugn and spun around to face Monseigneur Edwards, whose hands were dripping wet.

"Get out!" screamed the old man.

It was the boy's turn to scream in pain. Then, without another word, he fled the church, shoulder-barging his way past entering parishioners, then disappearing into the street. Vaugn watched Monseigneur Edwards, completely confused. Edwards watched Styx flee.

"What the fuck was that?" whispered Vaugn, so the curious congregation wouldn't hear him.

Standing behind Vaugn was Pierre, and he looked more pissed than normal. "*That was the effects of Holy Water,*" Pierre said. Vaugn turned around, still confused. "*It is time we talked,*" commanded Pierre. "*Maybe you'll listen this time.*"

***

Vaugn, Pierre and Edwards were standing in what could best be described as a small conference room somewhere hidden within the church. There was a striking similarity between this room's wall decoration and that of Lukas's hidden office. The walls were papered with pictures, documents, bank details and a timeline of events that reached back over three years.

In the centre of the orgy of information was a large map of the Straights. Pieces of string spider-webbed from pictures to associated locations on the map. It was a very amateur attempt at creating an operational case wall. Vaugn chuckled to himself as he rated the functionality of the wall. There was plenty of information on display but was terribly disorganised, in spite of clear efforts to the contrary.

It took Vaugn an instant to register the wall, and just as quickly as he had surveyed it, he ignored it. He spun on the spot and glared at Pierre and Monseigneur Edwards. Beyond the residual rage of being attacked by a teenager, his everlasting contempt for Pierre — and the bastard's secret keeping — was rising once again. Growing up, Vaugn always felt that Pierre purposefully kept secrets to maintain control of people and situations. This, Vaugn deemed, was more evidence to back up that theory. People were dying, and the old man was still unwilling to relinquish control.

"Explain. Now." Vaugn demanded.

PIERRE I

Pierre looked at Vaugn evenly. He freely admitted to not understanding Gabriel or his thought processes, but found it almost impossible to believe that his son was this stupid. He took a cautious step toward Vaugn. His face still ached slightly from the punch Vaugn delivered earlier and he wasn't keen to receive another.

"Explain. Now." Vaugn demanded.

"I already did," he spat, dismissively. "The day you ran away. Don't you remember?"

Pierre took one more step. He had predicted a religious refresher would probably be required, especially considering how defiant Vaugn was to religion as a child. What he hadn't anticipated was the regurgitation of emotions from that particular day. It had — surprisingly — hurt him when his adopted son left. All he ever tried to do was prepare his wards for the inevitable apocalypse. *How am I supposed to pass my knowledge down to two rambunctious scallywags with any degree of success?* Pierre thought.

"I tried to educate you about what I really was, what I was training you to be. What we are fighting." Pierre's mind kept trying to take him back to that day. As always, he fought against the useless emotions of the past.

"You didn't believe me. The supernatural world is very real, and we are charged with monitoring it and protecting innocents from nefarious acts. There is a form of evil and hatred beyond what you have seen," finished the wizened old man.

"Well I still don't believe you or any of this religious bullshit," Vaugn began as he walked over to the map on the wall for a closer inspection. ". . . But. . .I can't explain what that was out there," he said, pointing back to the church. "Just because I don't believe doesn't mean others don't either. . . it can still be used as a source of power and influence."

Pierre and Monseigneur Edwards looked at each other, discomfort etched into their disgruntled, aged faces. Their profiles held more suspicion and anxiety than seemed necessary for the occasion. With nothing but a look, Pierre could tell that they were sharing the same concerning memory of the day baby Gabriel appeared on the steps of Notre-Dame and entered their lives. The theories and concerns they both had about the young boy were the chief reason Pierre had always kept Vaugn at a distance. It was why Monseigneur Edwards had not spoken with Pierre in years and why the Soldiers of Christ had essentially exiled Pierre from their order.

If their gut feelings about Vaugn's parentage were true, his involvement in their world could be disastrous. But they had very few options. None of which they liked. At least Vaugn was a professional investigator, after a fashion.

"Explain it to me again," Vaugn said, surveying the data.

VAUGN II

The three men sat around a small table in the centre of the room. The priests were sitting quietly, smoking fat, potent cigars. A pile of papers was stacked in front of Vaugn. He had barely finished scanning through the pages when Pierre, obviously frustrated by the ongoing silent treatment and sporadic glaring looks from his wayward son, offered his insight into their investigation.

"We don't know which of them is the cook, but this Cipher character is the true power in charge. We believe La Bouffe was only brought in for finances and connections."

"And Cipher is a demon?" asked Vaugn, as broadmindedly as he could muster. *I can't believe I'm actually following this ridiculous line of inquiry. Bad shit happens because of bad or stupid people. The world's messy enough without throwing supernatural elements into the mix.* The notion of "evil personified" scared Vaugn precisely because of the dastardly deeds he'd witnessed so-called normal people perpetrate. The possibility of pure evil on top of that was terrifying to him.

"Yes, like that Styx punk from earlier," barked Edwards, through a haze of cigar smoke and wounded pride. Edwards had never had time for anyone who had no perception of religious belief. The world worked on more than just cold, hard facts, in his opinion. And he had seen so much evidence to back up his beliefs.

"Where are your pictures in these files?" Vaugn asked, as he glared judgmentally at Pierre. "You're integral to this case's development. What about Lukas? What about his girlfriend?"

Pierre failed to hide his confusion and Vaugn quickly picked up on it. "Your amateur investigation has planted you firmly in this narrative!"

As an investigator, Vaugn didn't work on analysis and examination in the same way someone like Clair did. He worked cases as if they were stories being told. He followed the emotional elements of a case to reveal all the details. He would play out scenes in his mind. Improvise the possible outcomes and, as he put it, "feel out the truth." It was this alternative approach that, when partnered with Clair's methodology, produced unparalleled results.

"Lukas didn't have a girlfriend! He mentioned one or two contacts that he'd made during his investigation. But he didn't have any romantic relations."

Vaugn laughed hollowly, as the two old priests' patience with his mocking tone finally ran out. He knew they believed that, due to their positions, status and age, they were owed great respect and reverence. Vaugn delighted in refusing them these things. "You want to take these guys down, and you don't even know the movements of your own people?!" Vaugn laughed. "So much for investigative priests. You couldn't organise a piss-up at a communion."

He got to his feet slowly. Exhaustion was finally starting to hit him. He'd not slept, eaten or drunk anything of substance in far too long. But there was still so much to do. *Clair's in the same situation. I've no right to complain*, he thought.

"Leave this to me." Vaugn said as he turned and moved for the exit. "Lukas seemed to know what he was doing, sort of. But you two are the definition of inept. Stay the fuck away from this!"

As he passed the two, he looked intensely into their dull, greying eyes. He felt sure that Pierre and Edwards understood his meaning and knew it was best to do as they were told on this occasion. Even a seasoned veteran should know to follow the chain of command.

"Stay away from me. Stay away from this investigation. Maybe these guys will ignore you. I'll sort this out," finished Vaugn suddenly remembering his partner. "Did you see Socrates when you entered the church?" he asked Pierre.

"No." replied Pierre eventually after some consideration.

The pit of Vaugn's stomach fell away. Socrates never wandered off. Vaugn ran to the exit, as worry and panic began to quickly grow. He needed to find his friend. Pierre and Edwards watched him leave in confusion.

"He's always been a shit, hasn't he?" asked Edwards.

PIERRE II

Pierre silently followed Vaugn out. Over the years, stories of Vaugn and Socrates had slowly spread around to the point where even Pierre had heard some of them. People knew it was more than a simple master/pet relationship. They were partners. Friends. A small part of Pierre was concerned for Vaugn's mental wellbeing. He wondered if Gabriel could survive the loss of his brother and best friend so close together? What would happen next?

The questions led to uncomfortable theories and worry in the old man. The genuine fear coming off Vaugn touched Pierre and, or the first time in decades, he felt honest affection and concern for his ward as Vaugn raced out of the church doors into the Straights.

VAUGN III

Vaugn pushed through the parishioners and cast his eyes in every direction. "Socrates?" he shouted. He spotted a tuft of fur and blood on the ground. His mind raced. *How could I be so inconsiderate?!* he thought, chastising himself. "Pup? Where are you?" he said aloud, panic seeping into his voice.

He caught sight of something else on the ground a few paces past the fur. Moving closer, he realised it was one of Socrates's ears. It had been ripped off. Vaugn was trapped in the vice-like grip of dread. "Socrates!" he screamed in vain.

Church patrons commented and took mocking pictures and video with their HUDs. Pierre exited the church toward Vaugn. Vaugn glanced into the shadows to his left and saw two eyes reflecting back at him. From how low they were to the ground, it was clear the husky was laying down.

"Socrates!" exclaimed Vaugn, as he ran to his friend.

Socrates slowly moved out of the shadow towards his partner. Blood had started to clot in his fur where his ear used to be.

"Oh God," whimpered Vaugn, pulling the husky into a strong cuddle.

Slowly, the small crowd of people who had been mocking Vaugn moments ago felt the anguish of the scene. Even Pierre couldn't help but feel sorry for the man and his dog. "You're gonna be okay. You're gonna be fine," whispered Vaugn.

After a moment of consideration, Pierre spoke, purposefully dropping the Old Tongue, "I know where the nearest vet is. I'll take you."

improvise

/ˈɪmprəvʌɪz/

verb

produce or make (something) from whatever is available.

planner vs improviser

LUKAS I

Two months ago.

A dense, musky smoke of cinnamon, calamus, cassia, myrrh and marijuana hung low in the air of a room that looked like a film set bedroom. There was a large four-poster bed situated in the middle of the room with elegant fabric drapes hanging between the posts. The walls had been lined with linens. The ceiling was the only obvious area of the room to show its true form. It was a stained mess of burn marks, various bodily fluids, graffiti and old age.

Lukas and Elizabeth were laying back on the bed, casually passing a lit joint to one another. Lukas had been introduced to this particular blend by Elizabeth. It had a very pleasing citrus note to it that they both enjoyed immensely. She had told him that during the early Seventies, she invested in a small marijuana hydroponics farm on the French/German border that was keeping her well financed. He found that smoking a joint while coming down from Chimera helped stave off the shock factor. They were deep in the throws of metaphysical, drug-addled conversation, considering the suicides associated with Chimera . . .

"The church categorised suicide as a mortal sin because of the allure of Heaven. People weren't happy and were being promised eternal bliss in the afterlife." Elizabeth mused as she took a fresh drag on on the joint. "I can see why they'd want to trade up. People — usually the destitute — were killing themselves in massive numbers. The church had to step in and say their souls would go straight to Hell." Elizabeth finished while passing the joint back to Lukas.

"That's what actually happens? It isn't some kind of religious propaganda?" He asked as he toyed with her luscious, vermilion hair.

"On Earth, as it is in Heaven. Apparently not just words." Replied Elizabeth knowingly.

"Really?" questioned Lukas as he choked slightly on the smoke in his throat. "So why do you think Cipher produced Chimera?"

There was a long, considered silence as Lukas handed the join back to Elizabeth and watched her take a measured drag, mulling over his question.

"They don't tell anyone anything, unless there's no other choice. Or if they lose their shit." Ruminated Elizabeth as she shaped the smoke with quick movements of her tongue. "Secrecy, and no wasted souls were the only two major rules laid down."

"Is he . . . are they trying to swell Hell's numbers, or something?"

"Why?" Questioned Elizabeth.

"Well . . ." began Lukas as a fresh wave of consumed high washed over him, "People say God has a grand plan. Does Lucifer?"

"They're not really the planning type," she replied. "It all seems more improvisational. Besides, what would they need a plan for?"

"I don't know. Trying to destroy Heaven or something?"

Elizabeth couldn't help laughing at the notion. "Ha! Certainly not any more. There'd be no actual benefit from the destruction of Heaven." Elizabeth concentrated for a moment as her high spiked once more. "Lucifer does shit randomly because of boredom. The Wall Street Crash in '29, Heaven's Gate in '97. Fucking with people's lives is purely entertainment."

There was a long silence. Elizabeth pulled Lukas closer to her.

"So if Lucifer doesn't want to get rid of Heaven, why waste no souls? How do souls benefit them?"

Elizabeth contemplated the question for a moment as she took in more smoke, until finally replying. "Continued existence and power."

"So . . . is there anything else out there that could threaten their existence?"

"Not that I'm aware of. Just like there's no benefit to destroying Heaven, there'd be no point for Hell to be destroyed either." Elizabeth looked as if a grand revelation had just occurred to her, " The war of Heaven and Hell is a fabrication of Humanity that just so happens to help both 'sides'."

But the notion of power, continued existence, and threats to those things lingered with Lukas. He felt that he was on to something. *The supposed return of the Son of God, the Devil being involved in claiming more souls. . . They were both events that would sway souls in one direction or the other. Why were both sides making more grand, obvious plays for additional power? Was something threatening them? If so, what could it be? What could be so powerful as to threaten the two titans, and would it be a threat to Mankind as well?*

"Have you ever actually been to Hell?" He asked Elizabeth.

"No. I was converted at the point of death." She replied distantly, before looking at him with an air of concern. "Why?"

Lukas was deep in thought.

"Lukas. What are you thinking?" She asked more forcefully.

It took a few moments before Lukas returned to his senses and realise Elizabeth was asking him a question. "Sorry, what?"

"Why are you asking about Hell?"

"I need to see what happening there."

Lukas felt Elizabeth pull away from him in an instinctual, repulsed manner. As he looked into her face, he saw the fear, the confusion, and the contempt in her expression.

"You're going too far with this!" She spat.

"Actually, I don't think I am. I think there's something much grander happening beyond what we can see. I can't do anything about it without going to either Heaven or Hell — preferably both."

"What the fuck do you think you're going to see?!"

"I think something, or someone is threatening them."

"What if there is? Are you going to stop it? How? And how do you plan on coming back from either place with whatever information you may, or may not find?!"

"I could try to see something about Heaven when I next take Chimera. I don't know if th—"

"—So you've already decided you're going to take it again?! It will drive you to death!" She paused for a moment and bit her lip. "Stop! Can't you just save yourself?!" She pleaded.

Even in his drug addled state, Lukas could hear the begging and pleading mixed in with the fury. He wished he could do as she wanted. . . but it wasn't in his nature. He knew that (to his detriment) he had to help wherever possible.

". . . I save myself by saving others."

There was a long, painful silence between the two of them. They had pulled away from each other.

"So . . . you plan to look in on Heaven and Hell, see what's going on there, pop back, and stop it?"

Another long silence followed. Lukas already knew that Elizabeth wasn't going to like his response. Eventually he swallowed hard, and replied.

"That would be lovely. But I don't think I will be coming back."

". . . fuck . . . I knew you'd say that. . ." she said as all her energy drained out of her.

"Do you have any ideas on how I could get information back here, from the hereafter?"

"No fucking clue. Possession? Fucking seance." She replied angrily.

"Do those actually work?"

"Again, no fucking clue."

Lukas nestled up to Elizabeth once more and took a fresh drag on the joint.

"What about shit going on here?" Elizabeth asked.

"I had a thought about that. . . my brother."

"Your brother?"

"If I was to . . . die . . . under questionable circumstances, he would fuck shit up trying to find out the what, why, where and how. All we'd need to do is point him in the right direction."

"The Vaugn Boys: Defenders of the world, huh?"

Lukas smiled and chuckled slightly. "More like, we don't like to lose. And we're really fucking stubborn."

Elizabeth lent over to the bedside cabinet and stubbed out the last of the joint. "Well, that's a bit of a shitty thing to toss at your brother. 'Hey, your brother killed himself. Oh, and you have to stop Lucifer from wrecking havoc on Paris, and the rest of the world. Good luck!'"

"Fair point. We'll have to set up some things for him. Help where we can." Replied Lukas as the gravity of the undertaking began to hit. "Wow, I'm a fucking terrible brother!"

Elizabeth leaned over and kissed his cheek gently.

"We can't tell him why I'm doing this. He'd want to follow me to the other side. He's never surrendered a fight."

awry

/əˈrʌɪ/

adjective

away from the usual or expected course; amiss.

awry

ELIZABETH I

Elizabeth silently entered the cold, stone room where Cipher was lackadaisically drifting from thought to thought, wandered through the corridors of his mind in pleasant harmony. She watched him as he meditated and was reminded of her first interaction with him, over a century and a half ago. She couldn't help but see many similarities to that time. Cipher had stealthily adapted himself into her town, much like he'd done in Paris. The slowly increasing death toll was the same. Even the use of prostitutes to gather information and victims was a repeat from their time in Cody, Wyoming.

Despite Cypher's fast-changing moods, Elizabeth could see he was still a creature of habit, just like anybody else. Unfortunately, those habits had oftentimes terrible repercussions. Like Lukas. Elizabeth considered Cipher his own worst enemy.

"Was there something you wanted, or do you simply like watching me?" asked Cipher with his current accent.

From his tone, she knew that her mere presence was pissing him off. A small part of her really enjoyed that fact, but her survival instincts kicked in quickly. It was one of the reasons she regarded herself as such a good spy.

"I'm sure you're getting tired of hearing this, but we have a situation," she said confidently.

Cipher let out a very audible sigh of frustration. She could see his lips moving ever-so slightly. He was attempting to calm himself by counting to ten. One. Two. Three . . . He slammed his fists down on the ground and bore more than a passing resemblance to a sulking child throwing a petty tantrum — or to Remy La Bouffe.

"Why is shit fucking up?!" he exclaimed.

Elizabeth didn't look impressed. "You're trusting in humans and getting greedy."

Cipher was known for taking his anger out of whomever was nearby. She had more than a few scars on her body thanks to his fits of rage. But it rarely stopped her. She couldn't resist telling him her honest thoughts. Cipher spun to face her, his fiery rage boiling anew.

"What would you do, then?!" he barked.

Elizabeth shrugged her shoulders, rebelliously. "Quit trying to control everything. Release Chimera into the wild and let the chips fall where they may."

Cipher watched her and carefully considered his reply, trying to control his anger. "What about my opponents? How would you handle them?" he asked.

"Am I your campaign manager now? It's not my job to organise everything for you. You're too much of a control freak to consider something like that, anyway," Elizabeth laughed.

"Then what is your purpose here?" demanded Cipher, his temper flaring again.

". . .I am here to serve," she said, begrudgingly. Elizabeth looked angrily at him; he knew just as well as she did that she had absolutely no choice in that matter. She was a prisoner of Cipher's Will until the end of days. Cipher smiled as that Will was enforced.

"Now . . . what was the situation you were referring to?" he asked.

Elizabeth took a step towards Cipher and grudgingly delivered her report. "Styx may have increased your problems."

Cipher took a deep breath, held it momentarily and then breathed out quickly. He caught a brief glimpse of frustration on her face; it soothed him momentarily. "What's that little shit done now?"

"You wanted to know if Lukas's death would prompt any retaliation, so we were keeping an eye on the old priest. All he did was call someone. Then, a few hours later, a new guy turned up at his doo—" she said.

"—What new guy?" interrupted Cipher.

"Lukas's brother apparently. Gabriel Vaugn. He works for Interpol," replied Elizabeth.

"Interpol. Really?"

"Styx wanted to make sure everything was okay, so he checked on La Bouf—," continued Elizabeth before Cipher interrupted her.

"—Get to the point!"

Elizabeth shrank away from him. She'd seen this monster at his worst and, in spite of her rebellious natural instincts, she knew it was best to keep back and keep moving. "As you wish. Styx confronted this man—"

Before she could finish her sentence, Styx stormed into the room, spouting very imaginative profanity. His eternally breaking, pubescent man-child voice screeched out to nobody in particular. Elizabeth may have been an old-school girl, but her professionalism was timeless. To her, Styx was a perfect representation of how human evolution had gone seriously wrong somewhere. She hated him just as passionately as he did her.

STYX I

Elizabeth and Cipher had made it abundantly clear to him that they hated his voice when he got this agitated. It was torturous, and a firm reminder that, despite Styx's real age, he remained an immature child. Most of the time, Styx enjoyed being underestimated and used it to his advantage. But instances like this made him wish he could be treated like a fellow adult, rather than a child.

It took him a few moments to realise he wasn't alone in the room. Elizabeth was wearing her typical, unimpressed expression. Cipher, on the other hand, looked at the young man with open disapproval.

"Oh," began Styx, reading their judgmental faces. "Hello," he finished, feeling foolish. Styx's face had thankfully stopped melting, but it was still very raw and unequivocally ugly to behold at this moment. His boyish charm had been desecrated and vandalised. A set of fresh claw marks ran down his right cheek — a parting gift from his encounter with Socrates. The cuts were from a single, powerful blow that started just above his right eye and continued all the way down to his jawline. The wound was still bleeding slightly and had left dried streaks down the young man's face.

"Bad day?" asked Cipher, filling his words with as much hate as possible.

"Nah, this is my new look. You like? I call it 'Mauled'," replied Styx, without a hint of fear.

ELIZABETH II

Sarcasm was something Elizabeth had learned early on to never use against Cipher. She couldn't tell if it was that he genuinely found it rude, unfunny or dismissive, or if he simply didn't understand when he was on the receiving end. The point was that it unquestionably pissed him off.

"Are you a fucking amateur?!" screamed Cipher.

Elizabeth may have been an old-school girl, but her professionalism was timeless. To her, Styx was a perfect representation of how human evolution had gone seriously wrong somewhere. She hated him just as passionately as he did her, so seeing the snotty little shit being reprimanded was a welcome pleasure. She always did savour those moments.

STYX II

"I take it you're referring to Gabriel Vaugn?" Styx asked, flatly. Even he knew when to submit to Cipher's tantrums. He cast a dark look towards Elizabeth. "Tattletale," he snapped.

"Don't start that kiddie bullshit!" Cipher snapped. "I want to know why you would purposefully antagonise an Interpol agent?! Why even confront him at all?! Why are you fucking with me?!" screamed Cipher, absolutely losing his shit.

Though a seasoned veteran of nefarious acts, Styx felt instant dread and began checking his surroundings for escape routes, should the worst happen. He glanced over at Elizabeth and saw her doing exactly the same thing. Styx began nervously prodding his wounds gently with his fingertips.

"As I'm sure your. . ." began Styx, before very pointedly coughing, "loyal whore here has already told you, this guy is Lukas Vaugn's brother. I thought it prudent to find out everything I could about him. He has quite a reputation for success and maximum destruction. He's also the guy investigating Remy La Bouffe. Even an idiot could see that guys like him need to be handled head on and quickly. Leave him to build momentum, and he becomes an even greater issue. And so I confronted him directly," finished Styx with confidence.

"The direct approach apparently didn't work out, though, by the looks of your face," snapped Elizabeth.

"If you had shared all the information about the Soldiers of Christ, I wouldn't be in this state!" barked Styx, pointing an accusatory finger at Cipher.

But before Styx had finished his tirade, Cipher cleared the distance between them and was jovially snapping Styx's left arm with a nauseating crack that made even Elizabeth wince.

"Don't forget your place!" commanded Cipher, with unquestionable authority.

Through sheer force of will, Styx resisted screaming out in pain. He remained forever impressed by his feat, while Cipher remained forever annoyed by it. The relationship between Styx and Cipher had never been a good one and was entirely a "business arrangement".

But, over the course of Chimera's operation, Cipher had grown more and more suspicious of the young boy and his motives.

Styx had proven himself highly independent, which had literally never happened before with an Immortal. It was because of this independence that Styx had managed to rise high within the Immortal collective, in spite of his age. It was also the reason Cipher had reached out to the boy in the first place.

***

Immortals had been roaming the Earth since a young female descendant of Adam and Eve was caught defiling the Tree of Life — with the aid of a Cherubim, no less. Though this woman was gifted with immortality, she was cursed by God. Banished from God's light and requiring the lives of others to sustain her eternity. She became a haunted and hunted legend. Drifting aimlessly through the millennia, watching the world evolve and change as she was no longer able to do. Time was not kind to her. Isolation, fear and hatred twisted her soul. She began experimenting.

One such experiment was the creation of her "offspring," which she accomplished by using, on others, the same basic ritual she had performed to gain her own immortality. The results were impressive. She had successfully created new kinsfolk to share the ever-after. A side effect of her experimentation was a shared consciousness, a hive mind, which proved exceedingly helpful in hunting, as well as for the protection of the collective.

All except Styx.

He had successfully kept a secret from his brethren since his "birth," and he defended that secret at any cost. It was this secret that Cipher could sense, though he couldn't quite penetrate it, and this was the reason neither trusted the other.

***

Finally, Cipher let go of Styx. "Well, there's no point in wallowing in your failures." He began walking towards Elizabeth. "We now have to move with increased speed. Elizabeth, would you mind rounding up some new subjects?"

Without a word, Elizabeth exited the room. She was quite happy to leave the scene; she had taken more than enough of Cipher's bullshit for one day.

She left "the boys" to play and disappeared to District Seven. In the short span of time Lukas had been in her life, she had learned one simple fact about herself: she enjoyed the company of strangers. She realised it was one of the reasons why she had continued her side business of prostitution throughout the ages. It was a way for her to take control and let go, all at once. It also reminded her of a time, long since past, when she had friends and a family. Memories she held dearly.

hellhound

/ˈhɛlhaʊnd/

noun

a fiendish person

hellhounds

PIERRE I

Pierre's church was tiny when compared to Notre Dame or even the Straights monstrosity, but there was a huge amount of character, reflective of Pierre's demeanour. It was old, cold and hard. The walls were made of stone so ancient it had witnessed the centuries leading up to the French Revolution without a care. The wooden pews were worn and heavy with the weight of time, faith and the potentially millions of people who had rested upon them. There were ornate, unimposing stained glass windows depicting various elements of the Bible. Attendees would often call Pierre's church "rural" and "lost in time".

There was a barely perceptible aroma of frankincense that had permanently fused itself to the paper of the church bibles. It rarely made itself known these days, but on occasion, it caught Pierre's senses and brought him comfort. If he could smell it, it meant someone had picked up one of the bibles and begun reading it.

***

Pierre was in the middle of a drab, sombre sermon in front of a half-empty church. His voice resonated off the stone walls, adding an extra layer of holy might to his words. He was well aware of his reputation for being "too accusatory and depressing" for the general masses. He enjoyed not having a packed church every day. He considered it a testament to genuine quality of those in his flock. The congregation was a diverse swath of society: young children, hipsters, mothers, fathers and the elderly. Some had put on their Sunday best, while others appeared to have dressed for a night out at the Black Moon Bar, although that particular dichotomy was not likely.

"Puis je vis un nouveau ciel et une nouvelle terre; car le premier ciel et la première terre avaient disparu, et la mer n'était plus . . ." droned Pierre.

But his sermon was suddenly interrupted by the clattering of the church doors as they swung violently on their hinges and burst open.

Pierre casually stopped preaching and looked to the doors beyond the vestibule. Given the theatrics, he assumed it would be Vaugn. But what he saw send his mind into tactical mode instantly. Felix Sauer was standing prominently between the entry arches. Flanking him on one side was a massive hulk of a man. A goon in the classic sense; muscle and bone and brutality etched into every scar of his mug. A mane of dirty, golden yellow hair clung to his face as sweat oozed from his pores profusely. His clothing was strangely regal, with red, yellow, black and white displayed prominently throughout his tough-but-fashionable clothing.

On Felix's other side was an uncomfortably nondescript, relatively slender man. To Pierre, the mans appearance was remarkably average in every regard. Average height, average length, dark hair. His eyes were the only things that stood out about him. Even at nearly the full length of the church, Pierre could see they were overflowing with malice.

The congregation watched in stunned silence. Pierre looked down angrily at the three men. He recognised Felix, but the other two men were a mystery. His instincts told him that he was in danger. From the investigations into Chimera, Pierre had managed to gather quite an impressive profile of Felix Sauer. It was because of this information he completely ignored the man. Pierre's focus was evenly shared between the two accompanying men. He could feel the violence and danger emanating from them, as if he was standing right in front of them.

"Don't let us disturb the performance," said Felix.

A longer-than-was-comfortable silence fell, as the congregation looked back and forth between Felix and Pierre. They had seen Pierre physically and emotionally destroy drunkards and brigands easily and without question on almost a weekly basis, especially when the Straights first opened. It was a mystery to them why he seemed to be holding back on this occasion.

"Please continue," Felix begged, mockingly.

Pierre realised there was no way to prevent the coming confrontation. Finally, he spoke to his flock once more.

"Well, on that peculiar note, I think we shall end the service for today," he said, unable to mask his confusion, anger and mild fear. "God be with you," he finished.

"And also with you," came the reply.

***

After a few uncomfortable minutes, the last of the congregation made their way out of the church. Felix, Menelaus and Agamemnon remained standing near the door, sarcastically wishing the patrons well as they left.

"Thanks for coming."

"Bye-bye."

After making sure that the last of his congregation had safely left his church, Pierre made his way behind the altar and into an antechamber off to the side. *Fuck!* He thought. Considering the strangers' brazen attitude and violent aura, Pierre was certain that trouble would very soon follow. *I need to prepare quickly. I can't let this fight go on for too long,* he coached himself.

As Pierre opened the door, Socrates ran out into the church and began growling at the three men. Socrates's ear had been well bandaged, but a small amount of blood was seeping through the swabs. As he did with Vaugn, Socrates positioned himself as a sentinel, between the threat and his charge. Pierre couldn't help feel an odd combination of concern and pride for the wounded Husky.

"*Don't be stupid, mutt. You're still doped from the drugs. Best to stay out of the way.*" Pierre commanded, even though he knew his command wouldn't be followed.

The three intruders saw the snarling dog before them. Pierre even heard them snicker as Socrates swayed on the spot slightly from the drugs. Menelaus stalked toward Pierre's chambers, while Agamemnon moved to confront the growling husky.

"Hey, pooch!" snarled Agamemnon with a violent grin.

Apparently Socrates needed no further confirmation of the man's intent. He, like Pierre, could sense Agamemnon's bloodlust. Even though they didn't like each other, Socrates couldn't help but protect the old man. The large dog pounced at his target and successfully sunk his fangs into the man's face, with a satisfying crunch.

Agamemnon punched Socrates in the midriff. Socrates let out a yelp of pain as his body flew to one side.

"Fucking mutt!" yelled Agamemnon as blood pouring from the fresh wounds on his face.

Blood was thumping in the old priest's ears like a war drum. He pressed himself up against the wall beside the only entrance to his chambers. Though time had been generally unkind to him between his active combat days and now, the training — and natural feral instincts — had kicked in and seemed keen to show him one last time, that he had fight left. He was fairly confident he could get at least one good surprise attack in before being drawn into a brutal melee battle. He sucked in a deep breath. Time seemed to slow around him, giving him a moment to consider battle tactics.

I don't have any longer range weapons, he thought to himself as he looked at the metal cross in his boney clutches. *Close-quarters combat would be suicide, so that's out. There's the dog too, though I have no idea how useful he's actually going to be.* He swallowed hard. *Gabriel would kill me too, if I let the dog die.* He knew the only logical option for survival was to run. Even then, he needed to first incapacitate — at least — three younger, healthier men if he wanted any chance of getting to safety.

As he finally exhaled, he looked up. *If you're watching, I could use some help,* Pierre prayed as the creaking of the old, wooden floorboards outside his room alerted him that one of the intruders was about to walk through the door. *And so it begins,* Pierre thought pridefully.

The door burst into the room, ripping itself free from the iron hinges that had held it in place for centuries. Menelaus walked confidently across the doorway threshold. "There is no door that can keep m—" Menelaus began to pontificate.

But his monologue was brutally interrupted as Pierre swung the cross — his make-shift holy weapon — with as much power as he could, intending to end this fight before it truly began. The cross landed perfectly in the centre of Menelaus's face, completely caving his nose inward. Blood and sinew burst forth like a grotesque firework from the mouth and impact point.

"*Fuck . . . you!*" The Priest snarled as he saw his target's eyes immediately go bloodshot. There was no doubt in the old man's mind that his victim was, at least temporarily, blinded.

The cross had sunk so far into the hulk's broken face that after a moment of wrestling, Pierre had to abandon retrieving it. Menelaus stumbled backwards into the church again and collided with his advancing brother, howling through the pain and flowing blood.

"Ahhh!"

Pierre had been unaware that the the second of the attackers was so close to his position that, when Agamemnon caught Menelaus mid-collapse and tossed him back through the doorway like a flailing human shield, Pierre was forced to jump backwards as he saw the abrupt redirection of Menelaus' body hurling right back at him. Menelaus fell to the ground between Pierre and Agamemnon fighting to remove the cross from his face, screaming like a wild beast. As Pierre landed from his jump, he immediately saw Agamemnon leap over his compatriot towards him with a flying Superman punch. Pierre was had no way of defending himself as the fist smashed squarely into his face, breaking his nose with a nauseating crack.

As Pierre's head whipped backwards from the force of the punch, he saw Menelaus finally dislodge the cross from his disgusting mug. More blood poured from the wound onto the ground. Menelaus foolishly attempted to reconstruct the bloody, boney mess of his face.

"Cabed by fuckib fath ib!" he blubbered.

Pierre finally hit the floor. *Shit,* he thought hazily looking up into the face of Agamemnon towering over him and cracking his knuckles. Menelaus wiped the blood from his eyes leaving blackish red smears on his cheeks like warpaint.

"Ib godda fuckib destroy you!" he bellowed.

From the sound of Menelaus' speech, Pierre assumed the cross had done some serious damage to his hard and soft palate. A rebellious smile grew on the old man's face.

"You hurt my little brother." Agamemnon whispered with a gravelly voice.

Whack! A brutal groin kick from Agamemnon knocked the wind out of Pierre. He rolled to one side cradling his balls and fighting to regain air. His vision was drifting in and out of focus as waves of pain reverberated through his system. Agamemnon turned his attention to his brother for a moment and assessed the damage caused by the cross.

"You're really messed up, brother. But you can have your revenge."

As his senses slowly returned, Pierre spotted his black cane resting against the wall a short distance away. Yes! He thought triumphantly before chastising himself for not remembering it earlier. He reached out for it hopefully but Agamemnon noticed the movement, laughed and stomped on Pierre's defenceless ankle, shattering it.

"Arrhhhh!" screamed Pierre, as bone fragments pierced through his skin.

A violent growl from behind the brothers momentarily drew their attention away from Pierre. As they foolishly turned to see what it was, Socrates burst into the room, teeth bared, bloodlust in his eyes, and howling like one of his long-forgotten wild wolf descendants. He lunged at Agamemnon, biting hard on the man's thigh and shaking it as violently as possible. Flesh and blood and clothing flew as Socrates embraced his role of the avenger.

Finally Agamemnon managed to shake the dog off. Socrates was pushed into the path of Menelaus, who easily picked him up by the scruff of the neck with his left hand. Socrates hung in the air, still lashing out in all directions with tooth and claw.

This distraction gave Pierre just enough time to reach for his cane. Good dog, he praised silently. Pierre took this opportunity to strike out at Agamemnon with his freshly acquired cane. To anyone else, it would have seemed like a futile effort with no chance of success. But Pierre Vaugn alone knew the true provenance of this particular item. It had been with him for close to sixty years and was his weapon of choice. The thin, black wood of the walking stick smacked into the side of Agamemnon's knee. Menelaus punched Socrates in the chest and laughed maniacally.

"Down motherfucker!" he bellowed.

The cane sliced through Agamemnon's knee like a hot knife through butter.

Pierre fought his way back to a weak standing position, as

Agamemnon collapsed onto his freshly stumped knee. Menelaus looked over and saw his wounded brother prone before the Priest. Pierre went to strike Agamemnon with a fatal head blow. But, just as the deadly attack was about to connect, Menelaus delivered a brutal boot to the side of the old priest's head. The limp frame of the old man was blown towards the doorway once more.

A moment of painful silence fell as Pierre and Socrates reeled from their injuries and tried to move out of the crowded antechamber. Agamemnon grabbed the detached portion of his leg and held it to its former position. Before Pierre's very eyes, the wound began to heal itself. *Fuck,* he thought to himself. *This is not going well at all.*

Menelaus grabbed Pierre with both hands, lifted the broken body up, and held him at arm's length with his powerful grip.

"Whedeber you're ready, brother," he said.

Agamemnon's leg finished re-attaching itself and he shakily got to his feet. He bent over and picked up the bloodied cross Pierre had weaponised earlier, and limped over to his brother and the body being served up to him in some twisted form of tribute.

Agamemnon leaned in close to Pierre's face. The abrasive, chemically odour, mixed with rotten onions that constituted Agamemnon's breath was one Pierre instantly remembered. The memory alone would have been enough to turn his stomach, but to have it blown straight into his olfactory organs was torturous. Apparently the involuntary, repulsed response of Pierre's face entertained the monster before him as a malevolent sneer spread across the face.

"I know who you were back in your heyday. One of the Vatican Spooks. The self-professed, Hell Hounds. 'The Humans monsters fear', am I right? Agamemnon whispered, "It would have been entertaining to fight you then. I wonder if you could have beaten me?"

Agamemnon stepped back a few steps from his prey. "Your attack on my brother was commendable," he continued, "But now you are weak. Now you are old, and the fight has left you."

The man rested his left hand on Pierre's shoulder as if he was doing his best to comfort a friend during a trying time. "This is a cheap victory for me. This is to be a painful death for you. However, you have my professional respect."

Without another word, or hint of warning, Agamemnon swung the cross, as if determined to chop down a thousand-year-old oak tree in one swing. The impact of the cross against Pierre's stomach threw him violently into the main church hall. A trail of blood and spit traced Pierre's movements through the air for a brief moment. Pierre's back smashed into the altar with a bone-crushing strike. Somehow — even Pierre himself wasn't sure how — he managed to catch himself on the edge of the structure before tumbling to the floor. Through the doorway the brothers watched incredulously as Pierre attempted to run away, hobbling for the main entrance of the church. Pierre continued to painfully move towards the church entrance, but could hear behind him — through the high-pitched ringing in his ears — at least one of the brothers already giving chase.

"Oh. Are you leaving?" came a voice from ahead of him.

Sitting perched on the back of the pew nearest the inner vestibule was Felix, smiling at the torture being presented before him. *I almost forgot about the third guy!* Pierre fumed through his pain.

Though he had expected to be caught quickly, the impact of Menelaus's barbaric rear tackle, and the ensuing exclamation of "Gotcha!" was still shocking and jarring. Menelaus and Pierre collided, violently impacting the small stone font at the entrance of the church. Pierre was bleeding profusely from a fresh wound to his head as the two men both lay on the ground, winded. Neither man had enough energy in the moments following the impact to move, or even make pained noises. All that Pierre could hear through his muffled hearing was the gleeful laughter of Felix nearby. Teetering just above their heads, the stone bowl of the font finally tipped over and spilled its contents. Menelaus's body immediately began to melt away. "Ahh, shit!" he screamed, uncontrollably.

Every fibre of Pierre's being begged him to just lie down and die. *Not yet. Not yet,* he commanded himself. With a grunt and wince of pain, he rolled onto his hands and knees, and slowly clawed his way towards the entrance, but the liquifying mound that was Menelaus lashed out and grabbed his trailing foot.

"Fuck you!" screamed the dissolving fiend.

Socrates pounced on Menelaus's remains and began savaging the demon's face, forcing him to let go of Pierre's leg. Pierre took a second to look at Socrates, as the husky continued ripping Menelaus's face apart.

"Good boy!" he said, not hiding his pride, nor using the Old Tongue.

Grey pointed to Agamemnon, who was using a large, metal candlestick holder as a makeshift crutch. It was empty, but looked vicious, more like a weapon than a symbol of worship.

"Please, kill him!" Grey barked.

disguise

/dɪsˈgʌɪz/

verb

give (someone or oneself) a different appearance in order to conceal one's identity.

sexual disguise

CLAIR I

The Straights of Paris had been unofficially broken up into eight districts a few years earlier. It had occurred in much the same way most large cities produce their own enclaves, such as Little Italy in New York. District Seven was the official bordello section of the Straights; fuelled by sex, drugs and debauchery. This "economy" went a long way toward explaining how D7, as it was colloquially known, had rotted quickly compared to the rest of the Straights. Like a hedonistic rock singer, it had aged poorly; many of the buildings resembled some post-apocalyptic neo-futuristic setting. Over the years, there was a growing rumour that Whisky had been looking into expanding his territory, "The Neutral Zone" as he called it, to include D7. If that was to happen, Whisky would be the largest single territory chief in the Straights, 'protecting' Districts five, six and possibly seven. His response was always the same, "Wouldn' tha' be in'eresting."

Many of the buildings were derelict and plastered with "Condemned" signs on their doors and windows. Nonetheless, the area was teeming with people, all larger than life, brash and bold. It had more life than almost any district of Paris. Cafés were full, prostitutes displayed their wares proudly, and street vendors drew huge crowds with their over-the-top performances. People were moving around the make-shift piazza enthusiastically.

Sitting at a small table outside of a retro 70's, vibrantly coloured café was Vaugn. He was looking across the way at a dilapidated, but very beautiful five-storey building, with ten gorgeous prostitutes and gigolos of varying ethnicities and body types on display. He sipped a cappuccino and absentmindedly played with his HUD using his free hand. Looking at the screen, he saw that he'd unconsciously called Pierre.

"Urgh!" he said, quickly cancelling the call.

"Mind if I join you?" came Clair's voice from over his shoulder.

As she moved around the table, she gave Vaugn a kiss on the forehead.

"Hey. Nearly called Pierre just then," said Vaugn. "I'm worried about Socrates."

Clair sighed as she slid into the seat next to Vaugn. There was a single white rose, an espresso and a chocolate piece waiting for her. She smiled to herself at Vaugn's go-to apology for causing her trouble. She appreciated the thought, though.

"Pierre said he'd take care of him. I know it's hard, but try to trust him. Despite everything, I think Pierre is actually trying. . . in his own way. . ." she said, knowing that her words wouldn't help. "Thank you for the rose, by the way. Given the current circumstances though, I don't think you really need to apologise."

She allowed the silence to linger a little more. Vaugn's stress began to melt away just from her presence. Vaugn watched her take this opportunity to drink her coffee. An uncontrollable, bright, happy glow sparkled in her eyes and shone across her face the instant the coffee touched her lips. It helped him to see her happy. When the cup was drained, she spoke again.

"That . . ." she began, "was a perfect coffee." She let out a satisfied exhale, gently put her coffee cup down and leaned forwards slightly. "You're not going to believe what I found in your brother's room!" she whispered excitedly as the sugar and caffeine comforted her.

At that moment, Vaugn spotted Elizabeth stepping out onto the street from a beautiful but dilapidated, fire-storey building. She began conversing casually with the other men and women whom he presumed were prostitutes. They seemed to tense up upon her arrival. The other men, women, and agender prostitutes were responding to Elizabeth's presence like soldiers springing to attention when a superior officer arrives unexpectedly.

Vaugn leaned forwards as the thrill of the chase began to swell inside him once more. "There she is!" He exclaimed.

Clair turned around to see who this "she" was that he was so excitedly about. Scanning through the fog of early-morning D7 patrons milling around in front of the café, she saw the showcase of sex workers; one female stood out more prominently than the others. Clair was no stranger to the multitude of sexual opportunities the world offered, but the sight of Elizabeth was extraordinarily alluring. It took her a few breaths to regain focus. "Hold on."

Before she could say anything more, Vaugn jumped out of his seat and began walking over to the workers.

"Vaugn, you need to hear me now!" She implored as she too got up and began following him.

"She knows about Lukas!" He called back to her.

Their conversation and Vaugn's bullish antics were quickly gathering attention. Vaugn moved through the milling crowds of people like a juggernaut; nothing seemed capable of stopping him. His eyes remained fixed on Elizabeth as she continued to command the people around her.

Clair was looking from Vaugn to the sex workers and back again when she noticed a figure standing off to the side of the open area. They stood out only in that they were not moving, nor were they awed by their surroundings like so many tourists, and they was purposefully hidden within the shadows. Vaugn pulled further ahead of Clair as she slowed her pace to take a moment to glean any more details from the unusual entity. The figure was almost entirely covered by a vintage World War Two Officer's overcoat. The collar of the heavy woollen coat had been turned up and gathered around the front, covering the lower parts of their face. Pulled down low over their forehead (but still with a slight, fashionable angle to it) was an old, but well-kept black top hat. As a result, Clair was unable to make out any discernible details of the person's features.

The figures head — and thus their point of focus — shifted ever-so slightly to the right; the movement was so minor that anyone would have missed if they had not been watching at that exact moment. But Clair saw it. Clair felt it. She instantly knew that the unidentified person was looking straight at her. As she tried to record every detail to memory, she watched as the figure's left hand slowly rose up to should height. . . and slowly waved at her from side to side. Then, in the blink of an eye, as Clair navigated past more people, the figure was gone. No sign.

Clair watched the shadows for three long seconds before refocusing on Vaugn. This time she was more concerned about their current position. The commotion Vaugn's brutishness was causing was getting everyone's attention and it made Clair feel increasingly unsettled and unsafe. Stretching out, Clair grabbed the trailing tail of Vaugn's coat and yanked him backwards.

"Stop!" she snarled at him as he spun on the spot. "You are going to listen to me! Now!"

ELIZABETH I

The growing commotion coming from deeper within the masses of morning tourists had not escaped Elizabeth's keen senses. She instinctively positioned herself a few paces in front of her workers so that she was between them and any possible threat. After a very short period of time working with Cipher, Elizabeth had realised she needed her own agents, and they needed to love and fear her. Protecting them meant she kept them, no matter what.

Taking a moment to survey the scene before her, Elizabeth completely understood Lukas's comment as she saw Vaugn plough through people towards her, closely followed by Elizabeth. She registered the danger this could cause for everyone. *He's going to confront me here and now! Madness!* she couldn't help thinking, *Doesn't he know how fucked up that would be?*

As a response to this thought, she remembered a piece of advise Lukas had given her. . . "Point him in the right direction. He'll do the rest. He can't help himself."

It was then that Elizabeth noticed Clair looking off to the side. Immediately, Elizabeth looked in the same direction and unfortunately confirmed her worries. She saw Styx standing nestled into the shadows in his overcoat and dumb hat. . . and he was waving at Elizabeth. . .? *What the fuck?* she thought.

Elizabeth turned to her workers, "Get out of the city. I will contact you when it's safe." Without another word, she began walking down the street, away from Vaugn.

As soon as Elizabeth started walking off, every single one of her workers quickly gathered their things from the front of the building and ushered themselves inside. No words were spoken; no looks of concern; they simply did what they were told. Elizabeth knew she needed to guide Vaugn somewhere more discreet; somewhere safer. Whether he would allow that to happen was another matter entirely.

CLAIR II

Clair was still glaring at Vaugn. "Stop and fucking think for one second!" she hissed at him. "Our movements are being watched."

"I know. One of them straight up confronted me." he whispered back.

Clair pulled him into a passionate kiss for a moment. She then turned his head slightly and whispered into his ear, "If that woman knows about Lukas, maybe scaring her off isn't the best move. It is the red-head you were charging at, right?" she asked, already knowing the answer. "Well she's leading us off. So cool your jets. . ."

Holding onto the back of his head, she moved so they were looking into each others eyes, ". . .Otherwise you will really piss me off," she finished.

Vaugn couldn't stifle a smirk. "Dominatrix."

"Shut your mouth and read these," replied Clair as she stuffed her notes into Vaugn's hands. "I'll find us a prostitute."

Clair took a moment to scan through the crowd and quickly found Elizabeth sauntering away. Clair grabbed Vaugn's free hand and began directing him through the masses as she pursued the red-head. As she and Vaugn began to clear the crowd and head deeper into the built up areas of D7, she couldn't help entertain two possibilities: they were either being led into a trap, or they were being led to safety. Given the information in Lukas's files, Clair doubted anything about their current situation was safe. *Vaugn needs answers. If I'm being honest, I too need to know what happening here,* Clair thought.

Clair and Vaugn continued following after Elizabeth, as she skilfully directed the impending confrontation away from prying eyes and ears. Meanwhile, Vaugn quickly read through the notes Clair had distracted him with. He couldn't help but be impressed with the organisation of the hastily-written clues — it was quintessential Clair. In general terms, Vaugn was already privy to this information as much of it was similar to the case wall Pierre and Edwards had showcased him earlier. But the intelligence of Lukas' meticulous, premeditative mine shone through, even in the abbreviated version Clair had provided. There was more focus to the data collection. The unnecessary information had been stripped away. Simply put, it was far more useful than Pierre's work.

"This is—" began Vaugn.

"—Shut up and keep reading." Commanded Clair.

Elizabeth continued to surreptitiously guide Vaugn and Clair away from the busy thoroughfare. Vaugn glanced ahead of him hoping to catch a fresh glimpse of Elizabeth. Just at that moment, she whipped into a side alley on her right and disappeared from sight. Seconds later, Clair lead Vaugn around the same corner and into the alley their target has dodged into.

"You read. I'll talk." Clair demanded, as she finally let go of Vaugn's hand and quickened her pace trying to catch up with the target. Clair ran right up to Elizabeth and rested her hand on the woman's shoulder. "Hey! Don't be so coy." Vaugn heard her say as he continued to speed-read the notes.

ELIZABETH II

Elizabeth was skirting a very difficult line. She needed to get out of thoroughfare quickly, but also look as casual as possible. These two following her, weren't making it any easier. *I just need to lead them round*— she began to think to herself as she felt a hand on her shoulder. Instinct took over. Elizabeth grabbed Clair's hand and twisted it painfully. The hand let out sickening cracks and grating sounds. As she turned to face the owner of the hand, she saw the woman grimacing through the pain of the iron grip as it crushed and twisted.

"Holy shit!" she exclaimed.

"Wait. We just want to . . . talk," Clair began. "Is there perhaps somewhere more private?" she finished, doing her best to mask the agony she was still suffering through.

Elizabeth looked from Clair to Vaugn — who was slowly catching up as he read through a small collection of notes. Despite the measured tone of Clair's voice, Elizabeth could tell from the anger in her eyes and the clenched fist at her side that this woman would be more than willing to fight.

"Don't touch me!" she demanded with as much forced calm as she could muster.

"Please." Clair asked politely.

It was as clear as day that this woman was forcing herself to remain as civil as possible. Elizabeth finally released her hand. "What do you want?"

"You were referred to us. Lukas might have mentioned us?" Clair said, nursing her wounded hand.

Elizabeth looked around suspiciously. She had learned, through painful lessons, that paranoia saved lives. "You must be Clair" she stated, already know for certain. She then continued walking down the alleyway, this time at a more passive, luring pace. Out of the corner of her eye, she saw the couple cast each other cautious glances.

"It's extra for two," called Elizabeth over her shoulder as she walked.

With a percipient glance over her shoulder, Elizabeth caught the ever-so subtle exchange of looks between the two people following her. Evidently they were silently agreeing between themselves that a trap might be about to spring. But there was no sign of hesitation in their movements. They followed on willingly.

Considering the brusqueness with which Vaugn had begun to charge at her in the piazza of D7, Elizabeth surmised that a more dominant approach would be the most effective to use on these two. *Get them to submit,* she told herself.

With her impressive gait and athletic legs, she had managed to travel about halfway down the alleyway, and almost three meters ahead of her quarry in no time at all. Then she turned on the spot and for the first time, properly looked upon her followers. She assumed a hands-on-hips power pose and spread her legs apart a little further than needed. It was just enough to move her short skirt up her thigh suggestively for any who might be watching — a little trick she had learnt over the years that came in handy to ensnare fresh clients.

"How do you want to play this?" she said, using her finely crafted arts of seduction. She highlighted the lilt of her rhythmical, Mexican accent and added a touch more bass to her voice than was normal.

Now, like so many times in the past, she was the effect of her vocal tricks take hold in Vaugn and Clair. A blink-and-you-miss-it smile crept onto her face as she watched them walk towards her cautiously, but with an undeniable eagerness in their eyes. *Things might just go— No! Don't fucking jinx it!* she chastised herself.

CLAIR III

Because of her analytical mind, and staunch belief in order over chaos, people who didn't know her, regularly assumed that Clair's mind was — somehow — incapable of sexual stimulation. This was simply untrue, and Clair freely admitted to having a very open, and active opinion of sex and sexuality. The analytical process of Clair actually made her to be a very successful Dom to Vaugn's Sub. Without words, she was able to read his wants and needs, and understand his pleasure and pain thresholds. She considered herself very good at controlling the sexual pace, tone and safety of most situations. But this was fairly new ground for Clair. Her alpha position was being challenged . . . and it was thrilling to even toy with the idea of finally submitting to someone.

The succubus dominantly presenting herself before them was absolutely tantalising, and Clair found herself having to pointedly focus in the presence of her. She didn't need to look at Vaugn to know that he would be aroused by this woman. *Who wouldn't be? Every single movement, every single gesture is designed to lure someone in with promises of gratification,* she thought. Nothing was wasted. As she drew closer, Clair began to recognise tiny elements of the woman's presentation that suggested a South American heritage. The dark goldenrod skin colouration, the deep, ebony eyes and full lips. But her earrings were what so strongly suggested some form of Mayan connection to Clair. There were two distinct symbols; one above the other. The upper symbol was k'awil (meaning spirit), and the lower symbol was k'in (meaning sun).

Each eager, nervous step forwards was a contest. *Easy Clair, don't get carried away,* she prompted herself whilst remembering they may yet be walking into a trap. As this thought crossed her mind, she came into reach of the statuesque beauty before her. She had no chance to react. Elizabeth's left hand whipped out and grabbed the back of her head. The next thing she knew was that she was being kissed ferociously by sexual desire personified. It was unexpected. It was rough. It was arousing . . . but it was also an act. Clair could sense the duelling emotions. This woman clearly loved and relished sex and her prowess within this field. But Clair could also taste a surprising twinge of discomfort on those luscious lips. Something else was going on here.

VAUGN I

Vaugn stood in the alleyway silently gawping. He was completely stunned. He hadn't seen that coming. *Holy shit. I . . . err . . . I'm scared,* he confessed to himself. Vaugn watched, paralysed, as his fiancé began moving her hands around the waist of Elizabeth. He watched as Elizabeth moved Clair's head to one side with the gentlest of motions and happily whispered something into her ear. Vaugn was still fighting internally to gather his senses again and so couldn't make out what was being whispered. But he did notice the reaction on Clair's face. Whatever hushed tones had been shared, it had excited his partner. Just then Vaugn felt his emotions, heart rate, and control return to normal. His creative mind began considering the narrative. *Wait, why's she putting on such a show?* he pondered.

What's with this song and dance routine? Is she worried we're still being followed? At that thought, Vaugn cautiously considered his surroundings. There were more than enough places from someone to be surveilling from. He then looked back at Elizabeth. With more control returned to hims thinking process, he could see why Lukas would be drawn to this woman. *But what's her story?* he wondered.

ELIZABETH III

Elizabeth finally broke away from Clair and traced her index finger across her lips, savouring the flavour of the kiss that still lingered there. Having seen the spectre that is Styx skulking around the piazza had sent Elizabeth's paranoia into overdrive. *That fucker is getting everywhere,* she thought aggressively as the momentary sanctuary of sexual desire faded away. Her eyes darted around the alleyway, up towards to rooftops of the surround buildings, then back towards the piazza. *Don't say or do anything unless you are completely certain of your surroundings,* she reminded herself. She knew that she would need to continue the act further, though it made her uncomfortable in light of her relationship with Lukas. Elizabeth dug down deep inside and pushed forward, turning to Vaugn.

"Such a frightened little Coati." She said playfully. "You will come with us now, my pet" she commanded with a devilish smile.

Elizabeth never broke eye contact with Vaugn but she felt the tiniest flinch from Clair. She assumed that Clair wasn't entirely sure how she felt about Vaugn being dominated by another person. But the next words from the cute French girl at her side were encouraging.

"Do as she says," Clair stated, adding a sultry tone to her speech pattern for good measure.

Elizabeth watched as Vaugn looked for some sign of reassurance from Clair. Evidently he wasn't a confident sexual partner, and was out of his depth right now. *Different to Lukas,* she noted. She felt terrible as she played up the sex. It made her feel like she was betraying Lukas's memory, and with his brother no less. But this was kind of the plan, and she soldiered on taking a step back from Vaugn and Clair.

"Trust me. You will enjoy it. It'll be a Heavenly experience."

Clair looked at Elizabeth suspiciously. "The Charon of sex."

Greek mythology references at the drop of a hat? Elizabeth thought, *She knows how to play my game. It's a shame we can't really have fun.* "I suppose so . . . But, as with Charon, the fare is steeper than it may appear," she said, cautiously.

Elizabeth finally reached out, grabbed Vaugn's hand and started climbing the emergency fire stairway of the building to her right. "Let us begin," she said, continuing her performance.

moment

/ˈməʊm(ə)nt/

noun

a very brief period of time.

a tender moment II

ELIZABETH I

One month ago; the Black Moon Bar.

Lukas and Elizabeth were sitting on their own on one of the highest platforms in the bar. He was in a bad way, with bruising under his eyes. He had a generally dirty and malnourished air about him. Elizabeth was holding his hand in hers and watching him worriedly.

It had been so long since anybody had treated Elizabeth like a human being. Lukas had seen past her position and her "nature". He had made her feel more normal than ever before. He looked at her and smiled painfully. Elizabeth was certain that she could see the life draining from him as he sat there.

"I wish I could make this all stop." She lamented.

"I know the moves . . . I'm always ahead," he chanted, like a mantra.

"It's killing me to see you like this!" she said.

As the words came out, she could hear their pathetic nature. Complaining about her pain when he clearly had a worse situation felt immoral, and stupid.

"You're already dead," said Lukas. "Can you die, anyway?"

Elizabeth turned away, angry. Lukas gently turned her to face him again. He was smiling contentedly. "You say that I turned you around. Well, you turned me around too. I was an idealistic fool before."

"The priest and the demon. Like a lame first line to a terrible joke. Or a fucked-up Romeo and Juliet." Elizabeth responded.

Lukas pulled Elizabeth into a ferocious hug. His body was failing him, but his spirit was still strong. Even now, he was trying to make her laugh. It was his sense of humour and open heart that made falling in love with him so easy to do.

He kept holding her in the hug, but his face showed concern again. "Do you remember what has to happen now?" he asked.

Elizabeth returned his concern from the other side of the hug. However much pain he was in now, it was going to get so much worse.

"You have to turn me in. You have to tell them that I stole the

Chimera plans," Lukas said. "If you don't, he will know you took them, and then we'll both be dead. Countless people will die because we failed!"

Elizabeth gripped Lukas more tightly. "I don't want to talk about this any more tonight. Can we just pretend this is a cute date between two consenting adults that results in cheesy hand-holding, longing looks and highly enjoyable sex?"

Lukas couldn't help laughing. "Hahaha! I think I can manage that."

predator

/ˈprɛdətə/

noun

a person who ruthlessly exploits others.

predator

VAUGN I

Elizabeth confidently led Vaugn and Clair down a derelict corridor within one of the many dilapidated buildings of D7. From the rotting decoration of the walls, the ornate wood crafting on the doors and windows, and the regal (if old, stained, and moth-eaten) carpets lining the corridor, this building could have once been quite an impressive hotel before The Straights had sprung up. Elizabeth had purchased the building about a year ago and seemingly done nothing with it. She never let others inside, and from the outside, there was nothing about this building that stirred up a desire to adventure within.

A pungent stench hung in the atmosphere, an overpowering combination of stale air, mould, various sources of rot, and the sweet-scented candles someone had lit in a foolhardy attempt to mask the rancid smells. Whatever was in the other rooms on this floor, their own unique stenches soaked through and stung the back of Vaugn's throat. Clair had to work hard not to vomit.

As the party ventured further along the corridor, the couple shared the occasional apprehensive glance an one another. In the time they'd been partnered up, Vaugn had successfully led them into several very dangerous situations. Clair had once asked him why he was so willing to charge blindly into situations and his response was perfectly fitting for him, "If it makes me feel live, then its worth it."

"Do you like to watch?" enquired Elizabeth to neither of them in particular and with no enthusiasm.

"Who says I'd let him watch?" she retorted, humorously. "Besides, you do as I say."

Vaugn meanwhile was lost in his thought process. He could see Clair glancing at him occasionally, but it barely reached him. *What's the deal here?* Vaugn thought, *Why did she emotionally engage with Lukas? Love? Maybe. Maybe she wants to get out of this, and hoped to use Lukas to achieve that end. Is she using us too, then? Probably, but does that really matter? No, not really.*

Vaugn continued to automatically follow Clair and Elizabeth silently as his mind continued to process, and question. *What's her* driving motivation? *Survival. Same as everyone involved in illegal activities. Is she being watched? Very likely. So she's keeping up appearances because she's concerned about her boss finding out about her. But which boss? La Bouffe, or this Cipher guy? And what are the chances they already know about her so-called relationship with Lukas? If she is being followed, and being this paranoid, then I'd say there's an eighty-five percent chance.*

He vacantly watched Elizabeth continue her alluring display, touching Clair's hand, leading them on. She was speaking, but the words were lost to him. *We're clearly being followed, Vaugn continued, and probably by the same group that she's associated with. So her being willing to even go this far suggests. . . what?* There was a brief pause in his processing, *She's running out of options. Why can't she get away on her own? What did Lukas want to help her? What can she get from us? She's taking us somewhere she considers safe.*

As Vaugn walked, he continued reconstructing the narrative in his head. Trying desperately to foresee the events as the 'story' dictated. *The biggest question mark is Cipher. Who are they and why don't I know about them? They're cautious, that's for sure. And they're apparently a force not to be reckoned with. Who can bully La Bouffe? Who can wipe out Strauss so efficiently? Why the religious connection? Why sell a product that drives the user-base to death? How does he benefit? What's his endgame?*

Before he knew it, Elizabeth was standing in front of a dirty, slightly burnt door. There was no indication this room was better, or worst, in any way than the other rooms they had passed to get here, but Vaugn noticed a slight, genuine smile briefly creep onto Elizabeth's face as she touched the doorframe. Their host pulled out a very common-looking keycard, inserted it into the reader and with a loud, abrasive 'beep', the lock on the door released. She pushed the door open, which let out a comically high-pitched squeal that snapped Vaugn out of his thought process and darkly reminded him of the squeals of joy from Clair's nephew and niece. A sweet aroma poured from the room and into the hallway, revitalising the two Interpol agents as it hit them. There were hints of citrus, ginger, cinnamon, and cloves; as if someone inside had been brewing a very strong Masala Chai tea for a few hours. It was delicious and exceedingly welcoming.

Elizabeth walked into the room, dragging Clair by the hand. Vaugn stood in the doorway, taking in the layout of the room. Taking up the majority of the room was an old, king-sized four-poster bed. The room itself was bizarrely decorated. Heavy white linen sheets attached to the walls draped from the ceiling all the way to the floor. The floor had a large, dog-eared rug covering the majority of the floorboards. There was a wardrobe on one of the walls that had probably been rescued from the side of the road after a rain-shower. Minimalist draws were positioned on either side of the bed. The room was fitting for the building they were in, but seemed at odds with Elizabeth herself. Vaugn couldn't help but feel as if the room was a stage. Someone's best attempt at copying what they thought a prostitute's room might look like in The Straights. Elizabeth turned and saw that he hadn't followed them inside. Vaugn looked at her for a moment and saw the frustration growing more visible now.

She's not a very patient one, is she? He thought.

"Come in. I won't bite . . . much." The dominant one proclaimed.

She grabbed Clair again and kissed her passionately. Clair looked stunned and it made Vaugn feel a little better. *At least I'm not the only one out of their depths, apparently,* he mused. Vaugn was bewildered, but also irresistibly turned on by the two beautiful ladies making out in front of him. Elizabeth gazed upon him once more and smiled, caressing Clair's breasts confidently. From the look on Clair's face, Vaugn could tell she still hadn't decided if she enjoyed what was happening or not, but she seemed determined to go with the flow as much as possible.

"Come and play with us." Clair said playfully before whispering, "That's an order."

Vaugn briefly noticed that etched into the door frame was a muddled mess of crudely engraved graffiti and many, many other forms of symbology. But he didn't pay serious attention to them, as he was more concerned with looked down the corridor for signs of trouble. He still had the nagging suspicion this was all a trap. But the corridor was empty. He took a breath, *Let's see where this takes us.* Then finally he crossed into the room.

"That's better," said the supreme beauty. Elizabeth gracefully stepped past Vaugn and slowly shut the door. "Now we can begin."

The door had barely closed when Elizabeth quickly spun Vaugn on the spot and began smacking the living shit out of him. With one enormous punch to his gut, quickly followed by two sharp jabs straight to his face, Vaugn was down, winded and bleeding from his nose and a cut under his right eye. Clair pulled her gun and aimed at the crazed prostitute.

"Calm the fuck down!" Clair snapped.

"Why didn't you come sooner?" Elizabeth demanded.

Vaugn cradled his stomach and gasped as he tried in vain to catch his breath. Tears were streaming down his face from the pain. "Why is everyone in Paris . . . so fucking strong . . . ?" he coughed.

Clair stood in front of Vaugn with her gun still aimed at Elizabeth's head, still trying to understand what had just happened.

"What the fuck are you talking about?" She countered.

"Why didn't you get here sooner?!" Elizabeth growled angrily as spit built up at the corners of her mouth like a rabid dog.

"We got here as soon as we heard!"

"Lukas is dead because of you and your selfish fucking bullshit!" Elizabeth spewed while looming before the couple and pointedly glaring at Vaugn. She then turned her attention to Clair and scowled. "You seem to be the smart one. Did you never fucking ask yourself why Lukas didn't just call his beloved brother for help?!"

The prostitute looked back to Vaugn, who had managed to sit himself onto his knees and was breathing erratically. "Are you really so self-centred you didn't wonder why the only way Lukas could think of contacting you was with his death? He was a fucking priest! You're the guns glazing hero, aren't you?!" There was a brief pause in her tirade. "Fuck you! If it wasn't for his express instructions, I would rip you apart."

Vaugn was unable to meet Elizabeth's burning gaze. He couldn't deny that he had had that thought repeatedly, but he wasn't ready to ask it aloud. A knot of embarrassment lodged in his throat for a moment. Even Elizabeth hadn't anticipated her own volatile actions when the full weight of Lukas's death finally hit her. "He didn't want you to have to deal with Pierre. He thought he could handle this and save you any discomfort . . ."

Elizabeth's rage eventually waned, being consumed by a deep, mournful silence. Vaugn was too ashamed to move. Clair slowly dropped her gun to her side.

"You ran away. You ran away from Pierre and left Lukas all alone. He loved you. He always loved you. And he never once blamed you. He knew better than anyone what a cunt Pierre is. And he was happy you escaped."

The weighty silence from Vaugn and Clair continued.

"After . . . after you joined Interpol, Lukas tried to keep tabs on you. Did you know that? But you didn't exactly make that easy." Elizabeth had to forcibly stop herself to take in a breath. "He managed to get occasional information through Pierre. When the suicides started up, he thought it would be his chance to show you his abilities. And prove to Pierre that he was 'good enough'. Fucking idealistic idiot . . .

"Pierre wasn't listening to him. He couldn't get ahold of you. If you and Pierre had just been able to get over yourselves, Lukas would still be alive."

Another long, painful silence followed.

CLAIR I

Clair began surveying the room. It was unusual. Like a film set, there was plenty of set dressing, but upon closer inspection, small faults in the details emerged. The most notable characteristic of the room Clair saw — or felt, to be more accurate — was that it was ready to be torn down at any moment. The floor-to-ceiling drapes were being held in place with simple pins. The furniture was cheap and dressed to look nicer than it was. This was a tear-down room, designed to disappear in an instant should there be a need. With that point noted, Clair began looking for more clues, and it didn't take her long to understand why the room was so heavily scented. . . it was covering the smell of some burning fluid. This room — and almost certainly the whole building — was rigged to go up in smoke at a moments notice.

She quickly glanced at Vaugn, who was still on his knees and looking sheepishly anywhere that wasn't towards Elizabeth. Returning her attention back to Elizabeth, Clair saw that the once strong woman, had dropped to a seating position on the end of the bed. Elizabeth was attempting to regain her composure with long, deep breaths, but she couldn't stop them from coming out jagged and shaken. Clair understood the exhalation's meaning. Elizabeth had been acting for so long, had grown so tired. She sniffed quietly, suppressing tears.

"You found his room, didn't you?" asked Elizabeth.

Clair nodded. "Yeah . . ."

ELIZABETH I

Elizabeth held out her hand to Vaugn, offering to help get him back to his feet. "Come on. Get up. You're no use to me like this. Don't you like blowing shit up?" She noticed a glint of joy alight in the Interpol agent's eyes as she mentioned blowing things up.

"You have a target in mind?" Vaugn asked with rejuvenated excitement and enthusiasm.

Elizabeth easily pulled Vaugn off his knees to a standing position. As she looked at Lukas's brother, she understood more of Lukas's plan. *Point him in the right direction . . . I see what you meant Lukas,* she thought with a hint of pride. Elizabeth then walked over to Clair.

"The formula . . . You found it?"

"I did, though I don't know what it's for," replied Clair.

"Chimera, right? Whisky mentioned it," Vaugn commented, his mind racing.

"You met Whisky?!" Exclaimed Clair as she turned her attention back to him, "The Master of Neutrality?"

Vaugn gave an unenthusiastic shrug in response. But the look he got back from Clair told him that he needed to elaborate. "Lukas was looking into it," Vaugn responded casually. "That's how these two met, right?" He asked, gesturing to Elizabeth.

"Did you finish reading my notes?" Clair asked expectantly.

Vaugn nodded once. "I think Pierre was stealing Lukas's data for his own investigation. The old man showed me what they — or rather, Lukas had discovered."

"He was a good data miner," Clair stated.

"Apparently so. What bothers me are the differences between Lukas's work and Pierre's version."

"How so?"

"There was far more religious iconography associated with it. Too much for it to simply be coincidence."

"Why does that worry you?" Clair asked pointedly.

"Just because I don't believe in that shit, doesn't mean there isn't power for others. Elizabeth," he began, looking back to her as she quietly sat herself back down on the bed. It dawned on him that much of Lukas's information probably came from her. "Yes or no, is this shit about Heaven real?" he finished.

"I'm sorry, Heaven?" asked Clair confusedly.

Elizabeth took in a deep breath as Clair looked from her to Vaugn and back, trying to understand what was happening. Vaugn's eyes never moved from Elizabeth. Elizabeth eventually exhaled and answered the question.

"You literally experience Heaven."

Clair turned to her, confused. "Like Ayahuasca?"

Elizabeth couldn't help but laugh. "Haha! That exactly what I thought at first. But it's more than that. Ayahuasca tears you down so that you may better understand yourself. Enlightenment. Chimera is. . . how can I put it? It's almost tangible. It doesn't reinvent you, it doesn't give you clearer understanding of yourself, or the universe, or any of that bullshit. It takes what you have, what you are, where you are and . . . I guess . . . allows you to experience your own personal afterlife. Lucifer, La Bouffe and Felix have created a marketable version of the actual Heaven!"

Elizabeth leaned over the bedside cabinet and pulled out a pack of cigarettes from the top drawer. She lit one and took a long, slow drag. Clair laughed at the idea. Vaugn took the theory more seriously.

"La Bouffe is financing the entire production and distribu—," she began to explain.

"—Hang on," Clair butted in, staring at Elizabeth in utter disbelief. "Lucifer?"

VAUGN II

The information Pierre had poured into his mind as a child was becoming clearer. He still didn't believe any of it, but it was forming a bizarre, semi-feasible logic if someone was so inclined to believe. Elizabeth blew an engulfing plume of smoke and watched the cloud gently drift away from her. From the pensive silence emanating from Vaugn, it appeared to her that he might be more open to religious dogma than Clair.

"He's using a warlock called Mr Felix Sauer to merge science and spell-craft. I still don't know why. I don't know the endgame."

"Whoa, warlock? Vaugn, you can't believe this shit!" Clair protested.

"If people are experiencing Heaven, why are they killing themselves?" Vaugn asked with a measured tone. He glanced over to Clair who was wearing an utterly disbelieving expression. *She's losing it,* he thought. He noticed that she had pulled out her notebook and was writing feverishly without looking at the page.

Clair glanced at him desperately, "Explain this to me! You seem to be understanding the gravity of this more than me. I'm worried one, or both of us is losing their mind. . . I need you to explain it."

The history of religion that Pierre had drilled into him and Lukas as children was returning to him so fast it was hurting his brain. "Lucifer's collecting souls," he said in no uncertain terms. "Suicide's still considered a mortal sin. Those souls . . . Lukas's soul is damned to Hell, if you believe that shit. It makes sense in a twisted way. Show people Heaven and they'll want to make it permanent. Would you want to come back to your life here, after seeing Heaven? But why is he collecting souls, and why now?"

"Don't know. Whatever it is, he's keeping it to himself," replied Elizabeth.

There was another long, meaningful silence before, "I need to try it," Vaugn said.

Vaugn's comment stunned both women. Clair was used to him making bold, idiotic moves. But this was on a whole other level. Elizabeth, on the other hand, was suffering a mild form of PTSD. Lukas had said the exact same line — and in almost exactly the same tone.

"Are you insane?" both women asked at the same time.

"Probably, but that's beside the point. I need to understand," he replied, without a hint of fear.

CLAIR II

Clair had seen Vaugn's file, and he had told her of his past, so she was as close to an expert on him as it got. He had lived on the streets for a number of years and gotten embroiled in various criminal activities, not least of which was the drug industry. He had been the unwilling guinea pig for many new recreational drugs entering the streets — he fell into a drug-fuelled hell. But in that terrible crucible, his iron will was forged. It was the catalyst for him joining Interpol. As he had put it, "I will suffer the pain so others don't have to." She stared angrily at her fiancé.

"I've seen the destructive effects of Chimera on Lukas and hundreds of others over the course of mere months. Nobody survives in the end. I'm not convinced of your chances." Elizabeth said flatly.

Clair spun her attention to Elizabeth and moved towards her angrily. "You might have known Lukas. But you don't know Vaugn. You don't have the right to question his chances."

Elizabeth looked us a Clair lazily. "So you think he can pull of a miracle? Is that it?"

The question completely derailed Clair's fiery passion and aggression. "I . . . yes . . . no! . . . Yes! I don't know!"

"I need to understand. I need to see," Vaugn interjected calmly.

Elizabeth reluctantly moved to the bedside table once more and began searching through the top drawer. Meanwhile, Clair grabbed Vaugn and whispered into his ear, "What are you doing?!"

"What I need to. This is the stuff that destroyed Lukas."

Before Clair could comment again, Elizabeth had sidled up to Vaugn, holding a hypodermic needle, just as she had for Lukas on his final trip. Vaugn looked into her face and saw nothing but sorrow. His gaze dropped to her hand, and landed on the needle.

"I'm ready." he said gravely.

"Bullshit." replied both women.

Elizabeth grabbed Vaugn's hand and began crushing it. Vaugn instinctually tried to pull his hand free, but her strength was incredible. With skill and precision, Elizabeth jabbed the needle into a now-exposed vein in Vaugn's arm. It was a technique she had used multiple times on Chimera "test subjects". Before he knew it, Vaugn's heart was pumping Chimera through his system. Elizabeth released his hand and took a few steps back.

Vaugn wiped his thumb over where the needle had penetrated his skin and looked nervously at Clair. Elizabeth was watching him carefully, looking for the first signs of Chimera.

Vaugn looked back at her, confused. "How quickly does it take to start working?"

Elizabeth too was becoming confused. She saw no indication of Chimera taking effect. She studied the empty needle in her hand. "You're not feeling anything?"

"No"

"You're not experiencing anything?!"

Vaugn looked at Clair. "Do I seem different?"

Clair shrugged. "No more than usual."

Elizabeth grabbed Vaugn's head and began inspecting his eyes closely. His pupils were dilated. His skin felt warmer. His heart was thumping like a bass drum in his chest. Chimera was effecting him physically, but it wasn't affecting him psychologically. She had never seen this non-reaction before.

"I don't understand" she said numbly.

"It's not working, is it?" he asked.

"It's working . . . it's just not affecting you."

"What the hell does that mean?" snapped Clair. "Is he going to be ok?"

"I don't know." She replied honestly.

ELIZABETH II

Without any word of warning, Elizabeth pinched Vaugn on the back of his hand. She got the exact response she was expecting: he had clearly felt the pinch, but he seemed to enjoy it. His eyes casually looked from the pinch to Elizabeth. There was a content smile on his face. Elizabeth began to understand the situation.

"What was that?" he asked, happily.

"Well, that's new," she commented to herself than the others.

"What's new?" demanded Clair, continuing to make notes.

Elizabeth felt strangely satisfied. "Chimera's working. But he's more fucked up than you could possibly imagine."

"What does that mean?"

"It means that this man is happiest in conflict. Pain is his pleasure. Chimera shows you exactly what your personal Heaven is. Simply put, this existence is Heaven to him."

Elizabeth's HUD suddenly let out an annoying whistling tone in her ear. She motioned with her fingers and a message popped up on the display. It was from Cipher.

"`I'm coming to get you.`" It read.

Elizabeth's professional facade immediately returned. "You need to leave, now. Cipher's coming." She forcibly began shuffling the couple towards the door. "We just had an enjoyable encounter, so look satisfied. I do have a reputation to uphold," she said, with an air of pride.

Clair put her notebook away and smiled awkwardly. "I think we should go see Pierre again," she said in a determined tone. "And I want to meet Whisky."

Elizabeth opened the door and impatiently held it open, waiting for the couple to exit. "Happy customers, remember. Big smiles and sore balls."

awkward

/ˈɔːkwəd/

adjective

causing or feeling uneasy embarrassment or inconvenience.

awkward

VAUGN I

Vaugn and Clair were hurriedly extricated from Elizabeth's room, right into the path of a man dressed in an exquisitely tailored suit. Even before their bodies collided, the man's offensively pungent, sickeningly sweet stench stung the back of Vaugn's throat. Everyone took an unexpected few steps apart. Vaugn looked into the face of the man before him. There was a devilish smile growing on the man's face.

"Hi there," he said, with more than a hint of a knowing, cheeky tone.

". . . err . . . hi," replied Vaugn.

Clair and Vaugn both recognised the man standing in front of them. This was the man in all the surveillance pictures. The mysterious Cipher. The man behind it all, and — if Elizabeth was speaking the truth, and a person was to believe in such icons — Lucifer themselves. Cipher began walking toward them seemingly without a care in the world. Vaugn grabbed Clair's hand defensively, ready to pull her to safety at a moment's notice.

"I guess I'm next," he said excitedly with his Texan drawl. "Though I do hate sloppy seconds. Still, she is a legendary whore, and legendary seconds are still infinitely more scrumptious than even the best meal. Am I right?"

Vaugn watched as Cipher passed them with a polite smile on his face. This man was not what Vaugn had expected. He appeared too carefree.

"You won't be disappointed," said Vaugn, projecting as much confidence as he could.

Cipher stopped and looked at Vaugn. "Oh, I know! She's a peach, isn't she?"

Elizabeth opened her door and leaned out. "I thought it was you."

"Elizabeth! You look delicious, as always!" Cipher said with hunger in his voice.

Cipher gently grasped Elizabeth's hand. "It's such a wonderful morning, I thought we might have breakfast outside," he said.

Anyone overhearing the conversation would have thought he was simply a young man inviting his date out for a romantic meal, when, in reality, there was malice and threat layered into every word. Cipher smiled politely at Vaugn and Clair, as Elizabeth allowed him to lead her down the corridor.

Vaugn was still staring at Cipher as the two reached the outside door. He reached into his coat and pulled out Lukas's old sunglasses. He had a theory about these glasses and needed to test it. Now seemed to be a perfect opportunity. He stepped toward Cipher and Elizabeth, positioning Clair behind him.

"Did you know Lukas Vaugn?" he asked, aggressively.

Vaugn put on the sunglasses, and his jaw dropped. "Wha—?" He wasn't entirely sure what he'd been expecting. "What the hell?!" whispered Vaugn, as he wrestled to believe what his eyes were telling him.

Clair watched him, quizzically. He took off the glasses, attempting to retain his composure. The Interpol agents stared at Cipher. There was coldness and violent intent barely hidden behind his eyes. Cipher remained silent for a moment, observing the couple.

"He . . . er . . . asked if you knew Lukas Vaugn," Clair said, politely trying to cover Vaugn's momentary stunned state.

Cipher looked at Vaugn, suspicious. "I heard he died," he said, flatly. "Such a shame. They say that death comes in threes. I'd be worried if I were in the Vaugn family."

CLAIR I

Cipher made no attempt to hide the threat. He didn't even try to hide his smile. For the first time in the encounter, Vaugn was scared, a chill running down his spine. Clair looked at her partner, concerned at how he might react to the remark. After taking a moment for his words to sink in, Cipher turned on the spot and continued walking out. Finally, he broke the silence as he left, "Have a good day, you two!"

Vaugn and Clair were left alone in the corridor. She watched Vaugn.

"Are you okay?" she asked.

Ignoring her question, Vaugn slowly walked towards the exit.

"Where are we going?" Clair demanded.

Vaugn remained silent, as Clair attempted to anticipate his next move. Finally, he looked back at her over his shoulder and said what she feared he would. "We have to follow them."

Clair's heart sank. This was one of Vaugn's characteristics she really hated. He was forgetting any form of strategy in favour of raw emotion and going berserk. She was determined to protect him and force him to take a moment. "What about Pierre?!" she exclaimed.

"Cipher is right there! We can end this now!" he barked, turning to properly face her. She noticed that — at some point — he had pulled his gun out.

"Oh yeah? And how do you end Lucifer, dear? With a simple bullet? Is that something Pierre taught you?"

"He's . . . he's . . . I need . . .," stammered Vaugn, trying to find the right words.

"What? What do you need?" she begged. "I want to help, but we need to be smart! We need more information. We need a plan."

Vaugn rubbed the hand holding his gun across his temple in frustration. Clair darted forward and snatched the weapon out of his hand.

"Don't do that! You idiot!" she snapped.

She clutched his gun in her hands and glared at him. Her patience with his bull-headedness, and stupidity had run its course. She was not willing to lose him in the craziness that was surrounding them.

"You're not going to die for this. I'm not going to lose you to stupidity. Be smarter!" she ordered.

decision

/dɪˈsɪʒ(ə)n/

noun

a conclusion or resolution reached after consideration.

a tender moment III

REMY LA BOUFFE I

Maria La Bouffe was stretched out on the recliner chair underneath the window of her Uncle's office. She was energetically flicking through her social news feeds with one hand, while reprogramming her make-up in preparation for her regularly scheduled live feed.

Sitting at his desk, Remy La Bouffe gazed dolefully at his niece. The events of the last few months weighed heavily on him, and he felt entirely out of control. His flesh crawled as the phrase 'out of control' echoed across his mind. *This deal is getting worse the whole time. I was an idiot to rely on someone else. Strauss would have quit given enough time. Maria would be safer. I wouldn't have fucking ulcers. Have I become a loser?* But the internal debating was enough to stun him back to consciousness.

"Maria, I need to speak with you." he said gruffly.

"Well, I'm about to go live for my audience," she replied. "You don't mind, do you?" she asked disingenuously.

For the briefest of moments, Remy remembered a happier time; when he was free to broadcast at his own whims. When he was completely in control of his own life, and those around him. He fondly remembered a time when he was feared and respected. But it seemed so long ago now, and he had no idea how it had happened.

He cast her a dark look, "Actually, I do mind. Turn off your HUD, dear." He swallowed hard before getting the next word off his tongue, "Please."

"I have hundreds of thousands of followers! They're expecting a live broadcast. I have a responsibility. I'm not giving this up." Maria explained while giving her uncle a rebellious glance and continuing to adjust her appearance.

Remy let out a long, deep sigh as he bit his lip in a vein effort to control his frustration. The vague complaints about "terrible lighting" coming from Maria felt like nails on a chalkboard. He scrunched his face up in defiance. He cast her a quick glance, but she was absolutely focused on herself. He slapped his palm down on the desk top as angrily and loudly as he could manage hoping the little outburst would have pulled his niece into line. It only infuriated him further seeing no reaction whatsoever.

"I'm still not sure about this shade" she commented to nobody.

Remy let out another purposefully loud huff of disapproval. He still wasn't getting the reactions — or respect — he deemed were worthy of him. *Fine,* he thought aggressively. *We'll do this the hard way!* He opened the top drawer of his desk and produced from it a small, black remote button. Without a word, he pressed it and watched for the reaction on his niece's face.

Maria felt a shock of pain across her eyes and ricochet into her skull. A static shock reverberated through her HUD and stung her brain. As she massaged her forehead, she glanced over to La Bouffe, who doing the same thing.

"What the hell was that?" she demanded in a tone that reminded Remy of himself at the same age. "Why isn't my HUD working?"

Remy let out one more woefully sign, "EMP. We need to talk. And it cannot involve anyone but us."

"You're really weird, Remy . . ." Maria stated as she swung her legs off the recliner to properly face her Uncle. "Fine! What's so important?"

As he looked at his Niece in this moment, he was struck with combatting emotions. There was so much about her that had clearly been inspired by him, and he felt an enormous amount of pride for that. But, at the same time, he saw so much of himself in her that he couldn't help feel a strange sense of guilt. *Have I fucked up your life?* he considered before answering his own question. *No, everything you've done and become has been your choice. whatever happens in the future isn't my fault,* he rationalised.

"You have a choice to make," he began, making sure to use the most simple language he could. "Ignorance is bliss. Knowledge is power. Which do you choose?"

Maria looked at her Uncle with a disbelieving smirk on her face. "Since when did you give anyone a choice?"

Remy remained calm and controlled as he fine tuned his question for her. "Bliss or Power? You can't have both. I don't want you to know the information I need you to know. But you need to know the information I don't want to tell you."

"What the fuck does that mean?!" She blurted out with a cackle.

"If I don't tell you everything, I'm worried you won't survive. If I do tell you, I'm worried you won't survive."

Maria shuffled forwards on the seat to get a little closer to her uncle. She was still massaging her forehead. Apparently she wasn't used to having the HUD turned off remotely, if at all. The odd combination of pained look in her eyes, and humorous confusion on her face spoke volumes to Remy.

"What are you talking about?" begged Maria with a growing sense of fear and excitement in her voice.

Remy finally got out of his chair and walked over to his niece. Groaning, he knelt down in front of her, gentle clasped her hands in his and looked her right in the eyes. A moment of quiet fell between the two La Bouffe's. Remy was not one to show any form of tenderness like this and it shocked him, just as it did her.

"I'm not going to make this decision for you. You probably wouldn't let me anyway." the elder La Bouffe began. "Whatever you choose, your life will almost certainly be in danger. So choose. . . But know that it is your choice. So I ask you again, bliss, or power?"

Maria considered her uncle's words for a moment in silence. She leaned back in the chair and stared at the ceiling. La Bouffe smothered his face with his hands and forced himself to breath slowly and deeply. After a moment he took a seat next to Maria. Neither knew just how long they remained silent. Neither moved for what felt like an age. Eventually, Maria sighed loudly and pulled herself back into a seated position.

"Well . . ." she said, getting up and walking towards La Bouffe's desk. She ran her fingers gently over the edge of the wood surface. She surveyed the office around her. Then she looked back at Remy. La Bouffe looked up into the pretty face of his niece. He saw her innocence leaving her eyes before she even spoke. He knew her answer before she said the words.

"I wouldn't be a La Bouffe if I didn't take the power, would I?" she said, a growing smile on her face.

La Bouffe couldn't resist smiling also. He wasn't willing to make the decision for her, but that didn't mean he didn't have a preference or wish. ". . .Good girl."

"Tell me everything. How did you lose power?" Maria asked keenly.

Remy didn't answer straight away because he was going to tell her the truth. And the truth was unbelievable. Eventually he replied, "I made a deal with the Devil."

burden

/ˈbəːd(ə)n/

adjective

the main responsibility for achieving a specified aim or task.

burden

LUKAS I

One week ago; the Black Moon Bar.

"Do you understand what I'm asking you, Whisky?" Lukas asked solemnly, already knowing the bartender was painfully aware of just how dangerous the waters he planned to swim in were.

From Whisky's increasingly tired appearance over the last few months, Lukas fully believed that things were not going well for the barkeep. Elizabeth sat by Lukas's side, holding his hand and studying every age line, scar, and imperfection of the skin. As Lukas cast her a brief glance, he recognised the look on her face; it was the same expression he had undoubtedly worn a thousands times since he had admitted his plan to Elizabeth. They were taking great pains to remember as much detail about each other as they could, knowing that a dreadful clock was ticking down on their time together. Lukas looked back at Whisky meaningfully.

"Do you 'ave any idea 'o ya' really dealing with?" Whisky laughed humourlessly as he wearily leaned against the bar looking at the young priest with the practiced assertion of his many years.

"I do," interjected Elizabeth, "Intimately."

The rest of the Black Moon Bar was its typical busy, loud self. In spite of the live band — one Lukas hadn't bothered catching the name of — that was playing some. . . interesting. . . original pieces, the throngs of bar patrons seemed to be heavily invested in the music, and frequently joined in on the chorus. Lukas took a moment to calmly consider his surroundings, taking in as many of the faces of the patrons as he could. *At least the band is offering suitable cover for us,* he mused. From his brief assessment of the members of the audience, there didn't seem to be any known spies.

Profiles on the apparently limited "staff" for the Chimera labs and security had been one of the first pieces of information he and Elizabeth had gathered. It was a non-negotiable point Elizabeth had made right at the beginning of their relationship. She had demanded that he discover, and memorise the names and faces of all the people directly under Cipher's command associated with Chimera. Almost immediately, Lukas understood why it had been such a priority.

Cipher seemed to have everyone following everyone else.

Lukas reached over the bar and rested his hand reassuringly on Whisky's shoulder. He looked sincerely at the old bartender and strangely couldn't remember a time when Whisky had not been a part of his life. They had only known each other a short time, but it felt like eons.

"Think about Solomon. You can't keep doing this to him, or yourself."

Whisky knew the severity of their collective situation, but his fear had morphed into a soft anger. He glowered at Elizabeth. "'ave you told 'im what this stuff does?"

"Of course!" she replied with more than a hint of frustrated agreement.

Lukas put his arm around Elizabeth but kept his eyes locked on Whisky. He had thought Whisky was strong willed enough to stay the course, but his recent actions had planted doubts in the young priest's mind. With that thought, he suddenly realised that he'd not acted like a traditional priest in weeks. Perhaps it was time for Lukas the priest to reemerge — even if just for a moment.

"You regret your involvement in Chimera. I understand that. But if you want to 'save yourself', then you've got to work with me." he said emulating the confident speech intonation of his father for a moment.

There passed a long, heavy moment of quiet between the three conspirators, each weighing their position against the clear and present danger. They had so much potential happiness to gain from their rebellion, but the threat was very real and absolutely ferocious. They all took big swigs of their drinks as a way of washing their negativity away, even if only for a moment.

"I can't do it alone," Lukas finally admitted aloud.

WHISKY I

Whisky crossed his arms over his chest, worried. He had a moment of pure clarity. He could see their next actions and how they would ripple into the future. He could see exactly how everything was going to happen — their complete demise. Then, like a bolt of lightning, images of Solomon and Alex flashed into his mind and blew away all despondency.

"Fine! I'll arrange the meeting with Cipher."

CIPHER I

A day later; District Seven.

The piazza had been converted into a large Makers Market for the long weekend. It had been quite the spectacle on the Friday, and Saturday night. But this being the final day of official trade, some of the stalls had already packed up and left, others were still in the process of tearing down their spots. Apparently the half-dismantled state of the market wasn't enough to dissuade potential customers. People were still buzzing this way and that, being attracted by the multitude of varying vendors who were still willing to trade.

Standing around the very beautiful, but dilapidated, five-storey building were men and women displaying themselves, including Elizabeth. Evidently Elizabeth had made some kind of deal with a few of the temporary traders because there was far more pomp, circumstance and overall flair to the presentation of the human merchandise. A male and female couple were decked out in the most unusual outfits as they danced their hypnotic, alluring routine. Occasionally they would showcase their clothing, then point over to one of the nearby vendors and offer gracious applause. Another was parading from one side of the building entrance to the other making a show out of supplying sample tasters of some kind of home-brewed alcohol to the near-mesmerised crowd before the building.

Watching them carefully was Lukas, sitting at a table outside a classic café. In a bizarre twist of fate, Lukas was sitting in exactly the same spot Gabriel would occupy a month later. He saw Elizabeth standing to one side of the building, largely keeping out of the the main presentation area. Even she was displaying a new product. A simple-looking, chic, indigo-coloured dress. But every time Elizabeth moved, the colour rippled across her whole body. The fabric refused to move. Lukas watched her move gracefully to the music that was playing in the piazza. She made the colour ripples of her dress dance in perfect time to the music. It seemed so simple, so easy, and yet the effect on anyone watching her was hypnotic.

After a moment, Elizabeth glanced up from the captivated audience before her and watched Lukas watch her. She smiled, blew him a kiss, and gestured to her right where a spindly young man was holding his hand together and smiling proudly. The young man said something, but Lukas was too far away, and frankly didn't really care what he had to say.

# #

Walking up behind Lukas came Whisky and Cipher. "That's our guy!" Whisky announced, but not with his trademark level of excitement.

Cipher slowly walked around Lukas's chair. He reached his hand out and rested it gently on the back of the chair and allowed his fingers to graze the top of Lukas's shoulder. As he moved past the chair, Cipher allowed his hand to drop casually to his side. His eyes were not on the young man, instead scanning the crowd suspiciously. He knew Chimera was starting to grow into a legend around Paris. Legends always led to curious parties.

"Spend any more time staring at my girls, and I'll have to start charging you." Cipher said jovially, still without looking at Lukas.

Whisky and Cipher finally sat in the vacant seats opposite Lukas. Cipher made sure to block the view Lukas had of Elizabeth. Cipher took a dramatic, deep breath, and finally sized up the young man in front of him. Being one who cared absolutely nothing about how people perceived him, Cipher didn't even try to hide the disappointed expression from his face. *Oh. Another dullard,* he considered. He saw no hint of potential entertainment from the man; he was instantly bored.

"What do you want?" asked Cipher, without a care in the world.

fragment

/ˈfragm(ə)nt/

verb

break or cause to break into fragments.

fragment

CLAIR I

The streets were filling up with people of every variety: business folk in expensive suits, kids in school uniforms, hipsters and so on. As Vaugn and Clair approached the church grounds, she was speaking animatedly about all the data she had found in Lukas's office. Vaugn absorbed as much as he could, but it only served to highlight how little he really knew about who his brother had become over the years. Still, it kept him focused and controlled.

Standing outside the church was a very twitchy old woman, looking around anxiously and muttering to herself, "Just utterly disrespectful. What is happening to that family?" As they reached the church doors, Clair was the first to notice the woman. She was bundled up warm in spite of the mild weather.

"Are you ok, M'am?" she asked politely.

"No respect!" The old woman muttered more definably.

Clair walked over to the woman and gently touched her arm. "Are you alright?"

The old woman jumped and let out an exclaim of surprise. Apparently she had been lost in thoughts and unaware of the couple making their way towards her. "Ah, what? Who are you? Are you with them?"

"With who?" Vaugn asked as he drew up next to his fiancé.

"Those hooligans!" The woman hissed.

Vaugn stepped closer to the woman. "What hooligans?"

"The one's who interrupted Father Vaugn, of course!"
"Are they still here?"

"I saw two of them run out of there not too long ago. The screams coming from inside where terrible!"

Without another word, Vaugn darted toward the church entrance. The tip of a metal spike was just sticking through the thick wooden door. Below it was a small puddle of blood. As he reached the closed door, Vaugn's foot slid in the liquid, making him momentarily lose his balance. Vaugn caught himself and looked down. He saw the mess. His hand rested on the door.

Vaugn's heart was beating so loudly in his ears that he didn't hear

Clair come up beside him.

"Vaugn?" she asked hesitantly.

Vaugn touched the end of the spike. A small stream of blood had seeped through the wood of the door and snaked its way down to the end of the spike. Blood dribbled down Vaugn's finger where he had touched it. He had the sinking feeling that he wasn't going to like whatever was behind the door.

Vaugn pulled on the doors with all his might. The heavy oaken doors swung open slowly, revealing Pierre pinned to the inside by a make-shift trident. A much larger puddle of blood had formed beneath Pierre's body and had oozed into the cracks in the stone floor.

"Dad!" screamed Vaugn, Pierre's face inches from his own.

His eyes dilated and shook as they tried to make sense of what they were seeing. After what seemed like an age where time stopped and nothingness reigned supreme, his senses finally returned to him. He desperately wrestled with the steel pole holding Pierre in position, trying in vain to remove it from Pierre's corpse.

"Fuck you, Dad! You're not doing this to me!" he wailed.

Clair watched Vaugn struggle for a moment, then attempted to help.

"No! Don't touch him!" Vaugn yelled.

Clair looked hurt by the violent rejection. She watched him wrestle for a moment, then turned, and ventured into the church, surveying the damage. It looked like a war zone. Many of the pews had been destroyed. The altar had been decimated. The stone bowl that once contained holy water was now in three large pieces all over the floor. The water itself had spilled everywhere. Collapsed on the floor amongst the rubble of the stone bowl were the remains of Menelaus's melted, lifeless body.

"What the hell happened?!" she asked, in awe of the destruction.

At her voice, Socrates hobbled into the main hall, carrying a lump of flesh. He limped over to Clair, triumphantly showing off his new toy. He was limping from his front right paw, but it didn't slow him down much. Congealed blood in his fur gave his ruff a dreadlocked appearance. Yet, through the obvious physical damage, there was a happy sting in the Husky's step.

"Socrates!" exclaimed Clair. But then she saw what the husky was holding. "What's that?"

Vaugn collapsed to his knees, weeping in silence. His hands clung to Pierre's robes. Exhaustion had taken him over. He had nothing left and couldn't stand. As his knees hit the ground with a gut-retching thud, Clair's focus turned immediately to him again.

"Vaugn!" Clair ran over and dropped down beside him, pulling him into an awkward embrace.

They stayed that way in painful silence, as Vaugn's body vibrated from exhaustion and shock. Clair knew there was nothing she could say to help. Holding Vaugn in her arms, she intimately understood the pain he was suffering and the futility of words. She only barely registered that the old woman had ventured to the entrance of the church. Even she understood that saying nothing was the far, far better course of action. Without direction, the woman turned on her heels and moved on silently.

Then, as was his way, Socrates strolled up to his partners with the remains still in his maw. The grotesqueness of the flesh alone would probably have been enough to break open the scene, but the fact the remains were still attempting to speak made it a certainty.

"Let go!" screamed a voice as Socrates forced the fleshly gift in front of Vaugn's face.

The eruption immediately broke the emotional embrace, and Clair looked at Vaugn for a moment, wondering why he had seemingly shouted at her. But his expression was just as confused as hers. Clair and Vaugn turned their attention to the husky and what was dangling from the husky's mouth.

"Socrates? What the hell have you got?" she asked nervously whilst attempting to take the thing away. But Socrates growled playfully and dodged backwards a step quickly, just out of reach.

"No. This isn't a game." Clair explained as she, once again, attempted to snatch at the thing in his mouth. This time, she managed to get a grip on it and pulled.

"Drop it!" She commanded.

"Good luck, lady. I've been trying for fucking hours!"

Dumbfounded, Clair looked at the fleshy piece in her hands and finally realised that it was a face. Not only was it a face, but the remaining eye was looking directly at her and was, very clearly, pissed off. On top of that, it was still alive and talking.

"What the fuck?!" She exclaimed.

Clair immediately released her grip and shook her hand automatically, in an attempt to shake off the wholly discomforting sensation. "Urgh!"

VAUGN I

Vaugn looked round and saw Clair and Socrates momentarily playing "pull" with something grotesque. He got up awkwardly, slowly.

"Socrates, let go of that thing!" Clair commanded.

"Yeah! Let go of me!" pleaded the remains of Menelaus.

Vaugn looked vacantly at the scrap of flesh. He was so tired, resembling a Chimera victim, which — in that moment — he realised he sort of was. But anger was beginning to reignite in his stomach. As Vaugn walked over, Clair looked into his eyes, pleading for answers and help.

"A little help with your dog?"

"It's a Demon," Vaugn said matter-of-factly, before glancing at the happy husky, "Socrates. Drop."

Socrates instantly let go of Menelaus's face. Clair grabbed the limp piece of flesh in her hands and held it out to Vaugn. He grabbed it and raised it up in front of him. The remaining eye focused on Vaugn. There was an incredible amount of hate reflected in that eye.

Somewhere in the periphery of Vaugn's senses, he heard Socrates let out a disappointed huff and whine.

"You're the fuckrag's son, huh? You a pussy like your brother?!" he screamed, irrationally.

Vaugn looked around him and, for the first time since returning to the church, took in the damage that had occurred within the holy walls. Not far from where he stood, he saw the sundered remains of the font. He walked over to the largest piece which still contained a small amount of fluid. Clair watched Vaugn silently, wrestling to understand everything that had happened in the last few hours.

"What are you doing?" growled Menelaus, with an undeniable note of fear in his voice.

Vaugn scrunched up Menelaus's face in his hands like a used tissue and dropped the ball into the remaining holy water. As soon as the fleshy remains touched the water, it began to melt away.

"Ffffuuuucckkkk!" screamed Menelaus, as the last vestiges of him melted away.

"I'm doing what needs to be done." Vaugn said dryly.

CLAIR II

Prior to their first meeting, Clair had been well informed as to Vaugn's unusual habits, tactics and general quirks. When they actually met, she remembered feeling a little scared, and apprehensive. She found it terrifying to not have a plan in place for an occasion, and everything she had heard suggested that Gabriel Vaugn was an improviser. On that first meeting, she was right to be worried because he had forced her to join him on stage at karaoke for a duet as a "fun way to bond!" as he put it.

But right now, with the quietness emanating from him, Clair was instantly terrified of, and for Vaugn. He was broken. She could see that he had purposefully detached himself from everything. There was a rumour everyone in Interpol had heard about him. His look and attitude made her scared that it might be true. As he walked off towards the back of the church, Clair found herself doing something she had never done before . . . she prayed. She prayed that he would suddenly do something madcap, something stupid and silly.

"Vaugn, what are you doing?" Clair asked nervously. "Gabe?!" Vaugn disappeared into the back of the church and she knew that her prayer would go unanswered.

gremlin

/ˈgrɛmlɪn/

noun

an unexplained problem or fault.

gremlin

STYX I

As Styx entered the Chimera lab factory, he was — as usual — hit by the powerful, lingering scents of the various burning chemicals, the ever-present sewage stench, and the sulphurous twinge to the surroundings.

"Ah!" Styx exclaimed with false comfort, "nothing welcomes you home like the smell of old farts."

As he looked around the lab, he couldn't help but notice that his comment hadn't gathered any attention, or even the slightest of giggles. Everyone in the lab was uncomfortably quiet and working at a feverish pace. Most were actively working to keep their heads down and focus on their jobs. A few of the newer faces Styx didn't recognise kept glancing up at Cipher with shocked expressions. He had seen this sort of atmosphere before.

He then saw Cipher standing on a metal gallery surveying the factory floor with a broad grin on his face and blood splattered on his left cheek. He immediately understood what had caused the spooking. He let out an understanding huff, but knew better than to say anything.

Lying beside Cipher was a freshly — and brutally — cleaved right leg. After seeing the gore, Styx was about to pick the smell the blood out of the other powerful aromas in the air. The blood oozed through the walkway grill and onto the floor below. Styx finally walked up the metal stairway to his right that lead up to the gallery where Cipher stood. As he got closer, he kept glimpsing back down to the leg. He couldn't help but find it funny that Cipher was such a slave to his emotions. I wonder if the other side have these problems, he considered, knowing better than to mention such things aloud.

As he crested onto the gallery, Cipher had apparently either not noticed his arrival, or was purposefully not looking in his direction.

"Grey didn't find the formula?" asked Styx.

The silence was threatening enough to make even Styx falter in his steps. He mentally shook off the fear and fought to keep moving forwards. He wasn't going to show any weakness.

"No." Cipher eventually replied.

As Cipher slowly turned to face him, Styx grimaced slightly. The bastard was smiling slightly. "It cost him his leg." Cipher finished as he cast a quick glance down at the fresh flesh.

Styx looked at the leg lying on the gallery floor once more. Cipher seemed strangely at peace. Violence had a way of calming them both. They were each born in brutality; it seemed fitting that brutality soothed their souls. Having too many similarities with Lucifer wasn't exactly what Styx was hoping for. Still, Styx felt that ripping a leg off did need some kind of explanation.

"It may be a dumb question-"

"-From you?" Jabbed Cipher mockingly.

Styx cleared his throat in protest, then continued, "Why would you do that? Couldn't you have done . . . anything else?"

"I made him kick his own ass."

Cipher was unable to contain his twisted sense of humour and giggled childishly. Styx smiled in spite of himself. He looked out across the lab floor. The men and women in white coats were still busying themselves working through the final stages of Chimera's creation. The mood had not improved.

"What now?" Styx asked.

Cipher picked up Grey's leg as he pondered the question. After months of planning, scheming and executing, they were finally on the home stretch. Cipher wound the leg back over his shoulder, like a baseball player stepping to the plate. "We need to tidy up loose ends. If the father didn't have my formula, then it stands to reason the brother must have it."

Cipher didn't even need to ask his question. Styx was already well aware of his employer's demands. He turned and descended the stairwell once more, without a word. Cipher swung the leg like he was hitting a pitched ball. As the swing reached maximum velocity, he released the leg and sent it flying across the factory. It collided with the far wall, and left a blood splat.

"Home Run!"

The squelching sound of the impact caught everyone's attention, but the deathly silence returned an instant later.

conflict

/ˈkɒnflɪkt/

noun

a serious incompatibility between two or more opinions, principles, or interests.

a good man goes to war

CLAIR I

With Vaugn somewhere in the back of the church and Socrates having followed him, Clair was alone in the ruined hall. She looked at the limp body of Pierre — still pinned to the oak doors — and did what she did best . . . analyse the situation. From Vaugn's silence, it was highly probable he was going to do something reckless; something stupid, and almost certainly something dangerous in retaliation.

She knew exactly what she was supposed to do. It would piss Vaugn off greatly, but with the way he was acting Clair didn't really care. Since their chance encounter with Cipher, she had been barely keeping him from going off the rails entirely. Now this with Pierre . . . It needed to stop.

Clair activated her HUD. The menu bar appeared at the bottom of her vision. "Phone Nieves," she said with authority, turning her back to Pierre's body.

Almost instantaneously, Robert Nieves answered the call with his typically nasally, brusque voice. "What do you want, Bobak? What's your fiancé done this time?"

Having gotten used to his blunt attitude during her time at Interpol, Clair remained unfazed. "Captain, we need your help."

"Ha! You say 'we', yet I know Vaugn would rather, and I quote, 'cut off my own dick to use as a silly straw than get your help'. I'm curious what shit he's gotten himself into now that you feel he needs my help."

"Did you hear about the priest who committed suicide?"

"What of it? One less idiot in the world."

"He was Vaugn's brother."

A long, awkward silence followed until Nieves eventually spoke again. "Oh."

"We came to Paris to find out why he killed himself. Long story short, he was a guinea pig for a new drug called Chimera. It's the reason for the recent suicide rate spike. We found out from the Lyon operation that La Bouffe is financing the development and distribution of Chimera. Vaugn's father has just been murdered, and now Vaugn is out for blood."

Another long silence followed.

"Shit," Nieves responded. "He's going to do something stupid isn't he?" asked Nieves, already knowing the answer.

"I need you to send a team to District Seven in the Straights. He needs more backup than just me and Socrates."

"And why should I help? Vaugn and you have actively fought for almost complete autonomy over your cases. Neither of you are willing to support me."

Clair couldn't think of a good response to the accusation. It was very true. They had worked very hard to be their own bosses. The way Vaugn operated, it was best if they didn't have to deal with Nieves often.

"Tell you what, I'll give you a choice . . . If I hear of either you or Vaugn — or that shitty dog of his — causing any trouble whatsoever in Paris or the Straights, legal action will be taken against you both. Your careers will be over and you will go to jail," Nieves continued.

"Or," Nieves continued, "You can forget Vaugn. Come back to Interpol properly. You're an amazing asset. It would be such a waste of your talents to throw it all away because of an out-of-control rebel. Clair, please."

Clair didn't say anything. Nieves was making a lot of sense.

"I'll give you one hour to think about it and let me know. Be smart."

He call ended, and Clair was left deep in thought. Finally she let out a long, stressed sigh and headed off in the direction Vaugn had disappeared.

***

By the time Clair reached Lukas's room, which was still a mess following her earlier ransacking, Vaugn was carefully laying out a collection of guns, a hip flask, a twelve-inch blade with a black handle and thin silver cross and an old phone on the small bed. Vaugn was in the middle of checking one of the guns, while Clair stood in the doorway, watching him. Socrates was nowhere to be seen.

She stepped towards Vaugn. "We need to talk."

"Now's not the time," he replied, sharply.

His response fanned her anger quickly. "No!" She snapped back.

Vaugn looked at his partner, stunned. It was rare that Clair snapped. Any time she did, he knew it was a serious situation. He quickly but carefully placed the gun back on the bed and took one step backwards.

"What's your plan here?" she demanded.

"Guns blazing," came the instant, flat response.

"Not this time. I spoke with Nieves—"

"—Why?" Vaugn butted in, "He's a fucking asshole!"

"You're about to charge headlong into a 'guns blazing' attack on who? . . . Lucifer? Maybe I missed the part where you just so happened to learn that guns can kill the fucking devil!"

"I have to do something!"

"Not this! This isn't going to bring back Lukas or Pierre!"

"I know!" he replied, breathing heavily.

An emotional silence fell between them.

"You have no back up. If you do anything, Nieves is going to have us both arrested. Are you willing to sacrifice me, as well as yourself, and Socrates for this?"

"I can't step aside. We need to stop this. Chimera is due to ship out any day now. If we let it hit the streets, countless deaths will be our fault."

"I understand that. I'm asking what your plan is." She pleaded.

"It's what Lukas would expect me to do," reasoned Vaugn.

"You are known for doing the stupid thing." she admitted.

Clair looked at Socrates, who had appeared from the chasm behind the wardrobe, carrying a large, canvas duffel bag. He trotted over to Vaugn's side and dropped the bag beside Vaugn's feet. She instantly recognised it from her examination of Lukas's room earlier. Her stomach dropped and she fought back the urge to grab the bag and just run. Vaugn turned around to check the open bag's contents. It was full of explosives.

Vaugn looked from the bag back to Clair and smiled, "Told you he'd expect guns blazing."

Clair looked from the bag to Vaugn. "What about me?"

Vaugn gently grabbed Clairs hands and pulled her closer in. "Tell Nieves you'll agree to whatever his terms were."

"What about us?"

"Would you be okay marrying a criminal?"

Clair laughed. "Can I call you a vigilante instead? It's sexier than 'criminal'."

self-imposed

/ˌsɛlfɪmˈpəʊzd/

adjective

(of a task or circumstance) imposed on oneself, not by an external force.

a self-made prison

WHISKY I

Three days earlier.

Renowned worldwide for its indisputable character, passion, and individuality, Paris truly stood apart from all other capital cities. Many commented about New York, or London, or Rome being in the same league; they weren't. But since the arrival of Cipher and his behind-the-scenes machinations, something about Paris — not just the Straights — had begun to change.

There was a gloom, a fear creeping through the streets. A bizarre duality had begun to form. It was akin to the development of split-personality disorder or dementia. It first started off as a growing frustration and annoyance within the people of the city, but it quickly translated to anger. Then anxiety gripped the city, as it attempted to bottle up the newfound rage.

Rain had been falling nonstop for nearly thirty-six hours. The streets were flooding, and a rising tide raises all ships — or trash, in this case. A syringe here, discarded beer cans there. The trash of society was being "resurrected" by the water, and it showed an ugly side to "beautiful" Paris; telltale symptoms of an infestation deep within.

Walking down one such rain-drenched street was a motley crew of men: Cipher, Whisky, Lukas, and three other decrepit, cloaked characters. Cipher was leading the sombre procession down the street. He was being followed by the three cloaked figures. Bringing up the rear were Whisky and Lukas. The extreme rain perfectly matched the sombre mood of the group, with the exception of Cipher, who was actually "performing" Singin' in the Rain as he made his way down the street.

As Whisky walked with Lukas he couldn't pretend to be excited about the current situation he found himself in. He glanced over to the young priest, and couldn't help feeling somewhat resentful. Lukas had shown such confidence, intelligence and certainty. *You were suppos'd t' know wat you were doin',* he thought. *Now look a' us. . . more th'n likely to no' see the sun rise.* As quickly as the thoughts had arisen, Whisky was smacked with a painful sense of shame and guilt as he saw Lukas walk under a flickering street light.

The light revealed the full degradation of the young man's physical form. There was a grotesque beauty to him; the darkness of the night compared to his pallid complexion. Lukas was cadaverously thin. Just looking at him, Whisky knew there was something inside the young priest devouring him entirely; body and soul. Lukas was attempting to appear strong, but every jostle of his frail form even from simply walking down the street was obviously hurting.

"You okay?" Whisky enquired.

"Can't you tell?" came the strained reply.

Concern for his young friend returned to him. He already knew the truth, but to ask was all he could do. He felt rotten. *This is my faul'*, Whisky thought. *I'm sorry Lukas. I should 'ave deal' with this. I' wasn' your shi' to clean up.*

CIPHER I

Cipher skipped over, threw his arm heavily around Lukas's shoulders and jovially patted him on the belly, as if they had been fast friends sharing a long and vibrant friendship. "He's the picture of health!" he chortled happily as he skipped on ahead towards a narrow set of stone steps leading down into the Catacombs. He spun around like a circus ringmaster rousing a crowd, exuding so much excitement and having a wonderful time.

"Welcome to my humble home!" Then, in almost pantomime, over-the-top fashion, he looked around with false wariness and comically held his finger to his lips. "Oops! That's supposed to be a secret!" he exaggeratedly whispered.

The three cloaked male figures walked obligingly down the stairs in hushed quiet, as Cipher stepped to one side. He encouraged them in, acting as a gracious host. Whisky and Lukas hung back momentarily.

"The sewer?" asked Lukas.

"Its home to me. Ironically, it helps keep the 'vermin' out." Cipher turned and smiled knowingly at Lukas. "Metaphorically speaking, of course!" he finished, judgmentally.

Lukas and Whisky finally descended the stairs. The permanent, faint stench of death enshrouded the party. Cipher watched happily for a second as each of the humans before him physically reacted to the odour. Then, he too descended the stairs, following closely behind with a malevolent grin; his eyes targeted Lukas.

At the bottom of the stairs, Elizabeth held open a huge, brushed-steel door that had separated the over and under worlds moments ago. The hallway beyond the steel entrance had a strangely clinical, science-fiction vibe to it. The walls had been painted pure white and were heavily lacquered — for easy cleaning and maintenance, no doubt. The floor was polished concrete, and fluorescent lights hung garishly from the ceiling. As Lukas passed Elizabeth, he purposefully paid her no attention.

"Gentleman!" proclaimed Cipher, as if he were the maître d' at a fashionable event. "I've decided to show you the birthplace of

Chimera for two reasons. . ."

Behind the loosely formed line of men, Elizabeth quietly pulled the door shut. Cipher pushed his way through the small travelling party to the front and positioned himself about ten feet ahead of them whilst keeping his back turned. Cipher continued. . . "Firstly, none of you can function in the real world anymore, so you're of little threat or consequence. And secondly . . . we're going to kill you and enjoy it."

"What?!" Whisky exclaimed, unable to maintain composure.

He finally turned to face the men. The visage of Cipher had completely changed. He was truly — and in every sense of the word — demonic. His flesh was blister-red and appeared to be drenched with sweat. His eyes were pitch black, with no signs of life in them. Not even the garish, overhead lighting could dent their impenetrable blackness. His teeth were unusually small and sharp, bizarrely monstrous.

One of the cloaked men stared at Cipher's face in shocked silence and horror.

"Fuck! I'm crashing hard," commented another of the cloaked figures with a cracking, weak voice.

"I think that shit's real!"

The only person in the 'line-up' of men who didn't visibly respond to Cipher's appearance was Lukas. All he did was to slide his hands into his pockets.

"Please be aware this isn't entirely your fault," Cipher calmly explained to the three cloaked men.

"Granted, every step that brought you to this location was *entirely* your choice. But this *moment* is because of Whisky, and because of this man." Stated Cipher as he finally pointed at Lukas whilst not breaking eye contact with Whisky. "You've been ever-so helpful, and entertaining. . ." continued Cipher, ". . .But you bought a Soldier of Christ into my business," he spat angrily.

Cipher then turned to face Lukas, who remained still and quiet. Lukas slowly lifted his head to look into Cipher's demonic face. He didn't flinch and remained strangely confident. Even now, Cipher couldn't help but feel impressed by the deteriorated form of Lukas.

"Worse than that, sir, you let a Vaugn in," Lukas stated, with complete determination, and an odd sense of professionalism.

Cipher had heard so many forms of threat across the eons of his existence. But this one legitimately caught him off guard. "Is that some kind of threat? I'm genuinely confused."

"Let me show you!" roared Lucas with a menacing grin. He charged at Cipher, with a ferocity and energy nobody would have imagined him capable of mustering in his present state. Cipher smiled excitedly. He clenched his fists, as Lucas geared up to strike.

"Let's see what you've got, young Lukas," said Cipher, mockingly.

Lukas savagely swung his hands towards Cipher's head, a small glass bottle of clear liquid clasped in each. Light glistening off the glass momentarily caught Cipher's eye.

"What's th—"

Cipher was unable to finish the question however, as the bottles viciously clapped on either side of his head and shattered in glorious fashion. Instantly, his skull began bubbling and melting. Because of the momentarily distraction, Cipher could do nothing but scream in pain as his face boiled. With the ferocity of the clapping bottle attach, Lukas screamed in pain as broken pieces of glass perforated his flesh. But the pain seemed to help focus him and the attack continued.

Elizabeth watched in silent amazement, as Lukas punched Cipher in the face with his bare hands, over and over again. She watched as Cipher collapsed to the ground. Lukas spun to face Whisky and the other potential victims. Whisky had cowered back to one of the farthest walls, gripped by the same primal fear as the junkies. The fear they were feeling in that moment was elemental, like a newborn experiencing a violent thunderstorm for the first time.

"Get out of here!" he screamed.

Without having to be told twice, the three other men rushed past Elizabeth, fumbled with the lock, and vanished into the drenched night. Despite their inebriated state, every single one of those men later remembered that night with crystal-clear recollection.

Lukas turned his attention back to Cipher, swinging his boot into his opponent's face, his years of amateur football finally paying off. His foot connected perfectly with Cipher's head, the force of the blow throwing it violently backwards. A loud — and very satisfying — snap screamed from Cipher's neck. A spurt of blood shot from Cipher's mouth and nose.

Lucas continued pummelling Cipher with his fists. But the power in Lukas's attacks was quickly fading, evidently his body was unable to maintain the onslaught for much longer. His opponent kept trying to get up off the ground after each weakening punch.

"That . . .," Cipher began to say between punches.

Another violent fist to his face.

". . . is . . .," Cipher continued.

Just as Lukas was about to connect with yet another blow, Cipher grabbed hold of the young man's leg with a vicelike grip.

". . . enough!" finished Cipher, as he felled Lukas like a tree.

# #

Elizabeth and Whisky, who were both standing by the open steel door, involuntarily winced at the obvious pain of the hit. The stone ground of the Catacombs was unforgiving, and pain rattled through Lukas's body, but he seemed unfazed. He jumped back to his feet, but was instantly confronted by Cipher right in his face. Cipher looked deadly in his plain-facedness, a cold expression promising nothing but violent delights. This was the face of the demon.

Cipher unleashed his fury on Lukas. He landed a mighty blow to Lukas's stomach with his left hand. Lukas doubled over in agony, as blood erupted from his mouth. He didn't have time to scream or moan before Cipher hit him again; fast and hard. Cipher brought his right forearm down on the back of Lukas's head, sending the poor man to the ground with a violent crash. The sound of the impacting attacks sent waves of nausea through everyone.

In the background, Whisky and Elizabeth watched Lukas getting brutalised. They knew there was nothing they could do. Lukas had made them both promise they wouldn't get involved.

Finally, Whisky turned and left. He didn't want to, but he had to think of his family, and dying would do them good. From the moment he turned his back to Lukas's plight, Whisky made a private promise to be a better man. To fight a smarter battle.

Elizabeth watched in angry silence. She refused to look away from the man she loved. She always knew this was how it was going to end for Lukas, and she refused to break now. She trusted him. She trusted his plan, and there was still so much left to do.

#

Lukas was bent over on all-fours dry-heaving. "Congratulations!" began Cipher as he grabbed a handful of Lukas's hair and lifted him easily off the ground. "You pissed me off," he continued.

Cipher hurled Lukas into the nearest wall with incredible power. The wall fascia actually cracked, as Lukas's body collided with it. Breathing heavily, Cipher took in his surroundings, remembering there had been quite a few people with his initially. Styx and three of the dwarfish creatures were standing at the far end of the corridor, watching the fight.

"Goodbye."

Without another word, the dwarfs charged at Lukas's frail body. Cipher watched and smiled at the damage he'd done to the human.

"Wait!" called Styx, as he sauntered towards the battleground.

The dwarves stopped in their tracks, looking from Styx to Cipher and back again. Cipher turned from his foe to glare at Styx.

"Why?! I want him dead! I want his whole fucking family dea—!" he began to rant.

"—Calm down before you do something stupid." Styx confidently chirped.

Cipher shot such a malevolent look that even the indomitable Styx felt a sliver of doubt and concern. "What do you mean by something stupid?"

There was a moment of silence, except for occasional spluttering and retching from Lukas on the floor. Elizabeth finally looked away from the priest and spoke as composedly as she could muster, given the situation. "Why waste the soul? Look at him. He's a heartbeat away from finishing your work."

Cipher looked back at Lukas's barely conscious form. The priest was still trying to get up off the ground, but with little progress. Styx glanced over to Elizabeth; she was, once again entirely focused on Lukas. Styx smiled, feeling his suspicions about her all but confirmed. She had genuine feelings for the priest, and that meant Styx had leverage against her.

"Waste not . . . right?" muttered Lukas before he passed out.

Cipher smiled, devilishly. "Good point. Take him away." The dwarves quickly grabbed Lukas and dragged him into one of the cells further down the corridor. As the body disappeared inside, Cipher wiped Lukas's blood from his fists, when he remembered Whisky. He turned, ready to threaten the bartender again, but saw all of the other "guests" had fled the scene.

"Oh, they're gone," he said, rather stupidly.

"Don't get rid of Whisky just yet. We have leverage over him. He could yet be useful," Elizabeth said.

"Beth's right!" agreed Styx, knowing full well she hated being called "Beth".

"Fine," Cipher said, stubbornly.

guardian

/ˈɡɑːdɪən/

noun

a person who protects or defends something.

guardian

VAUGN I

The Black Moon Bar was hectic, as always, but now there was a more sombre, Monday-morning vibe. Whisky was busy chatting up some ladies at the bar, while others were asleep in their seats, or thumbing through various social feeds, or news reports on their HUDs, or generally relaxing.

"So there was me, Strauss, 'n' La Bouffe locked up in 'ere for two weeks. Lemme tell ya, 'aving those two at the same table ain' an easy session." he guffawed to himself, "Bu' I managed it with style. They signed my proposal after jus' three days. Rest o' th' time was fuelled by excessive alcohol and drug consumption." said Whisky, comically. The ladies burst into laughter. They were clearly mocking him, but Whisky really didn't care; he was a glutton for attention. Any kind of attention.

Vaugn stood in the main entrance wearing a nightmarishly cold look on his face. Encasing his whole form was an old, dark tan-coloured, full-length leather duster. Perched on the bridge of his nose were Lukas's sunglasses. Slung over his left shoulder was the large, canvas duffel bag. From the way the coat hung and gathered around his frame, anyone would be able to tell that there was clearly something hidden underneath. Slumped on either side of the doorway were the two bouncers. They were each holding their hands to their faces and moaning quietly with embarrassed pain.

Vaugn surveyed the entirety of the Black Moon Bar. His eyes lingered a little longer as they gazed towards the upper levels. There was no sign of them currently being occupied. After almost a minute of measuring his surroundings, and still nobody having taken notice of him, he comfortably retrieved a shotgun from inside his coat. He aimed up at the bell hanging from the ceiling, took one final look around and confirmed that everybody had their attention elsewhere, and casually unleashed a shell with a simple click of the trigger.

Between the blast from the shotgun and the ringing of the bell, the whole Black Moon Bar was suddenly, painfully aware of Vaugn's presence. The ambient music had stopped. the noises from the gaming corner had abruptly ceased. The entire bar had gone silent and every eye was now on him. Whisky looked over to Vaugn. A smile grew over the old bartender's face.

"I guess i's time?" he said, happily.

Vaugn cast one more look up at the platforms overhead to see if anyone had come out of hiding. Someone had. Carefully looking over the edge of a high platform was a man. He was dressed in Army fatigues and drinking something that sparkled and bubbled in the fancy glass he was holding. The man was looking over the side and watching Vaugn with great interest.

"Everybody . . . get out," Vaugn said, with the utmost authority.

Vaugn stared straight at Whisky with unshakable determination. Everybody else also watched Whisky, who was still smiling. Nobody in attendance was quite sure what to do in this situation. Whisky had shown no mercy to anybody in the past. Vaugn heard the occasional murmur wondering who he might be. Vaugn did not look happy. He fired another shot at the bell. Still nobody moved.

"Did I fucking stutter?" Vaugn asked in an uncomfortably calm matter.

Finally, Whisky spoke. "You 'eard 'im. The bell rang twice. Everybody ou'! Now!"

WHISKY I

The Black Moon Bar had finally emptied. Vaugn stood away from the bar. Whisky remained on his stool, the long night catching up with him. But even his soulful exhaustion gave way to rising hope, as he surveyed Vaugn before him. For Whisky, Lukas had briefly represented hope and the possibility of liberation from Cipher. But that representation had apparently failed at the last minute.

Gabriel Vaugn, however, had a strength to him. Whisky saw in him a bizarre, holy brutality. It forced Whisky to hope again. It was almost terrifying. Vaugn cradled the shotgun in his arms and stepped closer to Whisky.

"Why didn't you tell me earlier?" he demanded.

"I wasn' really given a choice!" Whisky baulked, looking offended and slightly angry. "Y'er brotha tol' me ya needed ta discover tha story for ya'self."

"I think I've conducted myself exceedingly well, all things considered. But there are limits to everything, including my patience and politeness." Vaugn retorted.

Before Whisky had even realised what was going on, Vaugn had punched him squarely in the face. The force of the punch knocked Whisky from his stool. Vaugn reloaded the shotgun breathing heavily.

"Tell me where Chimera is."

"Why'd you hi' me?!" Whisky shouted as he pulled himself off the floor with a bleeding cut above his eye.

Vaugn levelled the shotgun at the old man. "Lukas is dead. Pierre's just been murdered. Lucifer, apparently, is claiming souls for some reason, and he's using Chimera," he spat.

"So you know abou' Lucifer, huh?" Whisky asked as he pulled himself back up onto the stool. He rubbed his face, attempting to alleviate the pain. "An' you say Pierre's dead too? I'm no' surprised. 'E always was antagonistic. Although I'm shocked you care. I though' you 'ated 'im."

"That doesn't mean I wanted him dead."

"So," Whisky began, "you'll be wan'in' revenge, then?" he asked cheerfully. He reached under the bar, rooted around blindly for something for a few seconds, then pulled out a folded map and slammed it down on the counter. Vaugn watched Whisky unfold the document and point at a location near the Factory District (District Two) of the Straights.

"You wan' Chimera? 'Ere it is," he said. Then he called, "Loki! Can you come down, please?"

VAUGN II

To whom the old bartender was talking, Vaugn didn't know. But then a shadow overhead caused him to look up. What he saw shocked him. The man he had noticed before was confidently walking over the edge of a top-tier platform.

"What the fuck is he doing?" Vaugn yelled, as he dropped his shotgun and scrambled foolishly, attempting to catch the plummeting body. More unsettlingly, as the person fell, they weren't flailing their arms or legs about. They weren't panicking in any visible manner.

Whisky watched and laughed. "Relax. He'll be fine!"

Vaugn looked over at Whisky in utter confusion. As he looked away, the falling man completed a perfect three-point landing in front of Vaugn. The man rose to his full height, towering over Vaugn by at least six inches. As he stood, he rolled his shoulders back to reveal the enormity of his build. Considering the dominant physical presence he exuded, the gentle smile on his rough, scarred face unnerved Vaugn. The tatty, heavily worn look of his very army fatigues further helped to reinforce the idea that this man was not the sort to enjoy the proverbial easy life.

"Hello, Gabriel Vaugn," he said, in a soothing, baritone voice.

Vaugn studied him briefly, trying to understand. No mortal would have been able to survive that drop, and Vaugn could literally feel an aura coming off the hulk before him—it was powerful, yet restorative. The exhaustion Vaugn had felt consuming him, ebbed away substantially within moments of being in Loki's presence.

". . . Oh God," sighed Vaugn. "You're an angel, aren't you?"

Loki didn't respond. Vaugn looked from Loki to Whisky — who had moved closer to them. Whisky unleashed a childlike grin. Vaugn looked back up at Loki, who was still smiling gently at him.

"Gabriel. If you are serious about going after Chimera and Lucifer, you need a plan. You will need my—"

"—Fuck you," spat Vaugn.

"Excuse me?" said Loki, a frown replacing the smile.

"Fuck you." Vaugn made sure to articulate the words as clearly as possible. "You're offering help? Did you help Lukas? Did you help

Pierre? Fuck it, did you help any of the Chimera victims?" Vaugn demanded, as he glared up into Loki's face.

"I have another task appointed to me." Loki replied flatly.

"Convenient," Vaugn responded.

"Since the arrival of Jonah, I've been working closely with the Soldiers of Christ to keep him safe." Loki said, looking blankly at Vaugn.

Vaugn glanced past Loki to Whisky, looking for some form of confirmation or denial. "Is he serious?" Vaugn asked incredulously. He looked back to Loki. "That YouTube miracle kid is more important than nearly a thousand innocent people?"

There was no response.

***

Vaugn, just like the rest of the world, was well aware of Jonah and his presumed miracles. The young boy's celebrity had exploded onto the scene and showed no signs of stopping. The footage of his "miracles" had been watched hundreds of millions of times online. They had been discussed and analysed on talk shows, news outlets and everything in between. He was a legitimate cultural phenomenon, and everyone had an opinion on him and what he represented.

Vaugn didn't like the kid. He viewed Jonah as a last-ditch effort to make religion relevant in the modern world. What he did find interesting was the fact that the Pope had made no official statements regarding the rumours of divine parentage.

Many, many reporters had attempted to discover who Jonah's parents were, but nothing ever came of these investigations. Some journalists claimed they had been scared off by members of the church. Others chose to say nothing because "confirmation was not what faith was based on".

***

Vaugn looked at Loki again and realised the physical immensity of the person before him. He wondered if he would have been willing to continue investigating Jonah if he'd been threatened by this guy in some darkened corner of Mozambique.

"So Jonah . . . he is the Son of God." Vaugn reasoned, "Nice to know you look after your own."

"Gen'lemen, you're on the same side. Please don' figh' in my bar," Whisky said, stepping between the two men. "I's one of the rules."

Loki motioned to the shotgun on the floor. "Give me your gun."

"What are you going to do with it?" demanded Vaugn.

"Bless them," Loki replied.

Vaugn laughed hollowly. Anger ran across Loki's face. He, like Vaugn, only had so much patience, and it had just run out. "You are such a pain in the ass. Stubborn, like your father!—"

"—Why am I not surprised you know Pierre.—"

"—Him too!" Loki said instinctively.

"What?" snapped Vaugn confusedly.

Loki quickly gestured the shotgun and duffel bag, hoping to change the current topic of conversation. "I blessed Lukas's equipment, like those sunglasses."

Vaugn pulled the glasses from his nose. "That's why I could see that . . . thing, when I looked at Cipher?"

"They let you see the truth of things," Loki stated. "If that's what blessed sunglasses can do, what do you think blessing your gun will accomplish? Or those explosives, perhaps?" asked Loki, angrily. "Do you want even a glimmer of success?"

The smile had returned to Whisky's face as the tension between Loki and Vaugn began to fade away. "Tha's be'er! Friends!"

smart

/smaːt/

adjective

  having or showing a quick-witted intelligence.

the smart one

CLAIR I

Through the many issues Clair and Vaugn had to work through in the early days of their team formation, there was one that pissed her off more than any other . . . she abhorred being left out of the action. Given her early research into Vaugn's background, she knew he had a habit of running headlong into trouble. But she didn't realise just how actively he fought to keep others away from harm.

On one particular occasion — about two weeks into their partnership — Vaugn had actually gone so far as to handcuff her, and lock her in her hotel room while he attempted to infiltrate a slave trading market on his own, in spite of intel informing them of a strong security presence. He later admitted this was a mistake and that, were it not for her timely arrival, he would most likely be dead. Clair chastised him so wonderfully that he vowed, there and then to never, ever do such a thing again.

***

As Clair sat in the church hall waiting for the local police to arrive, she absentmindedly fussed the long, soft fur around Socrates's neck, and fumed over her fiancé's actions. He'd sidelined it again. Her mind repeated the last request Vaugn had made before heading into proverbial battle. "Stay away. Stay safe." At the very least, he had taken the time to talk it through with her. But that didn't make it ok.

"Fuck it," she finally said. "I've got to do something."

She sat in silence for a moment, considering what that something should be. She swallowed hard and allowed her analytical process to take hold. Her mind moved, and reprocessed the conversation with Nieves again, and again. *How can I work this to safeguard Vaugn?* she thought. *Vaugn can't be associated with this. What are the chances that the connections to Chimera, Cipher, or La Bouffe come up?* . . . She let her mind continue working, but a part of her had begun to mine deeper when she thought about La Bouffe. "La Bouffe. . ." she voiced quietly.

She wasn't sure how long she sat there before four police officers arrived on the scene. Her attention was drawn to them when she heard one of the officers exclaim, "Merde sacrée! I've not seen this kind of damage since the height of the Strauss War."

Another officer walked right up to Clair. "Are you Agent Bobak?"

". . . The Strauss War. . ." she repeated mindlessly. "Huh? Oh. Yes, I'm Bobak."

"Are you okay?" The first officer asked. "Do you know what happened here?"

The Strauss War. That could work, she thought. "It was La Bouffe's men," she said, as her mind continued working.

It took her a moment, but she worked out exactly what she needed to do, and how to control the situation. She could use Pierre's death to help protect Vaugn. But she was going to need more assistance. Clair stood up and began walking out of the church. Socrates followed obediently.

"Excuse me, ma'am, but you can't leave just yet," Commanded one of the officers.

Clair stopped in her tracks and turned to face the officers. "My name is Clair Bobak. I'm with Interpol, and I'm currently working a case. I have to go."

"That may be. But we have to follow proce—"

"—What's your name?" Clair asked abruptly.

"Er, Bernard. Wilfrid Bernard" they replied.

"Wilfrid." Clair confirmed. "Well Wilf, I have actionable intelligence that this is only the beginning," she explained. "We've been hearing chatter about a surviving group of Strauss supporters looking for some payback."

"What does that have to do with a dead priest?" asked Bernard.

"Apparently Pierre Vaugn was helping them. Allowing them to use this place as a base of operations, so to speak. I believe La Bouffe's men heard about it. This murder is intended as a warning message." Clair stopped herself from monologuing. She allowed herself a moment to breath, and let the story sink in with Wilfrid.

"You can't make this public. It could start the war again." She laid it on thick, determined to control the narrative. "So I need to move now before this situation gets any worse. I will happily complete all the relevant paperwork later. I have full faith in you and your team to get to the bottom of this situation. But I need to move on now. Please."

As Clair finished her performance, Socrates looked up at the lead officer and growled gently, suggesting that all conversation was over . . . if they knew what was best for them.

***

Clair wasn't sure if it was her imagination, or a genuine feeling of dread in the air as she approached the entrance to the Black Moon Bar. The street seemed quieter, as if she was wearing noise-cancelling headphones. There was a tangible feeling of pressure in the air that reminded her of the quiet moments before a mission. The suspense tingled on her fingertips.

There was a fairly large crowd of people milling around outside the entrance to the Black Moon Bar, but it wasn't the usual, organised line. It was a frustrated crowd. As she drew closer, she heard snippets of conversation.

"—never been closed before."

"What's going on?"

"—heard a gun-wielding madman started shooting up the place."

At that comment, Clair failed to hide a grin, knowing they were talking about Vaugn. She and Socrates pushed their way through the crowd and walked up to the security team standing guard at the entrance. They were doing a terrible job of dispersing the crowd. She noticed that both bouncers were sporting fresh impact wounds to their faces. *Vaugn,* she correctly assumed.

"—how many times I have to say it—" the muscle-bound bouncer tried to explain to the crowd.

"—What's going on?" Clair interrupted. "I thought the bar never closed." she asked honestly. The bouncer looked away from a couple of Synth's that had been hounding him for more information. They analysed Clair for a moment, then noticed the husky beside her. "Is that Vaugn's dog?" they asked with a hint of worry in their voice.

"Is that a good or bad thing?" she replied.

"I was told to let his associates through as soon as they arrived."

So he knew I wouldn't be able to keep away, she thought with a smile. *I guess it's his way of trusting me.*

The bouncer stepped to the side and opened the door for Clair and Socrates. "Enjoy the Black Moon bar, Miss Bobak."

The pair had barely walked through the entrance before they were immediately ambushed by a loud, jovial roar. Standing between the bar and the entranceway stood Whisky, striking a power pose and wearing a big grin on his face.

"Clair! Welcome!" Whisky proclaimed excitedly. "This is a really unusual week I've been allowin'," he said, with a warm laugh behind his words.

Clair managed to hide her shock at the sight that was Whisky, by pointedly looking any everything else surrounding her. "How so?" She asked, recording to memory the shape, size and atmosphere of the multi-layered bar.

Socrates immediately moved to a corner near the entrance and hunkered down. His hackles were flared and his eyes never left Whisky. Evidently the husky was still unimpressed with the bartender, choosing quite solitude and the closest thing he could get to a snipers nest.

"I don' like t' involve myself with In'erpol."

"Why are Vaugn and I allowed such a rare privilege?" she asked, finally looking back to the mole-like proprietor. She stepped forward to shake his now-outstretched hand. Whisky clasped her hand firmly and shook it enthusiastically. The clammy texture of his hand in her's sent a slight chill down her spine.

"Because reasons," he laughed. "Come. How can I help ya?"

Without releasing her hand, Whisky led Clair to the bar. Clair sat on the bar stool she was offered. "There's a group of Strauss supporters who've organised and are looking for vengeance against La Bouffe."

"Oh really?!" Whisky's eyes widened at the news. "I hadn' heard."

"Apparently they're looking to blow up some drug lab, here in the Straights? Some kind of retaliation against La Bouffe? Or maybe for the death of that old Priest, Pierre. . . something?" Clair suggested, smiling coyly,

It took a moment, but then she saw the flash of understanding in the foggy eyes of the bartender. A big grin spread across his face and he couldn't resist unleashing a hearty, Ha! "I see wot y'r up to. I like i'," he beamed. "Then i' would be my moral duty t' le' everyone know, wouldn' i'?"

"Most certainly," Clair smiled back. "If anything bad was to happen, the people must know whose to blame, and why."

"I'll ge' my Speakeasies righ' on i'."

Clair didn't understand his meaning, but remained confident that her plan would go well.

"Wha'll you do, in th' meantime?"

"Me? I've been ordered to not get involved in Straights business." she said before remembering another task she needed to do, " I have to give my statement to the police." she finished with a deflated tone.

The smile faded from Whisky's face as he nodded sombrely. "I's a shame."

***

As Clair made her way back to Pierre's church, she felt that however Whisky was going to spread her tale, it was already in effect. There was an energy in the air now compared to when she had approached the bar. She wondered if it was merely a self-perpetuating placebo effect her own mind had created to help steady her frayed nerves. Whatever it was, she liked how it felt. It felt like hope. Everywhere she looked, there were groups of people chatting animatedly. But no matter their enthusiasm for the conversation, their voices remained hushed. It reminded Clair of her school years when classmates would spread nasty rumours about each other.

Occasionally she would hear random words of the conversation like, "La Bouffe," "Strauss" and "war". She was fairly confident her misdirection was working, at least sufficiently for plausible deniability. She allowed a smile to grow on her face as she touched her thumb and forefinger together and say, "Phone Nieves." *Now to report in,* she thought confidently.

volition

/vəˈlɪʃ(ə)n/

noun

the faculty or power of using one's will.

volition

VAUGN I

As Vaugn followed his HUD navigation to the apparent location of the Chimera labs, his mind kept returning to Clair and Socrates. In spite of his professions of determination, every step he had taken since leaving the church had gnawed at his resolve. He hated breaking promised to Clair, and making her mad. He wondered just how big of a mistake he was making. *Could I forget everyone and just live a good life with Clair?* he thought, *Could I stop fighting? Would that make me happy?*

The questions flooded his senses and stopped him in his tracks. *Could I be happy? What about that shit Elizabeth was spouting? This being my idea of Heaven? Wherever Clair is, wherever Socrates is, that's Heaven.* Vaugn pressed his palms to his forehead and tried to massage everything out of his skull. "No," he exclaimed aloud. "I'm not letting Lukas die for nothing."

As he berated himself in the middle of the street, Vaugn hadn't realised that he had reached his destination. He hadn't noticed the cobblestones under foot —the same stones Whisky and Lukas had travelled down not too long ago. He was too distracted by his internal argument to see a stairwell leading down into the catacombs about twenty meters ahead of him.

". . . Head in the game," Vaugn said to himself.

Vaugn gave his eyes one more heavy rub with his wrists. His vision blacked out momentarily before a brief, iridescent light display gave way to the world before him. Standing casually at the top of the stairwell, in the middle of conversation were three . . . entities.

As he looked at them, Vaugn found it impossibly hard to translate how they really looked. The one standing to the right of the entrance was unquestionably the most muscular of the three men. It wasn't a healthy-looking musculature, they were shredded to the point of vulgarity. Veins seemed as if they were on the verge of bursting over — quite literally — every visible patch of skin. Even the details of his eyes, nose and mouth were lost amidst ridiculous muscle definition so extreme it looked as if the fellow was suffering some kind of allergic reaction.

Vaugn's attention drifted to the 'creature' who was standing confidently in the front and centre of the cluster. As Vaugn began to study to gargantuan, rotund individual, he made eye contact with them. He wished he hadn't. Vaugn suddenly felt what it was like to be devoured from the inside out. As he looked into the person's cruel, ravenous eyes, he could feel their teeth gnashing, gnawing and greedily consuming anything, and everything within him. A chill shot down Vaugn's spine and he managed to look away. He didn't understand it, but felt certain that that chill had saved his life.

Finally, the tallest of these three weird people took two large, uncomfortable-looking strides forwards. His pose was painful to look at and reminded Vaugn of something out of a monster movie. He had an obvious hunch, but because his chin appeared to permanently rest on his chest, he stood leaning backward a little so he could make threatening eye contact. Even in his hunched pose, this monstrosity was well over seven feet tall.

"Hey! Fiare chier!" The Tall One shouted, pointing threateningly at Vaugn with a long, bony finger.

Vaugn felt the pit of his stomach drop away, a wave of light-headedness crashed over him. He could feel the muscles in his legs begging to either give out entirely, or bolt as fast as possible. He felt his resolve bending. As a myriad of thoughts of running began to invade his mind, he obstinately bit down hard on his tongue. The shockwave of pain rippled throughout his body and did exactly what he had hoped for; it reset his system.

"Va te faire foutre" the mountain of muscle shouted out.

Vaugn sucked on the wound to his tongue for a second, shaped the blood and saliva in his mouth, and spat it out aggressively on the ground. The three things watched curiously. The fat one tapped the muscular one on the shoulder, pointed at Vaugn and said something in a language Vaugn understand. It sounded vaguely familiar, but nothing specific was coming to mind.

"Is this where I might find Cipher?" Vaugn asked confidently.

The Tall One strained and turned to look at their associates. There was more conversation between them all for a moment. Again in a language Vaugn didn't understand. Again, it was ringing familiar bells in Vaugn's mind, but he still couldn't place it. The Shredded one stepped forwards cracking its knuckles and baring their teeth at Vaugn. From his coat pocket, Vaugn pulled out Lukas's sunglasses and slid them on. As his eyes adjusted, the three figures were revealed in the truest sense.

After a life on the streets, as well as some of the cases he'd dealt with, Vaugn was painfully aware of what true monstrosity looked like. Therefore, monstrous was not a word Vaugn would use casually. Yet he could not think of another, more appropriate descriptor. Each of their frames was essentially human in shape, but the flesh had been mutated, and ruined in innumerable ways.

The Gargantuan One was a heaping mound of congealed fat and sweat, and waves upon waves of skin-flaps. He had no discernible chin or neck. The fat folds hung everywhere on his body. Any movement created a ripple effect across his entire frame. The flesh itself looked like it was slowly cooking. Sweat was pouring off his body. The only thing that remained the same across both forms was the wheezing noise he made when breathing.

The Tall One's torso was smaller than expected, but his limbs were extraordinarily long — at least two times the length of his body. Even his fingers and toes were stretched and malformed. A sunken, pallid face sat atop a pencil-thin neck. There was a sallowness to the skin that made it look as if he were glowing a faint yellowish brown.

The Shredded One's true form was the most similar to his glamour. He still maintained his imposing physical prowess, but he was a living flayed man. Not a single shred of skin remained. The unprotected blood, muscle and sinew looked as fresh as if it had just been exposed. The visible tension in his muscles and jaw were the only indication that he was feeling any pain from his injuries.

The urge to turn and run crashed into Vaugn once more, but he fought it off quickly. He took a deep, steadying breath as he surveyed the creatures revealed before him. The intensity of their change had strengthened Vaugn's resolve once more. The questions that had been vexing his mind moments ago disappeared.

Without any sign of fear, Vaugn opened his coat to reveal a veritable arsenal of guns strapped to his body. He drew two handguns from their holsters and aimed them at The Tall One and The Gargantuan One. The Shredded One was standing back slightly, watching with a twisted smile on his flayed face. Vaugn glanced over to him and absolutely understood the meaning of that distorted grin — it was the same cocky, know-it-all grin Vaugn so frequently wore.

"This is where Cipher and La Bouffe are, right?" Vaugn asked. "The Chimera lab, yes?"

The Tall One and The Gargantuan One moved towards Vaugn smiling wickedly, and threateningly. With their glamours no longer visible to him, Vaugn had to fight hard not to throw up at the mere sight of their true movement. It was so alien, so painful to watch.

"Look at the scary little man with the pistols," mocked The Gargantuan One.

Vaugn swallowed hard and smiled devilishly in return. Without another word, he opened fire, ripping The Tall One and The Gargantuan One to pieces. The bullets and guns might have been small, but the carnage they wrought was unbelievable. The bodies of The Tall One and The Gargantuan One hit the ground like heavy, fleshy sacks. Black blood oozed from their ruined corpses.

The Shredded One instinctively cowered back from the decimation that Vaugn had delivered, taking a few paces down the stairway. "Oh fuck!" they whispered breathily. They then turned and bolted down the stairwell into the catacombs and out of immediate sight.

Vaugn exhaled heavily and holstered his guns once more. Finally he took Lukas's sunglasses off and looked at the bodies laying before him. They looked like the creatures he had seen before save for the bullet holes that now riddled their corpses. One was tall and malformed, the other was grossly overweight.

He looked down at the guns in their holsters, "Holy fuck this religious crap actually works!" he exclaimed.

He took a moment to collect himself, then put the sunglasses back on, started reloading his guns again, and walked down the stairwell toward the doorway.

CIPHER I

The stark contract between the considerable age, and original construction materials of the catacombs compared to the sparkling, up-to-date laboratory comprising the majority of Chimera's construction process was comically garish. It was like finding a flying car carefully parked inside Notre-Dame. Under Cipher's explicit direction, La Bouffe had spent a great deal of money retrofitting the modern labs into the tombs, and constructing the 'patient' cells to his particular specifications. This required an phenomenal amount of excavation — in a painfully short amount of time — to make areas large enough for their needs.

La Bouffe had offered the use of his pre-existing labs in far more common locations, but Cipher was particularly adamant about the location being in the Straights for some reason. Rather than question his new business partner's demands, he did what he usually did in tough situations. . . he threw money at the problem until it went away. He utilised shell companies to action the works and — at Cipher's insistence — had more philanthropic figureheads publicly address the undertaking as a charitable upgrade to the sewers for Paris's sake.

The northern portion of this room had been set up like a cargo warehouse. On the north-eastern wall were a set of heavy, double doors and a ceiling track that lead through the doors. It had been specially built so that when the mass-produced Chimera was ready for shipping, huge pallets could be moved quickly, and easily to the loading station further down the underground system.

There were fifteen men, and women dressed in lab coats and working furiously on their individual tasks at some of the twenty-four various work stations that were neatly laid out in six rows. They were essentially encased in a huge plexiglass 'clean room' which stretched from the floor of the first level, up the the floor of the second, and from the loading area, almost to the back of the large room. This room-within-a-room took up the vast majority of the first level of the lab. There were two entrances to the 'clean room,' one on the north side, and one on the south.

On the southern wall of the lab, behind the plexiglass was a set of double doors, leading off to more lab areas. On the eastern wall were five huge, floor-to-ceiling, metallic distillery vats with more than a passing resemblance to a beer fermentation plant.

A second level had been constructed with huge steel girders to allow research and development to be segregated from the production floor. There two sets of metal stairways leading up to the second floor on the north-east, and north west edges of the room. These stairways lead straight onto a metal gallery which circled the ceiling of the 'clean room' on level one.

The north end of the second floor, between the stairways was completely different from the rest of the lab. There were no plexiglass walls, or even windows. It was an ominous, cast-iron, sealed room. There was a permanent slight whiff of something having been burned inside, but the aroma was largely unidentifiable. There was a single entrance into the room, and only three people had access; La Bouffe, Cipher, and Felix Sauer.

On the far souther wall of this level were more double doors leading off, deeper into the honeycomb of passages, labs and "upgrades" La Bouffe had actioned.

Cipher was leaning comfortably on the railing of the south-side, upper gallery walkway, surveying the comings and goings of the "lab rats" through the clear ceiling. In a rare display of considering others, Cipher had advised La Bouffe that keeping his distance would probably be beneficial. So the crime lord stood a few paces away, offering an update to proceedings.

"—after this shift's ritual, the final stages will be complete and we can start making money!" he finished excitedly.

Cipher let out a big sigh, suggesting just how tired he truly felt, "Excellent."

So much preparation, he thought remembering the last two years, *But the end results will be worth it. I'll have the raw materials I need.*

They watched the workers in silence for a few moments before La Bouffe snapped to, shook his head and his nerves began to show once more. Cipher noticed the shiver and smiled to himself, *Yes, you are living on borrowed time.* As if sense the unspoken threat, La Bouffe automatically took a step further back from Cipher.

Cipher laughed, "Haha! What's the matter?" he asked, sensing the little man shy away from him.

"Why . . . why does it make you so happy . . . when they kill themselves?" La Bouffe cautiously.

"Two reasons," Cipher replied matter-of-factly, remembered the looks on the hundreds of Chimera victims' faces. He turned to face his associate, the smile broadening across his devilish face. "One: it's what I want, and two: it's so fucking ironic!" He was unable to contain his rising joy. "They follow the path I've laid out for them so willingly." He continued, "'I can't take it anymore!'," he mocked, overacting the part of a Chimera casualty, complete with flailing arms. "Cracks me up every time!" he finished as he burst into joyous laughter.

Cipher was still cackling to himself when The Shredded One from the catacombs entrance burst into the room, startling everyone in the labs. Cipher flashed a look in his direction. There was still a smile on his face, but it was more strained, as if he already knew he wasn't going to like whatever he was about to learn.

"Boss! We've got a serious problem!" The Shredded One bellowed with an uncomfortable, nasally voice.

Cipher let out a slow, deep, animalistic growl. He clicked his tongue in frustration, breathed in deeply, then spoke. "Can we change the language to 'challenge,' instead of 'problem'?" he asked, comically but with an undeniable air of violent dread.

The Shredded One went silent for a second, dumbly opening and closing his mouth as his slow mind tried to understand what he had just been asked. The smile vanished from Cipher's face, replaced with tired frustration. The Shredded One gave up trying to comprehend what Cipher had just asked, and carried on with his initial process.

"Someone's here! He just ripped Murmur and Abaddon apart like they were paper!"

"How? Aren't you guys . . . like, immortal, or something?" La Bouffe asked, stupidly.

Cipher stood perfectly still and perfectly quiet, though everyone could feel his rage growing. La Bouffe took another few paces back and clearly didn't want to be anywhere nearby when the rage exploded. He, like many others, had seen how Cipher handled emotional disappointment before. The silence stretched out longer, and longer, and longer.

For anyone watching, it looked like a handful of bloody entrails had suddenly materialised in Cipher's hands, coinciding with the unexpected disemboweling, and collapse to the floor of The Shredded One.

"Mr La Bouffe?" Cipher finally asked, in as measured a tone as he could, given his current mental situation.

". . . Yes?" La Bouffe said, weakly.

"I want you to deal with this," ordered Cipher as he tossed the guts over the side of the gallery. They hit the ceiling of the 'clean room' and everyone inside, looked up nervously at the thud. They saw the guts skit across, leaving a bloody trail. just as quickly, they turned their attention back to their work.

"Me?!" exclaimed La Bouffe, unable to hide his fear. He finally admitted to himself that he would never be the boss while Cipher was around. Remy La Bouffe finally felt his real position in the world.

Cipher leaned in close, "You have objections?" he asked, in a voice barely more than a whisper.

". . . N . . . No," said La Bouffe, pathetically.

Cipher smiled his evil smile. "Good. Now, please . . . kill that fucker!" he screamed.

VAUGN II

Vaugn had envisioned the journey underground to be the very picture of the descent into Hell. On his trek from the Black Moon Bar, he researched the Catacombs online. He saw the photos of skulls and bones jutting out of the walls; the pillars of death reaching from floor to ceiling, standing as monuments to those who have passed on. He was excited to see the entrance plinth that read "Arrete! C'est ici l'empire de la mort." He couldn't help himself building his childlike excitement up to mythological levels. He descended the spiral staircase for about twenty meters. Every step he took he could feel his pulse racing harder, and faster before the stairs ended and it opened up to the underground arcade.

"What?" He blurted out.

What he saw before him was nothing like the photos. Boring, sterile white walls, harsh fluorescent lighting overhead, and a modern, grey concrete floor. Confused, Vaugn brought up his HUD.

`No signal`.

"Shit. Did I get lost somehow?" he wondered aloud. "No. There were fucking demons guarding the entrance. I must be in the right place." Confusion and frustration oozing out of his words.

He was so jarred by the difference of expectation verses reality that he actually climbed back up the stairwell to confirm everything. As he crested the top of the stairs, his HUD reconnected to the network.

"Where am I?" he asked.

`"You are near the corner of Rue du Champ de Mars and Rue Duvivier"` The operating system replied.

"Where's the entrance to the Catacombs?"

`"1 Avenue du Colonel Henri Rol-Tanguy. Around three kilometres south of your current position. Would you like to be directed there?"` The operating system asked.

"No. Show me the map Whisky provided."

Immediately a picture of the map Whisky had provided was highlighted in Vaugn's HUD. "Am I at that address?"

"**Yes**" The operating system replied.

"Why is everyone referring to this place as the Catacombs then?!" he fumed.

"**Since the founding of The Straights, this sector of the sewers has garnered the nomenclature 'The Catacombs' by denizens of this area. Would you like to know more about the-**"

"—No." Vaugn snarled angrily. "Fuck sake!" He sulked, turned on his heels and descended the staircase once more.

***

After taking a few disappointed paces along the passageway leading directly off the bottom of the stairwell, Vaugn pause, still feeling crestfallen and disgruntled.

"This is it." he voiced. "This is Lucifer's lair. The Land of Chimera is a fucking hallway from a community college?" He stood in silence for a nearly ten seconds before, grudgingly moving on. "This is fucking bullshit!"

"Hello?" a voice echoed out from somewhere further ahead of him.

Vaugn instinctively pressed his back against the walls in a poor attempt to hide himself from curious eyes. He held his breath and listened intently. Thirty seconds of awkward silence passed. Then thirty seconds more.

"Are you there?" begged the weak voice.

Vaugn looked ahead of his current position and slid Lukas's sunglasses back onto his face. He could make out cell doors lining the corridor, but nothing seemed supernaturally unusual. He removed the sunglasses again. Nothing had changed.

"Hello?" he finally replied cautiously as he gingerly moved down the tunnels.

"Are you real?" the voice asked hungrily.

He passed three open doorways on the right, and three on the left. Glancing in, he could see the grotesque state each of the room were in. The stench emanating from them was nauseating, but it also told him that they had recently been occupied. "What is this place?" he asked in a hushed voice.

"Limbo" the voice replied weakly. "Are you real? Is this real?" The voice was getting stronger, bolstered by desperation.

There were three more open cells ahead of him; two on the left, and one on the right. The cell door furthest down the passage to his right was the only closed door. He approached it with extreme caution. The hairs on the back of his neck bristled excitedly. He reached out as far as his perception could manage with each careful step he took. He strained his senses until they started to hurt. He was determined to find any indication of a trap. When he was about eight paces from the door, he could hear soft weeping from behind the heavy, sealed entranceway.

Vaugn took the final steps to the isolated prison cell. "What do you mean, limbo?" he asked while wondering if this was where Lukas had been kept during the last days of his life.

On the door was a hinged steel plate — about thirty centimetres wide and fifteen centimetres tall — that swung down when released. It looked like an oversized post slot on the prison door. No doubt it was used by the captor to look in without having to unlock the door. Vaugn released the bolt locking it in position and carefully dropped it down. Behind the plate were two steel bars about three centimetres thick, and a pair of desperate, bloodshot and swollen eyes staring back at him.

"They won't let me die." the feminine voice cried.

The woman closed her eyes and tears rolled down her cheeks. Silently she stepped back from the door into the centre of the cell. All that Vaugn saw was a small, plastic tube in the far right corner of the room — just like the other, empty cells he'd passed before — and a physically ruined woman. Her teeth had been smashed out, her fingers had been cut off. She had blood all over her face from a bad wound on her head. Her head was shaved, she was totally naked, and painfully emaciated.

"They won't let me die," the woman repeated. "I just want . . . to die."

"Jesus!" Vaugn whispered to himself. "Chimera?" he asked, but was already certain of the answer.

She nodded feebly, "I was the first. They kidnapped me and experimented on me."

The woman moved closer to the door again, put her hands through the bars and reached the remaining stumps of her hands towards Vaugn's face gently. He stood his ground and let her touch his face. As he had expected, the stumps were rough from the scabbed over wounds and blood. But her touch was surprisingly gentle and uncomfortably caring. As she reached through the bars, he could see —even with his untrained eyes — the wounds were infected and puss-filled.

"What's your name?" he asked, gazing at her sadly.

"Will you kill me?" the woman whispered as if it was the sweetest, most romantic phrase in the world.

Vaugn looked at her earnestly through the slit. "Tell me where the lab and Cipher are, and you'll get your wish."

She snuffed back fresh tears. "Anamaria," she replied. "I was Anamaria Jeunet."

Vaugn recognised the name. Anamaria Jeunet had been kidnapped earlier in the year from somewhere in the Straights. No ransom had ever been made, and nobody had come forward to claim responsibility for her disappearance.

"You've been here all this time?" Vaugn asked astounded.

Anamaria pressed her face closer to the metal bars, "Do you promise?" she pleaded, "Do you promise to kill me?"

Vaugn looked deep into her eyes, took a deep breath and nodded. "I promise, you'll be dead by dawn."

Anamaria let out a tearful chuckle, "Thank you."

She smiled her cracked smile and pointed her bloody left stump up the corridor. "Keep going down the corridor. Turn left at the end, then left again at the next t-junction." She continued eagerly, "Go straight for about two hundred and fifty metres — the passage curves to the the right slightly. Take the next right and you'll see two huge wooden doors at the very end of the corridor. Go through. You'll see an enormous brick and steel furnace. Looks like a giant toad. There's a door at the back. Go through it and you'll be in to the labs."

After a thoughtful second, Vaugn swallowed and spoke, "Forgive me but . . . how do you know this?"

Anamaria laughed hollowly. "Ha. Cipher likes to show off. I took the opportunity to throw myself in the furnace. But he's too quick. He made sure I survived."

Vaugn reached through the bars and brushed some of the dried blood from her cheek. "Thank you, Anamaria."

***

After about ten minutes of winging his way down identical corridors and turns, Vaugn stood in front of a huge, old-fashioned furnace in the centre of an enormous hall. As Anamaria had said, the furnace did have an odd similarity to a mechanical toad. It also looked like a blast furnace, just on a slightly smaller scale.

Moving towards it, Vaugn couldn't shake the distinct sensation of being watched by a vicious, wild beast. The flames dancing gleefully inside inside the furnace and gave Vaugn the strange familiarity of someone licking their lips hungrily. It unnerved him, but not enough to distract him from his task. He gently placed Lukas's duffle bag on the ground, removed a large bundle of explosives from inside the bag, and positioned them underneath the burning beast. He then quickly headed for the door at the rear of the room Anamaria had mentioned.

As he approached the door, he could hear voices from inside.

"You have objections?" said one voice.

There was a muffled response, but it was too weak for Vaugn to make out.

"Good. Now, please . . . kill that fucker!" screamed the first voice. Vaugn cracked the door slightly and glanced in.

hazardous

/ˈhazədəs/

adjective

risky; dangerous.

hazardous materials

CIPHER I

Vaugn quietly spied through the ajar door. Vaugn saw the distillery vats lining the wall to his left, and the rows of work stations leading to the back of the large room. There were no more than fifteen people, all dressed in lab gear, and all too focused on their tasks to notice his presence. Their pace suggested that if they slowed down, there would be repercussions. Vaugn could tell they were petrified.

Standing on the upper gallery, at the far end of the lab were Cipher, La Bouffe and the dead body of The Shredded One. La Bouffe was still attempting to argue his case. "I don't even know what this guy looks like!" La Bouffe blubbered, "Would you really want me to kill the wrong man?!"

Cipher's eyebrows raised in surprise,"Did you really just ask me that?!" He laughed violently, "I don't fucking care who you kill any more!"

"I thought you wanted me to keep a lo—" began La Bouffe.

"—Oh!" Cipher exclaimed joyfully. It was then that Cipher's gaze caught Vaugn watching them from the doorway. "What a turn of good fortune! That's him over there!" Everyone in the lab stopped what they were doing and stared in the direction Cipher was pointing. Vaugn cleared his throat and casually began walking up the stairs to the second level.

"Were you looking for me?" Vaugn asked as casually as he could manage.

The lab assistants looked from Vaugn, to Cipher and back again. Without seeking any form of permission they all hurriedly began evacuating the area through whichever exit was nearest to them. What care and attention they formerly had for their job was lost. They felt the danger of the situation and nobody wanted to be around when the action started.

\#

Cipher watched Vaugn reach the top of the stairs. Since Vaugn had been spotted, they had not broken eye contact. He had watched this man walk confidently up the stairwell to meet his foes. They stood at the extreme opposite ends of the double-levelled lab with the work stations between, and below them. You arrogant little shit, Cipher thought excitedly. *I think I like you.*

"Hello again." Cipher chirped, "On a one-man crusade to avenge your family? How very noble of you."

The Interpol agent stopped at the opposite end of the gallery and tipped an imaginary hat. From the involuntary throat noise that escaped La Bouffe, Cipher presumed that his business partner had finally gotten a proper look at the intruder. Considering the quickly morphing look from abject fear, to confusion, then finally resting on fury, Cipher presumed La Bouffe recognised the individual.

"Holy fuck!" La Bouffe seethed, "Vaugn? Agent fucking Vaugn!" he exclaimed. "You fucking cum stain!" he spat.

Cipher was stunned to see a fire in the man's eyes that he'd not witnessed before. "Wow! What's gotten into you?!" he quizzed.

Anyone whose anyone knew of La Bouffe's temper, but Cipher had retained a permanent threat level over him for so long now to keep him in check, that this little outburst was actually mildly shocking.

"He's the fuckwad who blew up my apartment!" howled La Bouffe.

VAUGN I

A broad, obnoxious smirk grew across Vaugn's face. He had hoped to set more charges and extricate himself for this place without being spotted — but evidently that wasn't going to happen. He glanced around the room once more, looking for possible escape routes. In the south-west corner of the lab, behind Cipher's position were large ventilation pipes going form the first level, and tunnelling through the ceiling. *An exit?* he wondered. He had never met La Bouffe face to face before. So if this was to be his last stand, Vaugn decided to enjoy himself as much as possible with whatever time was left.

"It's true," Vaugn confessed smiling, before turning his attention to Cipher. "It was so much fun!"

La Bouffe fired wildly across the ten meter gap between. Vaugn instinctively dodged and weaved to his right, bringing him to the opposite side of the lab from the distillery vats. It wasn't hard to dodge the poorly-aimed shots and, as he moved he saw that La Bouffe actually kept shutting his eyes every time he pulled the trigger.

"Pas étonnant que vous soyez un tel coup de merde!" Vaugn laughed as he heard the unmistakable clicking of an emptied gun. Vaugn then turned his attention back to Cipher who was wearing the most unusual expression. It was somewhere between puzzlement, curiosity, and mild frustration.

"Why do you keep turning up?" Cipher asked. "Seriously, what are the od—?"

Without warning, Vaugn drew his guns and offloaded five carefully placed shots at La Bouffe and Cipher each. The blasts resonated against the walls, sounding like steel pipes being hit rapidly by cast iron crowbars. The first shot hit La Bouffe perfectly on the bridge of his nose, burrowed its way through his skull and escaping out the other side, finally embedding itself in the wall. The hollow point round had made a clean entrance, but as it vacated the skull had blasted a hole about five times its entry size into the back of La Bouffe's head. The next four shots were a tight cluster around where La Bouffe's heart would be. Vaugn fired off the exact same shots at Cipher, but they seemed to not hit. Not one.

Vaugn stood his ground, calmly reloading and watching Cipher. Cipher looked down at the ugly mess of wasted flesh and blood that was his former associate without a hint of emotional engagement. He turned his attention back to Vaugn.

"Thanks! Now I don't have to pay him!" he said, walking toward Vaugn again.

Why aren't the guns working on this guy? Vaugn wondered. *I'm sure I hit him.* And yet the dapper gent didn't seem injured in the slightest. He pulled the sunglasses out of their pocket once more and put them on. As he looked at Cipher, he saw the same monstrous figure that had chilled him in Elizabeth's corridor. But he also noticed that, even in this form, there were no signs of injury. He thought angrily, *I am so fucking out of my depth. . .* He looked at the ventilation pipes again.

I can't be more than a meter below the street at this point, Vaugn assessed. *If I get up to where the pipes meet the ceiling, I might be able to squeeze out.* His gaze drifted around the lab again, *I might be able to find a way out if I followed the lab workers out, but I don't know the route and would probably get lost.*

"Don't thank me too soon," Vaugn replied, as confidently as he could. Then he pulled a CB radio from one of his coat pockets. The look on Cipher's face was pure confusion by the appearance of the radio.

"A radio? A little low-tech, isn't it?" he asked with genuine curiosity. "Who do you think you're gonna call?"

"Definitely not Ghostbusters," he smiled as he cautiously began walking parallel to the west wall of the second floor, bringing himself closer to the ventilation pipes.

Cipher couldn't help but laugh, "Ah! I knew you'd say something like that!" But then his mood suddenly changed, and he was gravely serious again. "I'd suggest you don't piss me off. There's a limit to my forgiveness." he finished.

Vaugn feigned shock and blissful ignorance, "What have I done?!" Still he moved closer to the pipes.

With one simple step, Cipher pushed Vaugn's self-control to near-breaking point, and it showed. His eyes widened with fear as it clouded his mind. Every fibre of his being was begging, and pleading desperately to flee. *Holy shit,* Vaugn began thinking, *This guy . . . is . . . is . . .* but thoughts failed him and he was frozen to the spot.

"Your family has an incredible ability to fuck me off without knowing." Cipher began. "Who are you? Why are you here?!" The questions came out more like the rabid growls of a bear that was about to pounce.

Fuck . . . this . . . shit! Vaugn thought furiously. The paralysis that held him a moment ago bled away in an instant. "You might want to check your boiler," Vaugn quipped as he ran the final few steps to the ventilation pipes. As he ran, he pushed the button on the side of the radio. "Bye-bye!"

"What!?"

Cipher couldn't hide the fear in his voice as the sound of explosives going off in the other room set everything ablaze. Anyone within five kilometres of the blast felt the earth tremble.

CLAIR I

Clair was in the middle of describing to Parisian Police what had happened at Pierre's church, making sure to gently reinforce the narrative of gang warfare. She had managed to get Socrates on a leash at the behest of the Officers. But the husky was keen to chew on more demon flesh, sniffing around and gently growling.

"We opened the door and Pierre was exactly as he is now," Clair reported calmly.

The Officer nodded, "We just received reports that some of Richard Strauss's associates may be planning something. In your professional opinion," The Officer continued, "...could this be some form of retribution? Do you know if Mr Vaugn was involved in either the Strauss or La Bouffe parties?" the Officer finished.

Clair controlled herself as the rumour she had started was echoed back to her so quickly. But as she was able to reply, she noticed Styx standing in the doorway.

"Hey!" she exclaimed.

But then the ground quaked and the distant boom of an explosion echoed through the Parisian streets. Behind Styx, rising up above the rooftops was a plume of smoke. As she watched the small mushroom cloud develop, Clair had just one, worrying thought, *Gabe, what have you done?* After a second, she and Socrates darted off in the direction of the smoke.

trust

/trʌst/

noun

firm belief in the reliability, truth, or ability of someone or something.

trust at an all-time low

UNDERLINGS

Two days earlier.

Lukas was being dragged into what would become his final residence by the dwarfish creatures. His body still reeled from the battle with Cipher, but his fighting spirit remained as he kicked and fought as hard as he could against his captors, but with no real success.

The creatures tossed him into the cell like a rag doll, then shuffled out of the room and slammed the heavy metal door behind them. The resounding thud of the steel reverberated through Lukas's skull like a dentist's drill.

Lukas rolled onto his side — a feat more painful than he imagined. He guessed he probably had a broken rib or two from the beating, and he was not going to receive any form of care. He glanced around the cell; it was nearly pitch dark, but for a small crack of light under the door for which he was instantly appreciative. "At least I have some light," he thought to himself. He glanced up to the bars on the door. Through the opening, he could see a pair of young eyes looking back at him. The paradoxical eyes of Styx. Ancient and new. Smiling and evil. Friendly and antagonistic.

"Don't belittle your efforts. What you did was impressive," began Styx, with an unusually honest tone to his voice. "You actually hurt him."

Something happened during Lukas and Cipher's confrontation that hadn't been planned. Styx saw a normal man stand up to, and actually injure, Cipher. It emboldened Styx to the point that he had to meet the combatant. He needed to find out if he could replicate and develop what he'd seen, and succeed where the young priest had failed.

"I aim to please," replied Lukas, coughing up a mouthful of blood.

Styx smiled, recording this fresh event in his memories. Anyone or anything that could be weaponised against Cipher—or God, for that matter—was infinitely valuable. He happily admitted to himself that there was a power within the young priest. It impressed him that a relatively nondescript human could be capable of such potential.

But then Styx felt a familiar instinctual awareness, a tingling down his spine. He was being watched by something with a dangerous bloodlust. He turned away from the cell and saw Elizabeth watching him.

"Hey, Beth!" he said, happily, while considering whether he would be able to get away with killing her.

Elizabeth took a step towards him and commanded, "Don't call me that!"

Even though it was one of his favourite pastimes, Styx knew that now was not the time to piss her off. Something told him that she was seriously considering murdering him just as much as he was thinking of ending her.

"I suppose you're going to ask what I'm doing?" asked Styx, with his traditional, condescending tone.

"I already know," replied Elizabeth.

Styx looked at her, slightly concerned. "Really?"

***

Elizabeth and Styx had never worked together before the Chimera operation, though they knew of each other by reputation. The supernatural world was filled with secrets and deception. It lived in the shadows. Those who called it their world preferred not to get involved in the mortal world unless absolutely necessary.

The bloody history of mankind haunted the supernatural world: the Salem witch trials, the Spanish Inquisition, the Holocaust . . . all human responses to, or excuses for, supernatural occurrences witnessed by mortals who could not comprehend their insignificance. Mankind had repeatedly failed to understand their place in the grand scheme of things. Simply put, secrecy and shadows were the stock-in-trade of the supernatural world.

But that secrecy didn't mean it was without rumours and fables. Reputations were made quickly and proliferated like viruses. Styx and Elizabeth had more than done their parts to build their reputations. They were renowned in particular circles for their skills and attributes.

Before actually working together, they would probably both have been agreeable to the idea of teaming up.

Now, though? There was more chance of Hell freezing over.

***

If Elizabeth did know the extent of his plans, steps would have to be taken. Least of which would be to remove her from the situation. Styx's instinct to protect his secrets and to kill rose in equal measure. But how to do it was the question. Elizabeth's disappearance—especially now—would raise too many questions. Questions were what Styx was trying to avoid.

Elizabeth smiled politely as she walked past. "You're separate from the others," she stated, confidently.

A flash of genuine worry crossed Styx's face, but he attempted to remain calm and composed. *How does she know?* He thought. His mind raced, as he tried to find another way to handle this situation. Then, it struck him. One of the simplest and most effective methods of control was also one of his personal favourites, coercion. Styx smiled at Elizabeth as innocently as his devilish face could muster.

"What about you and this fella? And here I thought you didn't have a heart. Seems we both have our secrets, don't we?"
Styx walked off, as Elizabeth continued past Lukas's cell. After a moment, she finally replied.
"I'll keep yours if you keep mine," she said, without a hint of fear.

Styx spun on his heels. "What an interesting team we're gonna make," he said, jovially.

"And what treacherous waters we're playing in," finished Elizabeth.

"Makes you wonder if we've lost our minds, doesn't it?"

"I guess we'll see."

crumbling

/ˈkrʌmb(ə)lɪŋ/

adjective

breaking or falling apart into small fragments, especially as part of a process of deterioration.

crumbling down

VAUGN I

With the force of the explosion, the heavy doors separating the lab from the furnace room blasted inwards. They collided with the plexiglass 'clean room' and shattered the wall. The expanding cloud of fire carried the unhinged doors across the full length of the room. The blaze quickly made its way into the lab, consuming everything in its path. The distillery vats lining one of the walls quickly began to creak, and strain from the sudden change in temperature. The work stations nearest the blast's entrance point were instantly consumed, and became nothing more that additional fuel for the rampaging force. The glass cage in the centre of the room began to quickly melt and deform. The ceiling swelled like a balloon expanding.

Vaugn kept opening and closing his mouth as he worked on escaping. It seemed strangely futile considering his chances of survival, but he'd been around enough explosions to know it could mean the difference between a frustrating ringing in his ears, or the ear drums bursting entirely. The heat from the explosion was already burning the back of his coat and he was certainly in the process of being cooked alive. The pipe bend open with more ease that Vaugn had assumed. Without a seconds thought, he climbed inside. As he smushed himself through the hole he had made, he caught a brief glimpse of Cipher.

Cipher was completely ablaze as wave, after wave of flame washed over him again, and again, and again. But through the heat, and smoke and fire, Vaugn could still see Cipher's eyes glaring back at him with more hatred, and more fire than what was cooking them both right now.

"Mr Vaugn, you are really pissing me off!" Cipher roared as the 'clean room' ceiling finally burst and showered melted plexiglass all over the second level.

#

Anamaria sat in her cell, as flames devastated the cell door, and roared into her room. She smiled contentedly, ". . . Alex . . ." she said as the door blasted inwards.

The cell door impacted with her body and the blaze sped into the room a moment later. She was lost in fire.

# #

Vaugn had managed to squeeze himself fully into the piping and, as he had hoped, could see the light of the street reflecting into the piping less than half a meter above him. But then an unholy scream burst forth from the inferno that was the lab.

"Gabriel Vaugn!" Cipher howled with all the anger, and fury of someone who had just witnessed his endeavours go up in literal smoke.

A shiver ran down Vaugn's spine, as if someone had walked over his grave. Every instinct screamed at him to flee. *Fight or flight,* he thought. It was for less than a second, but to Vaugn it felt like a lifetime. He refocused again on his escape, refusing to look back. Revenge at the expense of the self was not an option. Clair would have never accepted it.

Vaugn stretched out his hands, knees, and back to either side of the pipe, applied pressure and painfully began to scale up towards the hole, and freedom. Every few centimetres he climbed, he had to strain, and twist his whole body to allow himself the required readjustments to then continue the ascension. He could feel the skin on his hands blistering. He could smell the burning flesh on his back as the pipe got hotter, and hotter. The sweat coming off his entire body was making it harder and harder to get the required pressure to keep climbing. But he forced himself on. After a gruelling thirty seconds of the worst workout Vaugn had ever suffered, his hands finally reached the metal grate that blocked his successful escape. He pressed against the pipe with his back and knees, grabbed hold of the grill and pushed with all his might. But nothing moved. Vaugn suddenly felt something grab hold of his trailing coat and attempt to yank him back down the pipe.

"Where the fuck do you think you're going!?" bellowed the familiar voice of Cipher.

As his body was being pulled back down into the fiery hell below, Vaugn's ruined hands clung on to the grill with as much strength as they had left.

"HELP!" he screamed, hoping there might be someone, anyone above ground and able to help.

"Nobody can help you!" Cipher screamed.

"PLEASE! I'M TRAPPED!" Vaugn screamed desperately.

"Est-ce que quelqu'un est là-bas?" came a young voice from above ground.

"Oui! OUI! Je suis ici" Vaugn yelled in reply.

Another hard tug on Vaugn's coat. Again Vaugn's hands managed to maintain their grip. Vaugn glanced down the pipe and could see the rendered flesh of Cipher's face glowering up at him, he could see the unsettlingly small, gnashing teeth snapping in his direction.

"PLEASE!" Vaugn begged as he looked back up through the bars.

So close! Please help me! he prayed. As he prayed, two young faces came into view. "How did you get down there?" asked the youngest of the two girls.

"What's happening down there?" asked the older girl, "The street's shaking!"

"Please help me! Can you get this grate off?" Vaugn pleaded.

The two girls looked confused, but quickly started pulling at the metal grate. Vaugn kicked down at the melted monster still biting at whatever it could get a hold of. He connected with a strong downward kick with his left leg. Cipher let out a pained, frustrated, "Argh!" The attack was just enough to force Cipher to let go of the burning coat-tails.

Vaugn repositioned his back and knees on opposite sides of the piping. "Ok girls," he commanded. "PULL!"

Together the two girls pulls as hard as they could at the metal bars. Vaugn pushed up with as much force as he could manage. One second, two seconds, three seconds of pushing. . .

"I . . . don't . . . thin—" The younger girl began to say.

But just then, the bars shifted. The girls toppled backwards and the metal grill clattered to the stone floor. Vaugn launched up the pipe a little from the pressure of his own efforts. Instinctually, he scrambled to get the rest of himself free of the hole.

As he extricated himself from underground, he snatched up the grill from the ground, spun round, and slammed it back into position. Only then did he allow himself to look back into the pipe. Still scrabbling his way up the pipe like a mad dog chasing a rabbit, was Cipher with blazing hellfire in his black eyes. Vaugn defiantly stuck his middle finger up.

"Fuck you!" he spat.

But then he remembered something one of the girls had mentioned, "What do you mean the street's shak—" Vaugn began. But as he turned back to face his saviours, he saw them running away as fast as they could.

"Courir!" Shouted the girls as they ran.

"Oh shit," Vaugn said automatically as he too could feel the vibrations.

Vaugn began running but the ground was determined to consume him whole, as huge chunks of the street folded into the ground all around him. He had to leap from rock, to rock to escape. His body was screaming in pain from the burns, and the effort of his escape. His legs were weak, and his burned hands weren't helping him much. But the desire to survive was still strong within him. He navigated himself through the collapsing earth. More than once he thought he'd reached safe ground, only for it to shudder upon his landing, then crumble under foot. *I am not dying now!* he kept repeating to himself. As he ran, and leapt, and scraped his way to safety, he could see others attempting the same — with varying degrees of success. Occasionally he caught glimpses of the two girls who had helped him escape. They were impressively nimble, and had about a two hundred metres lead on him. *Keep running!* he thought, cheering them on.

After two solid minutes of rubble-jumping, Vaugn began to find the ground becoming more solid. Many of the people who had be been trying to escape with him had been lost, but not all of them. Vaugn could see bystanders not too far ahead of him. They were standing in awe of the destruction. Vaugn was running across a portion of the street that had maintained itself for an impressive twelve seconds, but then he suddenly felt the shudder from underfoot.

"COME ON!" Vaugn bellowed, cheering himself on.

Vaugn sped forwards a few metres more before the street piece he'd been running toppled backwards quickly. He suddenly found himself trying to sprint up a rapidly inclining face. He huffed angrily and reached deep inside himself, trying to utilise every last drip of energy still in his muscles. Six seconds of increasingly obtuse terrain followed, but Vaugn reached the edge. He made a flying leap towards what appeared to be safe ground.

He crashed into a couple of onlookers who were helping another man clamber to safety, knocking them all to the ground. As they tumbled painfully to the floor, a loud cracking sound snarled underfoot. A second later and the ground continued to break away. He quickly got back to his feet, grabbed the three other people and continued to bolt away, a grin spreading across his face. He couldn't resist smiling. Adrenalin coursed through his veins. It thumped in his ears, and he felt energised.

After having dragged the other three people for about ten metres, Vaugn finally felt as safe on the ground as he could. Finally he allowed himself to turn back and see what he'd done. Even he had to admit that perhaps he'd gone too far this time. Oh fuck. . .

Slowly, a little giggle grew to be near-uncontrollable hysteria. Vaugn began getting strange looks from those around him. But he didn't care and wouldn't have been able to stop even if he wanted to.

CLAIR I

The ground surrounding the factory district was slowing its collapse into the sewers below. Buildings were still crumbling and collapsing, as foundations struggled maintain their form below. A massive crowd of people had gathered to watch with their curiosity piqued. The roads and paths of District Seven were cracked, and some sections were still falling into the chasm below, taking the occasional unfortunate soul with them.

Clair and Socrates had run from Pierre's church, all the way to the Straights when they had felt the rumbles, and seen the smoke billowing into the sky. She saw the bodies of bystanders falling into the abyss.

"Fucking hell!"

She drew her gun, began firing into the sky and shouting orders to the surrounding crowd. "Move back! Save yourselves!" Strategically fired into the sky, continually shouting retreat orders to the masses, Clair and Socrates wove their way closer towards the danger area.

They continued pushing their way through the crowd until they finally popped out on the frontline of the onlookers and could see the destructive panoramic before them. Popping off all around her, Clair could hear onlookers quizzing each other as to what had happened. Some were speculating it was planned demolition works, while others were proclaiming this was an act of retribution from surviving Strauss supporters.

"Holy shit!" exclaimed Clair, taking in the calamity.

She then turned to face the crowd again and fired her pistol again. "Move back!" Socrates joined in the crowd control by snarling and snapping in their general direction. It works quite effectively too.

Clair scanned the edge of the huge hole that had been made, taking in as many details as she could manage. But she was also desperately looking for any sign of Vaugn. Just off to her left were two young girls. They too were looking over the hole.

The younger of the two spoke, "Do you think he made it?"

The elder girl reached out and grasped the young girl's hand and shook her head slowly.

As Clair watched them for a moment, something caught her ear that was both incredibly confusing, and also hugely reassuring. Laughter. Excessive, uncontrollable laughter. She turned looking for the source.

"Vaugn?" she called.

There was no response. Clair looked down as Socrates darted off through the crowd with his tail wagging happily.

"Go find him!" Clair encouraged, then followed after him.

VAUGN II

Vaugn was still laughing uncontrollably on the floor when he was suddenly smothered by a giant fur-ball, otherwise known as Socrates springing out from the crowd of on-lookers. The weight of Socrates knocked Vaugn onto his back.

"Argh! Hey! Socrates!" he managed to giggle out.

Socrates was treading all over his partner, licking his face, and hopping on the spot with uncontrollable joy. Through the licks, and hops, Vaugn couldn't help let out more, and more groans of pain as he managed to get control of himself again. But as he regained composure, the pain wracking his burned, exhausted body began to make itself known.

Vaugn looked up and past the mountain of fur and spotted Clair pushing her way through the crowd. "Clair" he sighed with relief.

"Out of my way!" she was shouting, "I'm gonna kill him!"

But then, as their eyes finally caught each other, she shoulder-barged a young man out of the way and leapt on Vaugn, and hugged him tightly for a long time.

"Ooof!" Vaugn exclaimed, "Softly. A little softer, please. I'm a roast chicken right now."

"Bien fait pour vous" she said without relenting.

Slowly the crowd dissipated as the sound of Police sirens began to fill the air. Police officers were taking control of the area, and were shooing on-lookers back. News drones had started to fly into the area that used to be District Seven. The world was watching.

"You fucking idiot!" Clair chastised. Her body shook as adrenalin pumped through her muscles, though she refused to let go of her vice-like grip on Vaugn. Socrates was sitting down glaring at Vaugn with the unmistakeable look of, "I'm not letting you out of my sight" As the three of them shared this quiet moment, Vaugn and Clair had the same thought, though she was the first to voice it.

"This was too much," she said, grasping Vaugn tightly by the shoulders and forcing him to look her in the eye. "You can't keep doing shit like this and not listen to me . . . Involve me, at the very least!"

Socrates huffed in agreement. Vaugn looked back into Clair's eyes, silent tears rolling down his face. "I know . . .," he said through laboured breathing, and winces of pain. "I'm gonna stop. I'm gonna stop this all, for you."

"And for you!" Clair replied.

Vaugn laughed slightly, "Ha, yes. And for me." He then remembered there was still a lot of horrible work to be done. His soul sank, as the pain of his family's deaths returned to him. Any remaining shreds of survival exhilaration evaporated. "We still need to bury the dead."

"We'll tidy up our mess. Then we're both going to stop." Clair said matter-of-factly.

eternity

/ɪˈtəːnɪti,iːˈtəːnɪti/

noun

infinite or unending time.

for all eternity

STYX I

It was nearly midnight at the crater that once was District Seven of the Straights. Dust still hung heavily in the air, as well as the distinct odour of dynamite, rubble, and sewage lingered. The Police had erected a barrier around the perimeter of the new hole, but there weren't many actual Officers on duty. Most of the surveillance work was being handled by the Paris Police Prefecture drones that were flying overhead. Emergency services had vacated the area, and digging teams were not due to arrive for at least another hour.

But a small group of people consisting of Styx and five others, were standing in the centre of the crater where the underground lab had once been. One of the group, an older, handsome gentleman wearing a grey suit and bowler hat, stepped forward. "Wow!"

An older woman stepped a little closer to Styx, hesitantly. "Who did you say caused this?" she asked.

Styx remained focused on the ground before him, "Gabriel Vaugn," he said with an air of respect, "I think you should remember that name."

"So, what's the plan?" The bowler hat wearer asked repugnantly.

Styx remained perfectly still and just watched the rubble. The others did the same, except for the bowler hat wearer, who was fidgety and agitated. The man turned and walked towards Styx brashly.

"What are we waiting for?" he said, more commandingly.

Styx still didn't look away from the crater. "Waiting." He said simply, though he didn't quite know what for. But waiting was important, and it was a talent Styx had developed over the years.

The bowler hat wearer suddenly collapsed gargling, and holding his throat, which was bleeding profusely from a severe neck laceration. Styx smiled slightly. Death always had a way of cheering his spirit.

"Now, shut up and die." he said dryly, "You're annoying."

The body finally died and crumpled to the ground. Styx was holding a chunk of the man's throat in his hand. He raised it to his mouth and began consuming it, like some horrific apple. Blood dripped from his mouth and onto his chin. The four remaining figures surrounding Styx had all taken a few cautious steps away from the young man. They knew to fear Styx. They had no choice but to wait.

***

For two long hours they waited in silence. The question of Vaugn had planted itself deep in Styx's mind. *More research into him will certainly be needed,* the young monster mused.

But just as a smile began to form on his young face, Cipher suddenly burst forth from the rubble in a jet of earth, and stone, and blood. "I invoke the Eternity on Gabriel Vaugn!" he screamed in a language Styx had only heard about from much, much older creatures than himself.

Cipher's voice resonated so loudly that it echoed through the entire Parisian cityscape. Animals howled, and babies awoke from their slumbers screaming in response. The moment held, as Cipher pulled, dug and clawed himself free of the rubble.

"The Eternity?!" Styx exclaimed as he translated what Cipher had screamed. His four associates instantly felt his thoughts, "Stay back! He's not in control!" Styx quickly regained composure, and resumed his cast-iron grip on the group's collective minds.

Cipher glared at Styx with pure, unadulterated hatred. "Got a fucking problem with that?!" he screamed, inches from Styx's face.

Styx didn't look worried, more bored than anything. He held the silence for five full seconds before letting out a disappointed sign.

"You idiot!" He said as he shook his head, "Do you know what—"

"—I know what it fucking means!" Cipher exploded with rage. His fingers wrapped around an invisible foe, as he tore something to pieces in his mind. "I'm going to enjoy slowly ripping him the fuck apart!"

Styx stood perfectly still, unimpressed by the antics on display in front of him. This was one, if not the most annoying elements of working for Cipher. Abhorrent mood swings resulting in unnecessary mistakes and issues, Styx thought angrily. To Styx, the whole Chimera incident was a cluster-fuck of mistakes. Don't be a fuck child.

"And what about your other plans?" Styx said, mustering as level a head as he could manage. "I thought you were taking over the world. Not going on a stupid vendetta." Styx paused for a moment, just letting his words slowly penetrate to current animalistic psyche of Cipher.

"You've just effectively handicapped yourself." Styx commented neutrally. "Casting the Eternity means you now have to choose," Styx went on, as much for his own understanding of the new situation as explaining it to Cipher, "You can go after Vaugn, and get blissfully trapped in an endless cycle of torturing your enemy forever, but never fulfil you life-spanning plans."

A grim smile stretched over the battered face of Cipher, but Styx continued talking, "Or you can continue with you grander desires. Do anything, and everything else your twisted heart might want to, but you can never inflict even the slightest of physical pain against Vaugn for fear of initiating your Eternity."

"Eternal, base, violent gratification against your foe, or control of all existence?"

Realisation finally struck Cipher. The true weight of his words hit him. Cipher stood in silent turmoil for a moment, ". . . Fuck!"

beginning

/bɪˈɡɪnɪŋ/

noun

the first part or earliest stage of something.

seven months ago

WHISKY I

Paris…

The sun was slowly setting over one of the most picturesque vistas on the planet. The rain from earlier in the day had clung to the ground fiercely, though through the warming day it was starting to finally return to the heavens. The mist that was slowly, gracefully rising from the pavement and rooftops gave Paris a traditionally romantic atmosphere, but with a decidedly supernatural flavour.

Whisky was stretched out across a public bench next to the Pont d'Léna bridge and the River Seine — on the Jargins du Trocadero side of the river. He was happily watching the world pass him by as he smoked a cigar so far that it looked more like a sausage hanging out of his mouth. Displayed on the public news screens was the headline, "Turf warfare within Paris returns". The sudden return to violent, and explosive confrontations between La Bouffe and Strauss was a surprise even to Whisky. During the few short weeks in which the conflicts had reignited, Whisky had heard a few people mention a mysterious third party, aligned with La Bouffe. To know that there was another person working behind the scenes, but not know who they were was a real point of frustration for him. There was, however, a name that had been popping up occasionally… Cipher.

Hence his current position, sitting in his favourite spot, smoking a fine cigar and attempting to clear his head. The Eiffel Tower could be seen prominently across the water, as could the Straights, and Whisky's home. *Nowhere else in the world would someone like me be able to exist and thrive!* he happily mused.

He didn't know how much time had passed as his mind drifted from topic to topic, slowly calming and re-centring on his current position. But seemingly from nowhere, a man appeared next to the bench.

"Mind if I join you?" said the voice.

There was a South-American accent coming through. A healthy dose of baritone heightened the allure of the already seductive male voice. Whisky certainly wasn't the most astute fellow in the world, but even he found it hard to believe that someone could get so close to him without being made aware of their presence on some level.

Instantly he was on guard. He automatically ran through his 'security' check list in his mind; knife - left pocket; brass knuckles - right pocket; secondary knife - tucked into his left sock.

Whisky maintained his composure and fought the instinctive urge to look up at the man. He refused to lose face. He swung his legs down, maintaining his outwardly happy persona.

"There's plen'y of room" Whisky replied cordially.

The gentleman sat down. "You've chosen a good spot." He said as he let out a small sigh of pure satisfaction.

"'s the bes' view of m' home" replied Whisky as he leaned forward onto his knees and smiled broadly.

The gentleman pulled a cigar from the inside breast pocket of his jacket, and casually lit it. "You seem like a contented man" the man stated.

Whisky's funny smile broadened but he seemed to barely notice the gentleman beside him "I am."

"Uncommon these days."

After about two minutes of quiet contemplation and savouring of their cigars, Whisky finally looked over at the gentleman sitting next to him. Cipher was dressed in a preppy-looking polo shirt, and worn denims, with Converse trainers. To Whisky, he looked quite cool, but there was most certainly something 'off' about him. He made mental notes of everything regarding Cipher. In his many years working 'The Black Moon Bar' he had encountered almost every type of person. But in that moment, he knew that he'd never met anyone like Cipher before. Whisky instantly knew to be cautious.

Cipher was smiling politely and looked serene. "You're Whisky, right?"

"Tha's me!" Came the reply without a hint of fear.

Cipher offered his hand to Whisky. "Pleasure to meet you. I'm Cipher."

Whisky shook Cipher's hand confidently. The pieces of the jigsaw clicked together straight away in Whisky's mind. This was the mysterious third party involved in the turf war. "I've heard of ya."

Cipher smiled politely. "Impressive. Few people have. But then I understand you know everyone worth knowing."

"Everyone's worth knowin', Cipher" Whisky responded. "How can I help ya'?"

And so their conversation began.

LUKAS I

Meanwhile, on the opposite bank of the river, a fight was breaking out. Some of the church-goers were involved in an altercation (to put it politely) with some of the 'Black Moon Bar' patrons. Needless to say, but it wasn't pretty. Fights between the two very different sets of people were not unusual, especially after any new "miracle" videos appeared on YouTube.

On this particular occasion Lukas Vaugn was standing defiantly between two groups of vastly opposing beliefs and attitudes. Standing away from the fight, watching with great curiosity, was Elizabeth. She was watching Lukas

"Please!" He implored, "Stop fighting!"

But it was no use. The fighting escalated and Lukas was perfectly trapped in its centre. Pain, as it so frequently did for Lukas, followed. As the stiff kicks and punches began to fly, and Lukas prepared himself for a true battle, he was surprised to see the most beautiful woman he'd ever laid eyes on. She walked towards the fight with no seeming worry, or even concern. As she got close, the fighters seemed drawn to her; their attention quickly drifted away from the Priest.

She smiled at Lukas kindly, and held out her right hand. "I've been looking for you everywhere."

Lukas reached out and grasped her hand with his. So warm, he thought as a rejuvenating heat slowly crept up his arm. Then, without any further incident, Elizabeth lead Lukas off into the Straights.

"My name is Elizabeth, and that may have been the stupidest thing I've ever witnessed" she said with a happy energy behind her voice.

"Ha!" Lukas laughed, "You should meet my brother."

notes, acknowledgements and confessions

The story of Vaugn is, in no way, accurate to the existence we choose to call reality. I have taken so many liberties with pretty much all parts of this tale. If you're looking for an accurate interpretation of Paris, this is not the book for you. The Catacombs as depicted in The Straights don't exist. I used the real Catacombs as a launching point for an interesting setting. The Paris of Vaugn itself is near-complete fiction when compared to the real world.

I purposefully utilise many versions, variations, and bastardisations of religious iconography to tell my story. Some of them do relate to my own ideologies about faith, and reality. But the goal of my writing it first, and foremost, entertaining escapism. I apologise to anyone who might take offence, or get frustrated by my mutations.

Special thanks have to go to Shawna Gore, Brendan H Wright, and MK Gibson. All three of you went above and beyond helping this politely annoying, and annoyingly polite Brit as he fumbled in the semi-dark, trying to write this book. Your patience, guidance, and support made a huge difference to Vaugn, and to me. Thank you.

Thanks to everyone who read bits, and pieces of Vaugn over the years. You all made a difference, you all supported me as I began to find my voice, and tell the story I wanted to tell. Sorry to have kept you all waiting so long for the final version.

G.T., July 2019

www.ingramcontent.com/pod-product-compliance
Lightning Source LLC
Chambersburg PA
CBHW031251170626
46807CB00001B/84